CRY MY NAME

Roshan kissed her until kissing wasn't enough, until she was mindless, breathless with the same urgent need that drove him. Their clothing disappeared as if by magick, his or hers, it didn't matter.

She looked up at him, a low moan of pleasure rising from deep in her throat as he worshiped her beauty with his eyes and his hands, large hands that caressed her ever so gently, demanding nothing, asking for everything.

There was no hesitation in Brenna now, no hint of maidenly modesty, no murmur of halfhearted protest. In spite of the rain and the cold, her skin was warm, heated by the desire that burned within her. She was a woman, with a woman's needs, and he fanned the embers of her desire until she was ready for him, until she cried his name, her voice thick with passion and a hunger that could no longer be denied.

And he took her, there, upon the wet grass.

Took her innocence, and her blood, and in so doing, he bound her to him for as long as either of them drew breath.

Books by Amanda Ashley

DEAD SEXY

DESIRE AFTER DARK

A WHISPER OF ETERNITY

AFTER SUNDOWN

NIGHT'S TOUCH

DEAD PERFECT

Published by Zebra Books

NIGHT'S KISS

AMANDA ASHLEY

ZEBRA BOOKS
KENSINGTON PUBLISHING CORP.
www.kensingtonbooks.com

DARK EXISTENCE

Man or beast, I'm neither
Yet of both I am a part
The beast dwells within my soul
The man, amongst the ruins of my heart . . .

The beast so hideous a thing
The man but an empty shell
Awaiting salvation that never comes
Existing in eternal hell . . .

I long to see the sun again
As I long for love's embrace
But just as love can never be mine
The sun will never warm my face . . .

Lonely is my dark existence
I am cursed to roam the night
Though I feed to quell the hunger
I am starving for love and light . . .

Elizabeth Camp

CHAPTER 1

Drowning in an ocean of loneliness and bitter despair, Roshan DeLongpre sat in front of the huge stone hearth, staring into the fire. The flames were vibrant, crackling with life, brilliant reds and yellows, dazzling blues and greens. He saw each dancing finger of flame in perfect clarity, each subtle shade and hue. Fire. His greatest enemy next to the clear golden light of day.

Firelight. Sunlight. Both had the power to destroy him.

A sigh whispered past his lips. He was growing weary of his existence, so utterly, utterly weary. Each night was like the last. Life as he knew it had lost its luster; there were no surprises left, only an age-old instinct to survive.

Now, staring into the writhing flames, he wondered why he bothered. He had no compelling reason to go on. He could inspire passion but not love, command obedience but not affection. He could change his shape at will, move with incredible speed, defy the laws of gravity, dissolve into a fine mist or disappear completely. And yet, on this cool October night, his supernatural powers meant nothing.

Night. He stared out the leaded window into the darkness beyond. He had seen the moon's rising every night for almost three hundred years but was forever denied the majestic beauty of dawn's first light.

Perhaps it was time to watch the birth of a new day one last time.

Rising, he wandered through the narrow, dark halls of the house where he had resided for most of the last fifty years. It was a big old house located on a quiet street in a respectable part of the city. He'd had the interior remodeled twice; once simply because he tired of his surroundings and wanted a change and once when he had been thinking about selling the place and moving on.

Going into each room, he bid a silent farewell to the treasures he had collected during the course of his preternatural existence.

He paused now and then to run his hands over a few of the items he cherished for one reason or another—a small ivory statue of Venus, a life-sized grizzly bear carved from a single piece of redwood, a unicorn carved from a piece of onyx. He paused in front of his favorite painting. It depicted the sun rising over a clear mountain lake set in the midst of a pine tree forest. He gazed at it for several minutes, trying to remember what it had felt like to feel the warmth of the daystar on his face.

Moving into his library, he stood in front of the bookcase that reached from wall to wall and floor to ceiling. He had loved books ever since he learned to read, had spent years wandering the world to collect the ones that lined the shelves. Many of the books were rare editions; a few were first editions autographed by the authors. Some were so old they were in danger of disintegrating. A few were truly ancient, like the medieval Psalter that dated back to the fourteenth century. It was a beautiful work of art, carefully written and illustrated by hand. His collection also included a Bible handwritten by monks. Each page was in itself a work of art. He had other books and writings that were truly unique. Some were written on tree bark, others on bamboo or cloth or silk. One had been engraved on metal plates. He had a folding book that came from Burma. Called a *parabaiks*, it told the life of Buddha in words and pictures.

So many books. No ordinary mortal would ever have lived long enough to collect them all, let alone read them. But he had read them all at least once, some many more times than that. And this was only one bookcase of many located throughout the house.

He plucked a thick volume titled *Ancient History and Myths, Fact or Fiction* from a lower shelf. Dropping into a chair, he thumbed idly through the pages, skimming over the words and photographs until one particular image caught his attention. It was a small pen and ink drawing of a woman bound to a wooden stake. She was surrounded by a mob of angry men waving torches over their heads.

The caption under the drawing read: "The Burning of Brenna Flanagan, Accused of Witchcraft."

He stared at the photo, captivated by her uncanny likeness to Atiyana. His beloved Atiyana. He closed his eyes for a moment, remembering the only woman he had ever loved. Atiyana, dead at the age of two and twenty and their newborn son with her. He had not known another's love since her death, nor did he ever expect to love again, not now, when he was cursed with the Dark Trick.

Shaking off the memories, he turned his attention back to the book in his lap. The accompanying story claimed that Brenna Flanagan had been seen chanting and dancing naked in the moonlight numerous times. On one occasion, her neighbors alleged that dozens of toads had fallen from the heavens. On another occasion, they declared that lightning had split the skies, setting several cottages on fire. It was said that she had warned a local man to keep his pig from rooting around in her garden, and two days later the man had died. She had reportedly sold magic elixirs and charms to the locals, everything from love potions to a promised cure for spavins. Several young women claimed to have seen her flying through the skies.

Finally, the people in the village had had enough. Afraid that witchcraft would take over their small community, the way witches seemed to be overtaking the nearby towns of Andover and Salem, Brenna Flanagan had been arrested and tried, all in the same night. During the course of the hasty trial, she had been asked to identify the evil spirit she was in league with, and if she had made contact with the devil. She had denied being in league with the devil but her pleas had fallen on deaf ears. She had been convicted of being a witch. In Salem, witches were hanged, but the village folk wanted nothing left of their local witch. Brenna Flanagan had been burned at the stake and her ashes scattered in a mountain lake.

Frowning, his gaze settled on the drawing once more. Of course, it wasn't a true photograph, just an artist's rendition of the occurrence, and even though it was only a black and white sketch, she seemed alive somehow. He could feel the fear that sat like a lump of ice in the pit of her belly, the heat of the hungry flames as they licked at her ankles.

Rising, he searched his reference books, looking for her name, but to no avail. He found a great deal of information on the Salem witch hunts. From June of 1692 through September of that same year, nineteen men and women had been convicted of witchcraft, carted to Gallows Hill, and hanged. One man, over eighty years of age, had been pressed to death under heavy stones for refusing to submit to a trial. It had taken him two days to die, during which he had begged for "more weight" so that the end might come more quickly. In addition to the nineteen men and women, two dogs suspected of being "familiars" had also been executed.

Not one to be easily discouraged, Roshan fired up his computer. He knew that many of the old world vampires refused to embrace modern technology. They refused to learn new ways, refused to accept anything that had been invented after they had received the Dark Gift. Roshan was not one of them. He spent countless hours surfing the Web.

Going to the Internet, he typed Brenna Flanagan's name into a search engine. Moments later, her name appeared. The info on the Web didn't tell him anything new, but it did have what was purported to be a genuine portrait of the woman, supposedly painted by a man said to have been bewitched by her. A small notation said the artist, John Alfred Linder by name, had thrown himself off a cliff the day he learned of her death.

Roshan stared at the woman's image, completely mesmerized by what he saw. In this portrait, done in color, her likeness to Atiyana was even more pronounced.

She was a rare beauty, was Brenna Flanagan, with

hair as red as the flames that had taken her life, and beautiful green eyes flecked with gold. Eyes that held a soul-deep sadness. She had a small determined chin, a finely shaped nose, perfectly arched brows, and lips that begged to be kissed. Draped in a flowing white gown, she sat on a curved settee, her back straight. A large black cat with yellow eyes was curled up on her lap.

A witch, indeed, he thought wryly as he printed the picture. It seemed there was a cat in every movie and every story that involved witchcraft, though the only movie he could recall offhand was *Bell, Book, and Candle*, probably because he had long been a fan of the enchanting Kim Novak.

Cats were believed to embody demons that performed the witch's tasks. Roshan remembered a scene in the movie where Kim Novak held her Siamese cat in her arms while humming an incantation to make James Stewart fall in love with her, though he couldn't recall the cat's name. Py-something. According to the movie, witches lost their powers when they fell in love. He wondered absently if there was any truth to that.

Reading on, he learned that it was believed a witch could take on the form of a cat nine times.

A section on witches' familiars proved interesting. Such animals were usually cats, ferrets, dogs, or birds. A subsection talked about animals. It was believed that if a dog growled at an empty space, it meant a ghost was present. In Persia, dogs were associated with black magick and were believed to cause illness. Anyone who owned a dog could be accused of witchcraft. The ancient Egyptians believed that cats had souls. It was hypothesized that burying a rooster at the junction of three streams or at a crossroads would avert evil.

He looked at the date of Brenna Flanagan's death and felt an odd shiver run down his spine. All Hallow's Eve, 1692, the same night he was born, the night when the veil between good and evil, past and present, was said to be the thinnest.

He stared at her image until he felt the subtle shift in the air that signaled the coming of a new day, a faint tingling sensation that spread through every fiber of his body, warning him of the sun's rising. It was a feeling he had experienced every night for almost three hundred years, a warning that it was time to seek his resting place.

He glanced toward the window, which was already growing light.

Today would be his last day.

Today, he would put an end to his cursed existence.

He would leave the protection of his house and watch the sun climb over the distant foothills. He would walk in the light of a new day one last time, feel its golden heat warm his preternaturally cool flesh until the near-forgotten pleasure turned to pain and it destroyed him. Like Brenna, he would meet his end in flames. It would, he thought, be a fitting introduction to the fires of an unforgiving hell that surely awaited him.

Rising, he put the book aside and walked out the front door. Descending the steps, he glanced over his shoulder for a last look at the house where he had lived for the last half-century. It was a big old house, with huge rooms and vaulted ceilings. It was his favorite of all the places he had occupied in his long existence.

Turning toward the east, he lifted his gaze toward the horizon, watching in awe as the rising sun painted the heavenly blue canvas with brilliant slashes of pink and lavender and ochre.

It seemed fitting that his last sunrise should be the most beautiful one he had ever seen.

CHAPTER 2

The beauty of the sunrise was quickly forgotten as the sun's blinding light scorched his eyes and blistered his skin. The pain was far worse than anything he had anticipated, and he cried out in agony as his clothing began to smoke and his skin to burn.

He closed his eyes and Brenna Flanagan's image appeared before him. He groaned low in this throat, knowing this was how she must have felt when the flames began to lick her tender flesh.

"Brenna!" Her name was an anguished cry on his lips, a plea, a prayer.

He clenched his hands into tight fists. What madness was this? He couldn't destroy himself, not now. He didn't care what happened to the house or its furnishings, but he had made no provisions for the disposal of his library. He didn't want his collection sold at auction, or worse, sold for a few paltry dollars at a yard sale. He had spent centuries gathering his collection. It must go to a museum where it would be appreciated, where it could be shared with others who would recognize its worth.

And what of Brenna Flanagan? How would he rest in peace when there was still more to learn about her? He had barely scratched the surface. He wanted to find out more about her, wanted to know everything there was to know.

Hastening back into the house, he slammed the door against the glaring brightness of a new day.

He stood in the entryway a moment and then, with a strangled cry, he dropped to his hands and knees. Head hanging, panting heavily, he crawled down the hallway toward the narrow door that led to his lair. Made of the same wood and design as the wall, the door was less than three feet high. Its size and design made it almost impossible to find unless one knew where to look. It led down to a rectangular-shaped room he had built underground. One wall of his lair shared a wall with the basement. Another wall had a door in it that opened into a wall of earth. It was Roshan's bolt-hole. He could easily make his way up through the earth to the surface should the need arise.

Weakened by the rising sun and the excruciating pain that engulfed him, he hit the small lever that opened the hidden door and then, letting himself go limp, he rolled down the long, winding staircase until, with a gasp, he came to an abrupt halt at the bottom.

He lay there, too weak to move any farther. It took the last of his preternatural power to close and lock the door at the head of the stairs and then, with a low groan, he closed his eyes and surrendered to the darkness that dragged him down into blessed oblivion.

* * *

He rose with the setting sun, the burns from the day before nearly healed by the restorative powers of the Dark Sleep.

For the next two weeks, Roshan spent every waking moment searching for more information on the woman in the photograph. Brenna Flanagan. He haunted every library and museum within a thousand miles, scoured every search engine on the Web, saving every scrap of information that he found, though the available facts were pitifully few.

No one knew for sure where she had been born but it was presumed she had been born in Ireland. She had never married. It was said that she had never known love, that she had lived a solitary life and died a maiden, untouched by the hand of man.

"Who were you, Brenna Flanagan?" he wondered aloud. "Why did you live such a lonely life?"

Now, sitting in his favorite high-backed chair in front of the fireplace, Roshan was overcome with grief that one so young and lovely had met such a horrible fate. He stared at the flames crackling in the hearth, remembering how the sun's heat had scorched his own flesh. Her agony, endured to the point of death, would have lasted far longer and been infinitely worse.

Leaning forward, he braced his elbows on his knees and laced his fingers together. Like it or not, impossible or not, he was becoming obsessed with the need to see her, to know her. He was a supernatural creature, capable of feats beyond the powers and abilities of mere humans. He could change his shape. He could move faster than the human eye could follow. He had the strength of twenty mortal men. He could, simply by closing his eyes and willing it so, transport himself from one place to another, no matter what the distance.

"If I can transport myself across the world, why not into the past?" he mused aloud. Her past, of course. And if it was possible, would his going back in time change the future in any way?

He found the idea of time travel fascinating and he bought every book of fiction and non-fiction that he could find on the subject, and over the course of the next week and a half he read them all.

According to Einstein, space was curved, time was relative, and time travel was possible.

Stephen Hawking conjectured that the laws of physics disallowed the possibility of a time machine. One of his arguments was that, since we were not overrun with thousands of time travelers from the future, time travel was impossible.

Carl Sagan had several interesting ideas on the subject. His first was that it might be possible to build a time machine that could travel into the future, but not into the past. His second theory was that it might be possible to travel into the past, but that the farther back in time you went, the more expensive it got, and that the prohibitive cost had, thus far, prevented time travelers from making it back to the twenty-first century. Sagan's third idea was that time travel might be possible but you could only travel back to the time when a time machine was invented, and since we hadn't invented one yet, time travelers couldn't reach us.

Sagan went on to speculate that time travelers were already here, only we couldn't see them because they had invisibility cloaks, or that they were here and people did see them, only they were called something else, like ghosts or goblins or aliens. Sagan also mentioned the possibility that time travel was perfectly possible but would require a tremendous advance in our technology and that civilization would destroy itself before time travel was invented.

There was talk of black holes and white holes in space, and worm holes, which, if Roshan understood what he was reading correctly, were the hypothetical theoretical connection between the two.

One book put forth the theory that the past was totally defined, meaning that everything that had already happened or was supposed to happen was set in stone and could not be changed or undone. The author went on to say that if a man traveled back in time and tried to kill his grandfather, he would not be allowed to do so, that constant mishaps would prevent him from doing away with his grandfather, thus keeping the future intact.

A second theory held that if a man went back in time and killed his grandfather, it would immediately create a new quantum universe which would, in essence, be a parallel universe where the grandfather never existed and where the grandson had never been born. The original universe would still remain.

Another theory said that a man could not travel backward to a time when he didn't exist.

Even though Roshan didn't plan to use a time machine, the more he read on the subject of time travel, the more fascinated he became. He watched a number of movies about time travel—*Kate and Leopold*, *The Time Machine*, *Contact*, which had been written by Carl Sagan, and *Somewhere in Time*. The last was by far his favorite, perhaps because the hero in the film fell in love with a woman in a photograph. Not that he was in love with

Brenna Flanagan. Vampires did not fall in love with mortals. It was the height of folly to do so. No sane vampire revealed what he was to another, not if he valued his existence.

No, he was not in love with Brenna Flanagan. He would never love again, but she had given him a new interest in life, a goal, however impossible it might be to achieve, to look forward to, and that was something he hadn't had in far too long. For that alone, he would save her life, should he be able to do so.

But before he attempted something most mortals considered impossible, he would need to be at his preternatural best, so to speak, and for that, he would need to feed.

Leaving the house, he ghosted through the darkness, a whisper of movement unseen and unheard by those he passed until he reached his favorite hunting ground in the city. As a young vampire, he had hunted among the poor and downtrodden. Hiding in doorways, lurking in shadows, he had preyed upon the dregs of humanity. But as he grew older and wiser, he left the slums behind and went hunting among the rich, the elite, those who dined at expensive restaurants and frequented exclusive clubs. They drove costly automobiles or rode in luxurious stretch limos. They lived in million-dollar houses behind high walls and electric fences and thought themselves safe from the rest of the world.

It was so easy to breach their puny mortal defenses, to probe their minds while they slept, to call them to him. Under his spell, they left their lavish chambers. Drawn by his voice, unable to resist his power, they came to him, willingly offering themselves up to him so that he might quench his insatiable thirst. The blood of the rich was ever so much sweeter than that of the poor. The skin of the wealthy smelled of soap instead of vomit, their hair was squeaky clean instead of matted with filth, their breath was sweet and clean, not sour with cheap wine.

The house he chose this night was like all the others on the street—large and well kept behind a high stone wall. He vaulted over the barrier effortlessly and made his way to the rear of the house. A middle-aged woman slept alone in a room on the ground floor. A servant perhaps. He gently probed her mind for her name, then called her to him.

Moments later, she was walking toward him, a tall, slender woman, her bare feet peeking out from beneath a blue cotton nightgown. Eyes open but unseeing, she made her way toward him.

The scent of her blood called to him; his fangs lengthened as she drew near. She offered no resistance when he drew her into his arms. Her body was warm, pliant as he bent her back over his arm.

"Do not be afraid, Monica," he whispered. "I will not hurt you."

He brushed her hair aside, stroked the smoothness of her throat with his fingertips, then lowered his head to her neck. Her sweetness filled his mouth as his fangs pierced her tender flesh. In the beginning, after he knew what he had become, he had been certain that feeding would be repugnant, had feared he would perish rather than succumb to the hunger that compelled him to such repulsive behavior. Ah, how wrong he had been!

He drank his fill, erased the memory of what had happened from her mind, and sent her back to bed.

After leaving the estate, he spent the next few hours

wandering through the deep shadows of the night, listening to the sounds that mortals never heard—the whisper of a spider spinning its web, the sighing of the earth as it turned, the sleepy moan of a tree as it stretched its branches toward the sky.

It was a beautiful thing, the night, with a life and a soul of its own. He had wandered the world by the light of the moon, marveling at the wonders of the ages—the Great Pyramid of Giza, the Sphinx, ancient castles and cathedrals and bridges built by men long turned to dust. He had seen the invention of so many modern wonders—cars and airplanes, computers and satellites, bombs capable of wiping out the whole of civilization.

So many things that, in his time, had been impossible, undreamed of, or even imagined. When he had walked the earth as a mortal man, there had been no time or thought for anything but the work of surviving from day to day. There had been sheep and cattle to tend, seed to be sown, weeds to uproot, crops to be watered and harvested. In those days, he had worked alongside his father and his two brothers, toiling from sunup until sundown to provide food for his mother and his five sisters. There had been little time for anything else, until he had met Atiyana.

He shook his musings aside, his body tingling with the familiar warning that preceded the sun's rising.

It was time to return to his lair.

Brenna Flanagan's image lingered in his mind as he prepared to take his rest. That was not particularly strange, since she had been constantly in his thoughts, but what amazed him, even in sleep, was that her image stayed with him while he was trapped in the deathlike slumber of his kind.

He had not dreamed since the night the Dark Trick had been wrought upon him. One minute he was awake, the next he was lost in forgetful darkness, and when the sun quit the sky, he woke again, instantly mindful of his surroundings.

But on this night, for the first time since he had received the Dark Gift, he dreamed. He was aware of the miracle of such a thing even as the images unfolded in his mind. He was standing outside a circle of evergreen trees. Within the grove, he saw a slender young woman with fiery red hair and deep green eyes flecked with gold. As he watched, she began a slow, sensuous dance, her only covering the waist-length hair that fell down her back and over her shoulders, shimmering like veils of crimson silk in the silvery light of the full moon. A necklace of amber and jet circled her slender throat. She lifted her face toward the heavens, her eyes shining like priceless gems. Laughter rose in her throat, a sound of such joy and exuberance that, even trapped in the Dark Sleep, it brought a smile to his lips.

He moved toward her, darkness to her light.

She stopped dancing as he approached. A large black cat padded silently out of the shadows to rub itself against her legs.

Roshan paused when he was an arm's length away. The woman's gaze met his, bold and unafraid, a small smile curving her lips.

"'Tis you," she whispered.

Startled by her words, he took another step forward, one arm outstretched. "You know me? How can that be?"

But her answer was lost to him as the Dark Sleep dragged him down, down, into oblivion.

* * *

On waking, her picture was the first thing he sought. He gazed into her eyes. Green eyes. Slightly slanted, like a cat's.

'Tis you.

He heard the sound of her voice in his head. Soft and low, with a husky quality that he found incredibly sexy.

Going into his library, he searched the shelves until he found a volume on witchcraft. It spoke of casting spells and magick. There was herbal magick, candle magick, animal magick, and elemental magick. Some magick was best worked during a particular phase of the moon. There was talk of rituals and chants, of altars that could be adorned with dried or fresh flowers, seashells, crystals, pictures, and incense. Some chants were spoken, others set to music. Reading on, he learned that the purpose of the chant was to help the witch focus on that which she desired. It also helped to build the energy needed to cast the spell. Dancing was another way to build energy. He recalled that there were those who claimed to have seen Brenna Flanagan dancing naked in the moonlight.

Another section was devoted to the tools used by witches. The Athame was a black-handled knife made of iron or steel that was used to cast a circle or invoke certain spells. Since herbs shouldn't be cut with iron or steel, witches also possessed an herb knife made of copper or silver. Of course, no witch could pursue her art without a cauldron which was used for cooking raw ingredients and creating something new. Most witches owned a special cup, made of silver, wood, or clay, for use in certain rituals. The book also mentioned pentacles, necklaces, and wands. And brooms. He'd never really imagined witches flying around on broomsticks. According to the book, brooms were used to sweep away negative energy before casting a spell.

When he came to a chapter on the signs of the moon, his curiosity was naturally aroused, for the moon, after all, played a big part in his life. According to the author, the moon was believed to create different energies that affected day-to-day life. Aries was a good time for starting things. It was believed that things begun in a Taurus moon lasted longer; things begun in Gemini were easily changed by outside influences; Cancer was a time for growth and nurturing, a time to take care of domestic needs; Leo's emphasis was on one's self; Virgo focused on health. Libra smiled on friendship and partnership; Scorpio brought an awareness of psychic power; Sagittarius favored flights of fancy and imagination; Capricorn was heavy on traditions; Aquarius was a time for breaking habits; Pisces focused on dreaming and psychic impressions.

Each day of the week was influenced not only by a planet, but colors as well. The moon ruled Monday, bringing peace and healing. The colors associated with that day were gray and silver, lavender and white. Mars ruled Tuesday with passion and courage; warlike colors of red, white, black, and gray were associated with that day. Mercury influenced Wednesdays, bringing an inclination for study and travel; its colors were mild—peach and yellow, white and brown. Jupiter ruled on Thursday, leaning toward expansion and prosperity; Thursday's colors were lush—turquoise and white, green and violet. Friday belonged to Venus and curried love, beauty, and friendship. Colors associated with Friday were muted—rose and pink, peach and white.

He snorted softly. If he recalled aright, he had been

born on a Friday just before midnight. How did one associate love and beauty and the colors of roses with a man who stalked the shadows of the night, preying upon the lives of others? And surely any color associated with a vampire's life should be the deep dark red of blood.

With a shake of his head, Roshan continued reading. Saturday was ruled by Saturn, leaning toward longevity, home, and endings. Saturday's colors were dark—indigo and brown, blue and gray. Sunday was, of course, ruled by the sun, bringing healing and spirituality, strength and protection. Sunday's colors were benevolent—gold and orange, peach and yellow.

He thumbed through the rest of the book, reading the names of witches known in history and legend. Hecate, the Green Goddess of witches. Hecate was worshipped at the dark of the moon at places where three roads came together. It was said that she had three heads—horse, serpent, and dog—and thus she was able to see in three directions at once.

Morgan Le Fey, said to be a student of Merlin the magician. Nimue, also known as the Lady of the Lake. Circe, who lived on a magical isle in the midst of the sea. Medea, the goddess of snakes. Then there was a fifteenth-century Yorkshire witch known as Mother Shipton. It was said she possessed the power to heal and cast spells. He thought it interesting that she had also been a seer who had seen modern-day inventions such as airplanes and cars. Anne Boleyn, second wife of Henry VIII, had been suspected of being a witch because she had a sixth finger on one hand.

Caught up in the subject, he read further. Elisabeth Sawyer, who had been known as the Witch of Edmonton, had been accused of casting spells on her neighbors' children and on her neighbors' cattle because they refused to buy her brooms. At last, he thought with a wry grin, a witch with a broom. When Elisabeth, under duress, confessed to being a witch, she was hanged.

Another chapter dealt with spells. A sachet bag filled with rosemary, thyme, and sage was believed to be effective in attracting love. There was also a money-making charm. For this spell, a witch cut twelve pieces of paper into the size of banknotes. The paper was then to be put into a box, with thyme sprinkled between each piece. The box was to be tied with green string in thirty-one knots and buried no more than seven inches deep. If done properly, the box would contain real money when it was dug up exactly one year later.

He read that wood taken from an alder tree was used to summon spirits from the other world. Sitting back, he thought about that. Perhaps he could find a witch who could summon Brenna Flanagan's essence, but then, he wanted more than her spirit.

Closing the book, he thought of his own witch woman. Brenna Flanagan. Even her name appealed to him. He murmured it aloud, liking the way it felt on his tongue.

It was time.

Retrieving the picture he had printed earlier, he left the house.

Standing in the backyard, her likeness clutched in his hand, he let the night enfold him, its blackness drawn to the blackness within his soul, hiding him from the rest of the world.

He stared at her image, his gaze focused on her face as he chanted her name over and over again, and all the while he imagined himself spinning backward through time, each breath, each passing moment, drawing him away from the world he knew and closer to hers.

In the space of a heartbeat, thought became reality and desire became destiny. He was traveling through a long black tunnel. He saw the years falling away, the centuries receding as the modern world passed into the murky clouds of the past.

The twentieth century, fraught with wars and rumors of wars, with inventions people in his time had never dreamed of—televisions, computers, compact disc players, microwave ovens, jet planes, cell phones, frozen foods, penicillin, the Tommy gun, and the atomic bomb.

The nineteenth century had introduced the world to the steam locomotive, the printing press, typewriters and telephones, elevators and bicycles, Coca Cola, sewing machines and machine guns, and the Civil War.

The eighteenth century saw the creation of the piano, the steamboat, and the cotton gin, the fire extinguisher and sextant, submarines and parachutes, and the French Revolution.

The seventeenth century gave the world the air pump, the telescope, pocket watches and pressure cookers, Dom Perignon champagne, and the Salem Witch Trials.

He closed his eyes as he felt an abrupt cessation of movement, followed by a rush of dizziness.

When he opened his eyes again, his house and yard were gone and he was standing outside a circle of gnarled oak trees.

In the distance, he saw a small house with a thatched roof. A plume of gray smoke spiraled from the chimney. Yellow candlelight flickered in the window.

But it was the woman dancing in the moonlight who

caught and held his gaze. A woman with fiery red hair and knowing green eyes. A woman who was naked save for the shimmering veil of her hair and a necklace of amber and jet.

He stared at her for stretched seconds, unable to believe his eyes. She was more beautiful than any artist could paint. Her skin was unblemished by mole or scar, her slender figure perfectly formed. Dancing within a circle of white candles, she moved with a lithe grace that carried an air of unconscious sensuality combined with the innocence of a woman who had not known a man's touch. Moonlight combined with candlelight to bathe her in a halo of silver. Her hair fell over her shoulders and down her back like a river of molten red silk.

Captivated, he could only stand there, watching as she lifted her arms toward the heavens, then spun in a graceful circle, chanting, "Light of night, hear my song, bring to me my love, ere long."

Her voice wrapped around him, warm and mesmerizing with the same low husky quality he had heard in his mind while he slept, a sound that reminded him of firelight playing over velvet on a winter night.

"Brenna." Her name whispered past his lips, and with it a rush of desire the likes of which he had never known.

At the sound of her name, Brenna stopped dancing. In an instant, she whirled in his direction, her gaze searching the deep shadows of the night.

"Who is it?" She took a step forward, unconcerned by her nudity. "John Linder, is that you? Show yourself if you dare."

She waited a moment, but heard nothing. Deciding

she must have imagined it, she was about to turn away when she saw a bit of movement between one tree and the next. A chill ran down her spine as a dark shape separated itself from the shadows.

Her first thought was that she had somehow summoned the devil himself, for the creature walking toward her seemed to be a part of the very night that surrounded her. He was tall and lean with powerful shoulders and long limbs. His hair was as black as the inside of her kettle. Even in the dark she could see that his eyes were a bold midnight blue set beneath straight black brows. His skin was pale, though not sickly looking. More like that of a healthy man who spent little time in the sun.

She shivered as his bold gaze met hers. "Who are you?" she demanded. "What are you doing lurking in the shadows in the wee hours of the night?"

"I've come to see you, Brenna Flanagan."

His voice was soft yet compelling. The sound of it sent another shiver through her. "How do you know who I am?"

"I know all about you."

She lifted one delicate brow in disbelief. "How can that be, sir, since we have never met?"

He smiled faintly.

She noticed that his teeth were very white.

"Perhaps it was your magick that summoned me."

His voice, what was there about his voice that turned her thoughts down paths no unwed woman should even contemplate?

"Indeed?" She took a wary step toward him, her eyes narrowing, then widening in shocked recognition. Exclaiming, "'Tis you!" She took a hasty step backward, one hand covering her heart.

Roshan nodded. Perhaps it had not been his own powers that had brought him to this time and place. Perhaps it had been a bit of witchcraft wrought in the light of a full moon.

CHAPTER 3

She looked at him a moment more, then whirled around and ran, quick as a startled doe, into her house and slammed the heavy wooden door behind her.

Roshan stared after her a moment before following her. After traveling back five centuries to get here, he wasn't ready to let Brenna Flanagan out of his sight quite so soon.

Her cottage was set in a clearing not far from the grove. It was a small square structure built of weathered wood and stone. Smoke curled from a squat chimney. A single window was covered by a white curtain. There was a well to the left of the house.

Reaching her door, he knocked softly and waited.

There was no answer.

He knocked again, quietly cursing the supernatural restraint that kept him from entering a house without being invited by one who lived there, and prevented him from staying if he was asked to leave.

He knocked a third time, louder this time. "I know

you're in there, Brenna Flanagan. I'm not leaving, so you might as well answer me."

"What do you want?" she asked, her voice muffled by the heavy wooden door between them.

"I just want to talk to you."

"About what? Who sent you here?"

"No one sent me."

"Then what are you doing here?"

"I came to save your life."

She laughed derisively. "Then you are wasting your time, sir. As you can surely see, I am in no danger here."

"You're in more danger than you know. Why don't you let me in and I'll tell you all about it."

She was silent for a moment, thinking it over, no doubt. A full minute later, the door opened and Brenna Flanagan stood in the doorway wearing a white apron over a long gray dress. Her feet were bare.

"Come in." She took a step back, allowing him entrance to her home.

He felt a whisper of energy as he crossed the threshold into her dwelling. It was indeed a small place. The parlor in which he stood was furnished with little more than a couple of chairs and a small wooden table. A black cat was curled up in one of the chairs. Ears flattened, the cat hissed at him, its tail twitching. There were candles everywhere, most of them unlit. A fire blazed cheerfully in the small stone hearth. A black cauldron hung from an iron tripod. Herbs grew in narrow boxes on the windowsill. A broom rested beside the fireplace. Several colorful rugs covered the raw plank floor. He could see the corner of a bed through the partly open door across the room.

He looked at the fireplace again. According to what he'd read, witches who wished to keep their craft a secret often used the mantel as an altar. There were a number of baskets and jars on Brenna Flanagan's mantel, along with a cup, a bell, a pair of white candles, a censer, and a black-handled knife.

She studied him a moment before waving her hand in the direction of a ladder-back chair. "Sit down, then, and tell me how you know who I am and why you think my life is in danger."

"I am Roshan DeLongpre," he said, pulling one of the chairs from the table. "I saw your portrait in a book . . ."

"Such a thing is not possible."

Knowing he would never be able to explain it to her, he didn't try. How could he tell her he had seen her picture in a book he had read on the Internet? How did you explain a computer to someone who lived in an age of horse-drawn carriages?

"It was a portrait painted by John Linder."

Her eyes widened. "Who told you about that?"

"No one. It's as I said. I saw the painting in a book."

"I do not believe you. 'Tis impossible."

"Is it? You were wearing a white dress and"—he glanced at the cat sleeping in the chair—"you were holding a black cat on your lap."

"How could you know that?" She paced the length of the room then stopped in front of him, her eyes narrowed. "No one knows of that painting. And even if they did, why would anyone put it into a book? A book." She shook her head. "Nay, 'tis impossible. I will not believe it unless I see it for myself."

Reaching into his pocket, Roshan withdrew the picture he had printed off the Web and handed it to her.

She stared at the paper for a long moment. It was a replica of the portrait John Linder had painted, though it was much smaller in size. "What manner of wizardry is this?" she asked, her voice low and edged with fear.

He laughed. "You're the witch, not I."

Her eyes narrowed. "Who told you I was a witch?"

"No one told me. I read it in a book."

"A book? What book? Show it to me."

"I don't have it with me." Wary of leaving any trace of his visit behind, he took the picture from her hand, folded it, and returned it to his coat pocket. "What day is it?"

She frowned, obviously confused by the sudden change of topic. "'Tis the thirtieth day of October."

Roshan grunted softly. "We haven't much time then," he said, drumming his fingertips on the arm of the chair.

"What do you mean, we've not much time? Time for what?"

"To get you away from here before it's too late."

"You talk in riddles, Mr. DeLongpre. Please, speak plainly, or be gone."

"You're going to die tomorrow night, on All Hallow's Eve," he said bluntly. "Burned at the stake as a witch."

She stared at him, the blood draining from her face, and then she shook her head. "Nay, I do not believe you."

"You had better believe me," he said. "Your life depends on it."

Lifting the cat from the chair across from his, she sat down. The cat immediately curled up in her lap, starring at Roshan through unblinking yellow eyes.

"Did you ever make it rain toads?" Roshan asked.

"Who told you such nonsense?"

"Did you complain about one of your neighbor's pigs rooting in your garden?"

"You know about that, too?" she asked, her voice hardly more than a whisper.

"The man died a few days later, did he not?"

"He had a weak heart. Everyone in the village knew he was ailing."

"If I asked you to make me a potion, could you do it?"

She shrugged. "Perhaps."

"Women in Salem are being hanged for less."

She crossed her arms over her breasts. He saw the shiver she tried to hide.

Roshan grunted softly. Finally, he had said something that made her stop and think. Witch hunts had been running rampant in Salem, and all because of a bizarre set of circumstances that began when a young girl began acting strangely. She ran aimlessly through the house, hid under the furniture, and complained of having a fever. It was unfortunate that young Betty Paris's symptoms seemed to mirror those described in a popular book of the day. *Memorable Providences*, written by Cotton Mather, was about a washerwoman in Boston who had similar symptoms and was believed to be a witch. Talk of witches and witchcraft had increased when some of Betty Parris's playmates—Mary Walcott, Mercy Lewis, and Ann Putnam—started displaying the same strange behavior as Betty. When the local doctor failed to find a cure for the girls, he suggested that their illness might be supernatural instead of physical. From there, things really got out of hand. Dorcas Good, a four-year-old child, was accused of witchcraft. The child was arrested and spent four months in jail, during which time she saw her mother carried away to be hanged.

Before the hysteria was over, nineteen people had been hanged. But that had no bearing here, in this tiny village. Brenna's date with death would occur after Salem had come to its senses.

Brenna released a deep breath. "Thank you for warning me," she said, a distinct tremor in her voice. And then she frowned. "Are *you* a wizard?"

"No."

"Then how do you know these things?"

"It's a long story." And not one he had time to tell her now, even if he was so inclined. He could smell the dawn peeking over the horizon.

She was staring at him, her brow furrowed in thought, her eyes filling with suspicion. "Who are you?"

"I'm afraid I don't have time to explain it to you now," he said, rising. But it wasn't only the dawn's coming that urged him to leave the house. It was the nearness of the woman, the allure of her blood. It called to him, quickening his hunger, urging him to call her to him and quench his hellish thirst.

Afraid he wouldn't be able to resist the siren call of her blood, he bid her good night and hurried out of the house and into the darkness to seek his prey and a safe place to pass the hours of daylight.

Brenna stared after the stranger, puzzled by his hasty departure, troubled by his warning. Could it be true? Could her life be in danger?

She went to the window and peered out into the darkness. She would have thought him quite mad; indeed, even now she wasn't sure of his sanity. But he knew about the painting, something no one knew of save for herself and John Linder. Not only did the stranger know about the portrait, but he had somehow copied it onto a piece of paper that was whiter and finer than any she had ever seen.

Who was he?

Where had he come from?

How had he found her?

How did a portrait known to no one save herself and the artist find its way into a book, and how did the stranger have a copy?

She moved through her house, dropping the crossbar in place on the door, shutting the single window, snuffing the candles.

Meowing softly, Morgana jumped up onto the bed, circled four times, and curled up on the pillow.

Undressing, Brenna pulled on the shift she slept in and crawled under the covers.

Usually, she had no trouble at all falling asleep but every time she closed her eyes, she saw the stranger's image—his hair as black as hell's heart, his eyes dark and deep and mysterious. He had denied being a wizard but every instinct she possessed warned her that he was not an ordinary mortal.

After tossing and turning for an hour, she slipped out of bed and drew on her robe. A soft incantation brought the hearth fire to life. She lit a pair of white candles for protection and then filled her cauldron with water. When the water was still, she passed her hands over the bowl.

"Show me the stranger who came to my door, tell me why I feel I have seen him before; is he wizard or warlock, ghost or ghoul, show me the truth ere I act the fool."

Taking a deep breath, she peered into the bowl, her mind devoid of all thought save what she wished to see. A swirling mist feathered over the face of the water and when it settled, she saw Roshan DeLongpre's image reflected in the mirrored surface. He sat at a desk in a large room with high ceilings and white walls. He was leaning forward, staring at what looked like a small window. And even as she watched, he made some curious gestures with his hand and suddenly her image appeared on the window, and beneath her image there appeared several lines of writing that were too small for her to read.

He moved his hand again and a piece of paper emerged from a strange-looking object beside the window. And there, once again, was her portrait.

She leaned forward, her eyes narrowed, as Roshan went outside, her picture clutched in his hand. She stared at his image, thinking what a handsome creature he was, when he was suddenly enveloped in a swirling silver gray mist. And when the mist was gone, so was he.

She reeled backward, one hand pressed over her heart. "What dark magick is this?" she exclaimed softly.

Whatever it was, it was more than witchcraft, more powerful than any of the spells with which she was familiar. She could brew potions. She could cast charms. Sometimes she could even foretell the future. But to vanish from sight in a swirl of mist . . . She shook her head in astonishment.

Leaning forward, she stared into the dark surface of the water once again but it was clear now, the spell broken.

In the morning, she found it hard to accept what she had seen the night before. Mayhap she had dreamed the mysterious Roshan DeLongpre. Mayhap she had imagined the whole thing.

She tried not to think of him as she prepared her morning meal but time and again the image of his countenance appeared in her mind. She didn't know what or who he was, but he was no mere mortal, of that she was certain. And if he was not a wizard, then what was he?

He had warned her that her life was in danger. Dare she believe him? How did she know he had not been sent here to trick her in some way, to make her confess that she was, indeed, a witch? Burned at the stake. The very thought sent a shiver of dread down her spine. 'Twas a horrible way to die.

She shook the thought away. She was in no danger. Her neighbors did not fear her. Did they? Frowning, she turned to the task of making her bed. The villagers came to her when they needed help in finding an object that had been lost, or for potions to ward off the evil eye. They sought her aid in bringing rain to drought-weary crops or for charms and amulets to protect them against any number of disasters. They came to her for marriage and fertility charms, and for amulets to bring them good luck, or prosperity, or good health. They thought of her as a healer. Didn't they? She had never heard any of them call her a witch.

Troubled, she went to the well. What if the stranger was right? What if her life was in danger? She lowered the bucket and filled it with water, then returned to her house. Morgana trailed at her heels like a small black shadow.

Brow furrowed, Brenna filled a kettle with water and hung it over the fire to heat, the stranger's words echoing in her mind as she moved about her daily tasks. And all the while, she experienced a growing sense of foreboding. An omen, or merely her own anxiety fueled by a stranger's warning?

Time and again throughout the day, she went to the window looking for him, not certain if she was relieved or disappointed by his absence.

Toward midday, she went out to weed and water her gardens. Roses, violets, lavender, vervain, and rosemary were used in love potions. She grew peppermint, sage, garlic, rue, and wood sorrel for healing; mugwort, yarrow, and wormwood for divination. Juniper, mistletoe, basil, fennel, flax, rowan, and trefoil were protective herbs, and she grew these in abundance for use in sachet bags and protection wreaths.

Returning to the house, she went to her work area, where she kept her mortar and pestle, and began grinding the leaves of rosemary and lavender into a bowl, along with a handful of herbs. The love charm was for Nellie Beech's youngest son, Georgy, who was smitten with the youngest of the blacksmith's daughters.

Purring softly, Morgana brushed against Brenna's ankles, then sat at her feet while she worked. Brenna hummed softly, adding a bit of music to the charm, as well as the petals from a pink flower, pink being the color for love and affection.

Colors played a vital part in the casting of spells and preparing charms. The color green heralded fertility and prosperity; red was for passion and vigor, it was believed to increase wealth; orange increased sexual potency; blue brought peace and healing to the soul; yellow stimulated the intellect; brown was used in working magick for animals; black was for banishing illness or breaking spells. Brenna surrounded herself with the color purple to increase her own magical powers.

Late in the afternoon, John Linder came to visit. He was a tall, gangly young man with a shock of white-blond hair and sad blue eyes. John was shy to the point where it seemed almost painful for him to speak. He fancied himself in love with her; perhaps he was, but she felt only friendship for him, friendship and pity.

Today he came by on the pretense of needing a charm to cure a burn on the palm of his hand.

Smiling, she bade him enter her house.

Stuttering "Thank you," he followed her inside, removing his well-worn cap as he did so.

He sat on the chair beside the hearth, his cap clutched tightly in his lap, watching her every move as she mixed a bit of sheep's suet and the rind of an elder tree and boiled them together in a small silver pot.

When the ointment was ready, she removed it from the fire.

"How did you do that?" she asked while the ointment cooled.

Linder shrugged. "I . . . I burned it on the handle of . . . of a pan." A blush stained his cheeks. "I forgot it . . . it was . . . was hot."

Nodding, she applied a thick layer of ointment to his palm, then wrapped his hand in a strip of clean cotton cloth. "It will be gone in a day or two."

"Will I have a . . . a scar?"

"No."

Rising, he put on his cap; then, reaching into the pocket of his coat, he withdrew three brown eggs. "Th-thank you."

Taking the eggs, she placed them on the table. Those who came seeking her aid rarely paid in coin. "You are welcome, Mr. Linder."

He gaze slid away from hers. "Would you . . . ?" He cleared his throat. "Would you go . . . go walking with me . . . to . . . tonight?"

"I do not think that would be a good idea," she replied gently. The last time she had gone walking with him, he had kissed her. It was her first kiss. She thought it was probably Mr. Linder's, as well. It had been awkward and unpleasant and not something she cared to experience again.

His blush deepened. "Good day to . . . to you, then, Mistress Flanagan."

"Good day, Mr. Linder."

She stood in the doorway, watching him walk away. From time to time, in moments of weakness, she had considered marrying John Linder, not because she loved him, but because she yearned for a child, a daughter with whom she could share her gift, the way Granny O'Connell had shared her magick with Brenna when Brenna was younger. But it was only a foolish girl's foolish dream. Marriage had brought only misery and servitude to the women in her family. Early on, she had vowed that no man would rule over her.

Brenna lingered in the doorway, one hand resting on the jamb as she watched the sun sink behind the distant hills in a blaze of crimson and ochre and lavender.

She blinked and Roshan DeLongpre stood in the yard before her. Startled, she took a hasty step backward, her hand flying up in a gesture to ward off the supernatural, for surely that was what he was, to have appeared so suddenly out of nowhere. And if he wasn't a warlock, then . . .

"What manner of man are you?" she asked, disliking the faint tremor of fear underlying her tone.

He lifted one brow in wry amusement. "What manner of greeting is that, Mistress Flanagan?"

"Answer me, or be gone, sir!"

Roshan glanced over his shoulder. "Was that young Linder I saw leaving here?"

"Perhaps."

"He will not survive your death."

"What do you mean?" she asked, alarmed by his

words. Though she didn't love John Linder, she was fond of him, flattered by his infatuation, in awe of his talent.

"He's going to kill himself the day after you die."

She opened her mouth but words failed her.

"He must love you very much."

She didn't know what to say to that, and so she said nothing.

Roshan regarded her for several moments. There was always the possibility that if she simply disappeared, Linder would still throw himself off a cliff. It was a chance Roshan was prepared to take. The boy meant nothing to him. If it was John Linder's fate to commit suicide, so be it. It was Brenna Flanagan's life that concerned him. Now that he had seen her, he knew he could not let her perish.

"Who are you?" she asked at length.

"I told you. Roshan DeLongpre."

"What are you?"

He considered her question a moment, wondering if the truth would serve him better than a lie, and decided it would not.

"A friend," he replied. "I mean you no harm."

"You are no friend of mine, sir. And I believe you not." And so saying, she stepped inside and closed the door firmly behind her.

"Brenna, wait!"

"Go away! You are not welcome here!"

"Brenna, I've come here from the future."

"'Tis impossible."

"Nothing in this world is impossible," he replied. "You should know that."

"How far in the future?"

"When I left, it was the year two thousand and five."

Even through the wood of the door, he heard her gasp in disbelief. "What manner of magick brought you here?"

"I'm not sure. But here I am. And I want to take you back with me before it's too late." His own words surprised him but, once spoken, the decision was made. He had no intention of living through these primitive days again, nor did he intend to leave Brenna behind to suffer the plagues and poverty to come.

Brenna put her back to the door and closed her eyes. Dare she believe him? What if he spoke the truth? What if her life was in danger and he was the only one who could save her? With her own eyes, she had seen him in her scrying mirror, seen him conjure her portrait, a portrait no one knew existed save for herself and John Linder. Deny it though he might, Roshan DeLongpre must be a powerful sorcerer.

Dare she trust him?

No! Not now. She would not bid him enter her cottage after the setting of the sun, when a dark wizard's magick was strongest. If he could indeed travel through time, then he possessed sorcery far stronger than her own magick. And if he delved into the dark arts, as she suspected, she feared she would have no defense against him.

"Come back tomorrow," she said, "when we can speak in the light of day."

"I can't do that. We must leave this place now, tonight. Tomorrow will be too late."

"Do you think me a fool, sir, to go off with a man I do not know?"

"You know me," he said. "Why do you not trust me?"

"I know you not!" she denied vehemently.

"You recognized me when we met. You said, ''tis you.'"

Swallowing hard, she closed her eyes. It was true. She had dreamed of him one night, a dark dream filled with violence and blood and death.

His blood.

Her death.

She opened her eyes, overcome with a cold sense of dread and foreboding. If she went with him, she knew she would surely die, not at the stake, but by his hand.

Roshan paced outside her door, wondering how he could persuade her to trust him. He could not storm the house since she had withdrawn her welcome; therefore, he must somehow lure her outside.

Concentrating, he sent his thoughts winging through the night. If he could not go to her, then she must come to him. His mind touched hers and then, to his amazement, she pushed him out of her mind.

Roshan swore under his breath. In all his years as a vampire, he had never met anyone, male or female, who had the ability to shut him out. Truly, Brenna Flanagan was a most remarkable woman! And if he could not convince her that he spoke the truth, she would die before the sun rose on a new day.

"Brenna! Dammit, woman, listen to me! We have to leave this place, now!"

"Be gone from here lest I put a spell on you and turn you into a hop toad!"

He swore under his breath even as he fought back his laughter. A toad indeed!

Once again, he gathered his preternatural power around him. "Come to me, Brenna Flanagan," he called softly. "Let us walk together in the moonlight and share our thoughts and our secrets."

"Nay!" she retorted. "Be gone!"

Cursing softly, he resumed pacing back and forth in front of her cottage. What could he say to entice the woman to come out, or, better yet, to invite him inside?

How much time did they have before the mob came to drag her away?

"Brenna . . ." He frowned, overcome by a sudden urge to hop away, find a lily pad in a nice shallow stream, and catch flies. And then he laughed out loud. "It will not work, witch woman," he called loudly. "You can't turn me into a frog or a newt."

He heard a crash from inside the house and grinned as he imagined her throwing something against the wall.

"Come to me, Brenna Flanagan," he cajoled. "You know you want to."

Brenna blew out a sigh as she began to sweep up the broken crockery. Why had her spell failed? It had worked countless times before. It was a harmless spell, one that lasted only an hour or two. Why was he so handsome? Why did his voice appeal to her so? Even now, she could hear it in her mind, a deep dark voice that promised pleasure beyond compare if she would only yield her will to his.

But she could not, would not, put her life in his hands! She dared not trust this dark stranger with his hypnotic voice and fathomless midnight blue eyes. Warlock or wizard, she would not open her door to him this night!

For the next hour, he called to her, beseeching her to come to him before it was too late. And while he tried to coax her from the safety of her house, she conjured a dozen spells to send him away, her anger and frustration growing as each one failed.

Going to the window, she peered outside. She could see him, just there, pacing in the moonlight, a tall dark form that seemed to be a part of the night, a part of the darkness itself.

He moved with effortless grace, as if he walked on air instead of solid ground.

He walked in the light of the full moon and cast no shadow.

She was trying to absorb this bit of witchery when she saw flickering lights moving through the woods beyond her cottage. As the lights drew nearer, she heard the sound of voices.

Men's voices, filled with anger and laced with fear.

"Brenna, we're out of time!" And even as Roshan spoke the words, he vanished from her sight.

She drew back from the window, her heart pounding in her chest, as a man's voice demanded she show herself. A low growl rose in Morgana's throat as she rubbed against Brenna's ankles.

"Come out, witch! And bring your familiar with you!"

"Aye, come out and meet your fate, witch!"

Amid cries and curses, the men began pounding on her door. With a shriek like a woman in pain, the door exploded inward amid a flurry of splinters. Rough hands seized her and dragged her outside.

Kicking and scratching, Brenna tried to wrest free, but to no avail. Heart pounding in terror, she watched as they stripped a young tree of its branches. She screamed as they tied her to the stake and stacked the branches at her feet, along with a handful of kindling.

She glanced at the faces of the men, men she knew, men she had healed in the past. They refused to meet her gaze. In the glow of their torches, their faces looked grotesque, devilish.

She struggled against the bonds that held her as the pile of kindling grew higher. Her stomach churned with fear. Terror choked her until she could scarcely breathe.

Why hadn't she gone with Roshan? Where was he now, when she needed him? Why, oh why, hadn't she listened to him?

She cried out as the men circled her, putting their torches to the bits of wood at her feet. She stared in morbid fascination at the tiny flames that sprang up around her. Soon they would be licking at her ankles, catching at the hem of her dress. How long did it take to burn to death? She blinked the tears from her eyes. Oh, Lord, this could not be happening!

But it was. Nausea roiled in the pit of her belly. She felt lightheaded, as though she were about to faint, and then she prayed that she would faint, that she would be unconscious long before the fire consumed her.

The men clustered in front of her, all of them making signs to ward off the evil eye lest she try to cast some spell on them before death claimed her.

Heat seared her skin. Soon the flames would reach her.

She was sobbing now. Acrid smoke filled her nostrils. She cried out as the first tiny finger of flame singed her skin.

"Stop! Oh, please, stop!" She sobbed the words over and over again. It had to be a nightmare. She couldn't die like this, not here, not now.

The men stared at her, their eyes wide. One of them was chanting something. A prayer for her soul? Or some incantation to turn away evil?

She cried out in terror as the heat of the fire breathed against the backs of her legs. Soon she would feel the bite of the hungry flames against her skin. She opened her mouth to scream, felt her breath catch in her throat when she saw a dusting of silver motes shimmer in the moonlight, and suddenly Roshan DeLongpre was there, standing between her and the mob.

Power crackled in the evening air, like the sizzle in the atmosphere before a storm.

There was an abrupt silence as the men brandishing torches became aware of his presence.

"Who are you?" Henry Beech demanded boldly.

"Your worst nightmare." Roshan bit back a grin as he repeated a line he had heard in a movie.

He stared grimly at the flames slowly eating their way toward Brenna's feet and legs, shuddered as he imagined the fire moving over his own body. Preternatural flesh was especially vulnerable to fire. If he was going to save her without sacrificing himself, it had to be now.

Drawing himself up to his full height, he let out a roar; then, with preternatural speed, he was at Brenna's back, his fingers ripping through the thick ropes that bound her as if they were made of paper. Flames burned his hands, seared the skin on his forearms.

Cradling Brenna against his chest, he willed the two of them away from the smoke and the fire and the mob.

Brenna was still clinging to Roshan when the world stopped spinning. Glancing around, she saw they were deep in the heart of the woods that lay to the west of her cottage. It was a place she recognized instantly. She came here often to gather herbs and plants. She came here to celebrate the new moon. It was here that she came to cast some of her spells.

"Are you all right?" Roshan asked, setting her on her feet.

She looked up at him, her body still trembling with the aftereffects of her close brush with death. "Y-yes. I think my legs are burned a little. Are you hurt?"

He nodded. Had he been mortal, the burns would have been of no real consequence, but he was no longer mortal and the heat of the flames had blistered the skin of his legs and arms and burned the palms of his hands.

"Morgana!" she exclaimed. "They will kill her."

He shook his head in disbelief. "You're worried about a cat?"

"She is not just a cat. She is my . . . my friend."

"Your familiar, you mean."

"That, too," she replied candidly. "I cannot let them kill her."

Roshan grabbed her by the arm when she started walking back toward the cottage. "Hold on. I didn't risk going up in flames to save your life just to have you walk back into the fire."

She shook off his hand. "I am going."

"You stay here. I'll get the damn cat."

He didn't wait for her to answer. Dissolving into mist, he returned to the cottage, or what was left of it. The men had torched the house. There was nothing left of the stake but ashes.

Materializing, Roshan looked around for the cat. "Morgana," he called softly, "come to me."

A faint meow drew his attention. Following the cat's cry, he found her in a sack, hanging from a tree. Apparently the mob had decided to let the creature starve to death, if it didn't suffocate first.

Setting the sack on the ground, he debated opening it, then decided it would be quicker and safer to carry the cat back to Brenna while it was still in the sack.

The cat hissed and clawed at the inside of the sack until they reached Brenna. Dropping the sack on the ground, Roshan untied the cord that secured it.

The cat jumped out of the bag and into Brenna's arms, where it meowed loudly, no doubt complaining of its ill treatment. After a moment, it purred and licked her face.

"So, Brenna Flanagan," Roshan said, "do you believe me now?"

CHAPTER 4

Brenna blew out a deep breath. How could she doubt him now? Whoever he was, wherever he had come from, he had saved her from a horrible fate.

"How badly are you burned?" Roshan asked.

"Not too badly. What of yourself?"

"I'll be all right."

Nodding, Brenna knelt beside a large green plant with long spiky leaves. It had been a gift to her from a wandering traveler years ago. Breaking off a piece, she split the spiky leaf in half, then gently rubbed the thick jelly-like substance found on the inside of the leaf over the burns on her legs.

When she was finished, she looked up at Roshan, a question in her eyes.

He shook his head. Though painful, the burns would heal in a few days.

"It will ease the pain," she said.

Roshan frowned. It had been centuries since he had relied on any kind of human remedy.

"Do it," he said.

Lifting one singed pant leg, Brenna frowned as she began to smear the cool gel over his blistered skin. Odd, that his burns appeared to be more serious than hers when his ankles had been covered by his trousers and boots, and hers had been bare.

His trousers. She had never seen any quite like them, nor felt such material.

She couldn't help noticing that the fastening in front was most peculiar . . .

Feeling her cheeks grow hot, she quickly treated his other leg, then the skin of his forearms and his hands.

"Is that not better?" she asked, not meeting his eyes.

Roshan nodded. "Thank you."

"You . . . you . . . are welcome." She was shaking now, overcome by the realization of how close she had come to death. But for this man, she would be dead now.

"Hey," he said, drawing her into his arms. "You're all right. It's over."

She looked up at him, her body trembling uncontrollably. "You . . . you . . . saved my . . . my life. And Morgana's. I . . . thank you."

He gave her a squeeze. "Happy to help," he said lightly. But he knew he would never forget the sight of Brenna being bound to that stake, the flames licking at her ankles, the look of terror in her eyes.

He stared past her, wondering what his next move should be. He had done what he came here to do. Brenna was safe, at least for now. For a moment, he contemplated going to see his family. Tonight was the night he had been born. If he went to his father's house, would he see himself as a newborn child? Tempted as he was to go, it didn't seem wise. He looked at Brenna, wondering what the book *Ancient Myths and Legends* would say about her, now that he had changed the course of her life.

"All we need now," he remarked, "is a place for you to spend the night."

She wriggled out of his arms. "I could stay with John Linder,"

"No." He dismissed the idea out of hand. "Is there anywhere else you could go?"

But even as he asked the question, he knew he wouldn't trust anyone else to look after her. So, where could he take her where they would both be safe?

He thought about it for a moment, but there was really only one choice. "I'll take you to my place," he said, wondering if he could transport both of them into the future. "I suppose you want to take that cat."

"Yes." Brenna scooped Morgana into her arms. "Is your house nearby?"

"Not nearly close enough," he muttered.

She gasped when he wrapped her in his embrace once more. "What are you doing?"

"Taking you to my place, I hope."

"But . . ."

"Be still, girl, I need to concentrate."

Closing his eyes, he pictured his house as it had looked in the moonlight the night he had left. He focused all his energy on the house and the yard and his desire to be there, and all the while he imagined himself being propelled forward through time and space, each breath carrying him closer to home, closer to the safety of his lair.

Once again he felt himself moving through a long black tunnel, going forward in time, spinning through each century, watching humanity's achievements and failures as mankind endeavored to learn more about the world in which they lived and the people who shared it.

As he had before, he felt an abrupt cessation of movement, followed by a rush of dizziness.

When he opened his eyes, he was standing in the front yard of his residence. Brenna was clinging to him, her eyes closed, her heart pounding. The cat opened its eyes and hissed at him, then bounded out of Brenna's grasp.

"Brenna?"

Slowly, she opened her eyes. Slowly, she looked around. "What happened? Where are we? I saw things . . ." She shook her head, her eyes filled with confusion and doubt.

"Welcome to the future, Brenna Flanagan."

She stared at him in disbelief, and then she fainted.

With a shake of his head, Roshan carried her up the porch steps, the cat trailing at his heels, hissing all the while.

A thought opened the carved front door and he carried Brenna into the house, up the winding staircase, and down the hallway to the only bedroom that was furnished. It was a large room, with a marble fireplace in one corner. There were windows on three sides. They were covered with heavy dark blue draperies. The bed was a huge old four-poster covered with a patchwork quilt in shades of blue and brown and gray. He kept his T-shirts, socks, and briefs in the dresser across from the bed; his pants, shirts, and coats hung in the closet; his shoes were on the floor. A sitting room adjoined the bedroom. The bathroom was accessible from the hallway or the bedroom.

Turning back the covers on the bed, he lowered Brenna onto the mattress.

Meowing loudly, Morgana jumped up on the bed, circled twice, and curled up beside her mistress, her unblinking gaze focused on Roshan, a low growl rumbling in her throat.

Roshan lifted one brow as he scowled at the cat. You could fool people, but you couldn't fool animals. They knew him for what he was.

Brenna woke a moment later, her eyes wide and a little scared as she glanced around the room, noting the windows and the window seat, the high ceilings, the striped paper on the walls.

"Where am I?"

"My bedroom."

She glanced around the room again. She could have put her whole cottage inside and had space left over.

And then his words sank in. "Your bedroom!" she exclaimed. She was out of the bed and headed for the door before she finished speaking.

She skidded to a halt, a wordless cry erupting from her lips when she reached the door and found Roshan standing there, his arms folded over his chest.

"Calm down, Brenna."

She backed away from him and kept backing up until she bumped against the edge of the bed. "Who are you?"

"I mean you no harm."

"Who are you?" she repeated.

He took a step toward her, one hand outstretched.

Fear for her life made her reckless. She wasn't certain her magick would be effective when she felt so panicky. Hurried spells had backfired on her in the past, but it was a risk she was willing to take. Summoning her fear and the anger generated by it, Brenna pointed her finger in Roshan's direction, and muttered a hurried incantation.

Morgana hissed, the hairs raising along her back.

Roshan swore a vile oath as Brenna's spell slammed into him, driving him backward. He grunted as his shoulder struck the doorjamb. Her power sizzled over his skin, momentarily holding him in place. And then he was striding toward her again.

Brenna gasped. Any mortal man would have been rendered unconscious by her incantation. Before she could call forth the power necessary to try again, he was on her.

He glared down at her, his hands imprisoning her arms at her sides.

"Don't do that again." He bit off each word.

"Let me go."

He shook her until her teeth rattled. "Dammit, woman, I'm not going to hurt you."

She glanced pointedly at his hands gripping her arms, his fingers digging into her flesh.

He relaxed his hold ever so slightly but he didn't let her go.

She stared up at him, her jaw jutting out, refusing to give an inch even though he knew she was scared. The scent of her fear, mingled with the underlying scent of her blood, inflamed his hunger. His gaze slid down, over the smooth skin of her neck, lower still, to the rise and fall of her breasts.

Her eyes widened, her breath quickening under his regard. "Let me go." It wasn't a demand now, but a plea.

"Brenna . . ."

"Please."

Taking a deep breath, he closed his eyes lest she see the hunger lurking in their depths. He didn't want to frighten her more than she already was. He felt the prick of his fangs against his tongue, knew he was perilously close to not only losing control of his desire but control over the beast within him as well.

It had been a mistake to bring her here.

With a low growl, he shoved her away from him, jerked open the door, and stalked out of the room without a backward glance. The sound of the lock turning echoed loudly in his ears.

The house was too small to contain the wealth of emotions fomenting within him. He needed to go out, to put some distance between himself and Brenna Flanagan, but he knew himself too well, knew that if he went out now, he might not be able to control his hunger, and when he was out of control, people died.

Muttering a vile oath, he paced the length of the long hall between the living room and the back of the house. The hunger rose within him, overpowering every other thought, every other need as it clawed at his vitals, clouding his vision with a blood-red haze.

He didn't have to go out. There was fresh prey upstairs. A mortal woman from another century. He could take her at his will, savor each drop as he drained her of blood and life. He could easily dispose of her body. She had no one to mourn her, no one to miss her.

Ah, he thought. There was the rub, because he would miss her, his little witch.

What was there about Brenna Flanagan that drew him so? But for her, he would be naught but ancient ash by now, his remains scattered by an uncaring wind. One look at her portrait and he had been captivated. On the brink of seeking death, he had known he couldn't end his existence until he knew more about her. No matter what the cost, he'd had to find her.

He slammed his fist into the wall in an effort to diffuse his rage. He had traveled through time to save her from a horrible death. And was she grateful? No! She was afraid of him, had locked the door against him. Foolish woman! As if a lock and some puny slab of oak could keep him out!

He laughed, the harsh, bitter sound echoing off the walls in the quiet house. She should be afraid. Her very life was in his hands.

With an oath, he turned and headed for the staircase, only to pause halfway up. He stared up at the landing, his preternatural senses bringing him the scent of her blood, the rapid beating of her heart, the stink of fear that clung to her skin.

His hands curled into tight fists as he fought against the urge to break down the door she had locked against him even as the hunger whispered in his ear.

Sweet, it whispered. *She'll be all the sweeter for the fear running in her veins. You know you want her. Take her! She's yours, yours for the taking.*

"No!" He roared the word as he turned on his heel, grabbed a long black cloak, and bolted from the house.

Someone would die this night, but it would not be Brenna Flanagan.

Driven by the urgent need to hunt, he prowled the dark streets, his body quivering with the insatiable hunger that drove him relentlessly. He had been a vampire for two hundred and eighty-six years and in all that time he had been unable to completely subdue the beast within him. Try as he might to fight it, sooner or later his hellish hunger prevailed, overcoming whatever shred of self-restraint he had thought he'd gained, proving to him yet again that he was still a slave to the dark hunger that dwelled within him.

Knowing he was near the breaking point, he fled the city and headed toward the dark underbelly of the town where the drug lords and the pimps plied their trade. Every city had such a place, an area where the city's less favorable citizens banded together. Though Roshan usually preferred hunting in more pleasant surroundings, it was here that he came when his tenuous control shattered and the hunger would not be denied. Death was not unknown here. It often came swiftly in the ongoing struggle for power.

The sound of angry whispers drew Roshan's attention. Pausing, he lifted his head and sniffed the air, his nostrils filling with the scent of greed and whiskey.

There. Down the alley across the street.

His cloak billowed behind him like the shadow of death as he followed the scent of his prey, his whole body vibrating with a need that would no longer be denied.

Brenna pressed one ear to the door, listening for some sound that would tell her Roshan's whereabouts. At first, she heard nothing, and then she heard the slam of a door. She knew immediately that he had left the house and the slamming of the door had nothing to do with that knowledge. She felt a sudden void in the house and knew he was gone. The fact that she could be so aware of his absence frightened her in a way nothing else had.

For what seemed like the hundredth time, she found herself wondering who he was. What he was. He was no mortal man, of that she was sure. But if he wasn't mortal, what was he? She had grown up on tales of otherworldly creatures. Granny O'Connell had believed in all manner of supernatural beings—fairies and trolls, gnomes and goblins, werewolves and vampires, and a host of other frightening folk. Brenna had refused to believe in such beings. If they existed, where were they? Why had she never seen one? But Granny had believed and often posed the question, "If there be witches and warlocks, why not werewolves or other fey folk? 'Tis only another form of magick, after all."

Except for her own mother and her maternal grandmother, Brenna had never encountered any other magical or mystical folk. She didn't know what manner of creature Roshan DeLongpre might be but she knew, in the deepest part of her soul, that he was like no other man she had ever met.

Biting down on the inside of her lower lip, she pondered the wisdom of venturing outside his bedroom. She glanced over her shoulder and a sigh shuddered through her. His bedroom. His bed. What did he intend to do with her? Why had he brought her here? He didn't even know her. Why had he traveled through time to find her?

So many troubling questions—questions for which she had no answers.

One thing she knew, she could not stay here, in his house, in his bedroom.

Muttering, "Come, Morgana," she unlocked the door. After looking up and down the hallway, she hurried down the stairs, out of the house, and down the long road that led to a huge, elaborately carved wrought iron gate set in a high stone wall. She wasn't surprised to find that the gate was locked.

Lifting the hem of her dress to keep it out of the damp grass, Brenna followed the high stone wall, looking for another way out. Morgana trailed at her heels, meowing softly.

Brenna had never seen such a vast holding in her whole life. The house, bigger by far than any she had ever seen, seemed dwarfed by the grounds that surrounded it. There were trees and bushes everywhere. In the back of the house, she found a maze and strange trees cut in the shapes of animals both real and mythical.

She wasn't sure how much time had passed before she made her way back to the front of the house. She stared at the gate, wondering what magick she could use to open it. Calling Morgana, she held the cat in her arms while she tried a simple revocation spell, and then a nullification spell, but to no avail. Brenna tapped one foot on the ground, then frowned as a horrible thought crossed her mind. Was it possible that her magick was of no effect in this new time and place? That couldn't be it. Her magick had worked against him earlier. Had he used some magick of his own to thwart her escape? Perhaps she needed her wand to help her focus?

One thing was for certain. She did not want to be here when he returned. She glanced around, hoping to find a place to hide. If she ducked behind the bushes beside the gates, she might be able to sneak through, unnoticed, when he returned, yet even as the thought crossed her mind, she knew it wouldn't work.

Feeling pressure on her bladder, she glanced around the yard, wondering where the privy was. She didn't remember seeing one in the backyard, but surely in such a house as grand as this, some provision had been made! Putting Morgana down, she circled the house a second time until, unable to hold it any longer, she went behind a bush. Morgana followed, staring at her through wide yellow eyes.

Putting her clothes to rights again, Brenna picked up the cat and made her way back to the front of the house. When she put Morgana down, the cat immediately ran off into the shadows, no doubt in search of prey. She was a fearless hunter, and the bane of the birds, mice, and rabbits back home.

"Morgana, come back here! Morgana!" Brenna started after the cat and then, with a shrug, she went inside, leaving the front door open a little so the cat could get in when she was ready.

With nothing else to do, Brenna explored the rooms on the first floor of the house. The place was like nothing she had ever seen before, and not just because it was such a large house, but because of all the strange things it held, things for which she had no name. Things she was reluctant to touch for fear Roshan might return and be angry at finding her wandering through his grand manor. Of course, if he didn't want her poking around, he shouldn't have brought her here in the first place, or left her to fend for herself!

One room had numerous cupboards. There was a small round table and two chairs. It must be the kitchen, she thought, though it looked like no kitchen she had ever seen before. Feeling as though she was snooping, which she supposed she was, she opened the cupboards. All were bare. Perhaps, in this strange new world, people kept their food somewhere else.

She peeked into several other rooms—a parlor, a library with bookshelves that lined three walls from floor to ceiling, a room that was empty save for more bookshelves. He had more books than she had ever dreamed existed. She wondered why he had so many. Surely he could not have read them all!

And then she came upon the room she had seen in her scrying mirror. There, on a large desk, was the peculiar square window where she had seen her image. Only the window was black now. Was he a wizard, then? Did the strange dark glass act the same way as her scrying mirror? Moving closer, she peered at it intently, but she felt no power radiating from it, no whisper of magical energy.

Making her way up the stairs, she moved from room to room. She assumed they were bedchambers, though it was hard to say since all were empty of anything except more floor-to-ceiling bookcases and large comfortable chairs. The only furnished bedroom was the one that was his.

So. She had nowhere to go and no place to hide. No weapons with which to fight him save her magick. And that, she knew, would not be strong enough. How could she fight him if she couldn't even remove something as simple as a spell on a gate?

Returning to his room, she turned the key in the lock, then climbed into the bed, fully clothed except for her shoes. She drew the covers up to her chin and closed her eyes, but as soon as she did so, her mind filled with images of men with torches surrounding her. Men from families she had known all her life. Their faces looked grotesque in the light cast by their torches as they set fire to the kindling at her feet. The smoke stung her nostrils. The flames licked her skin. If Roshan hadn't arrived when he had, she would have died in the flames . . .

She opened her eyes and the images faded from her mind.

She was still awake when he returned to the house. Though she heard no sound, she knew the moment he entered the dwelling. Sitting up in the bed—his bed—she stared at the door. The door that she had locked against him.

The door that now swung open, revealing Roshan standing in the corridor. He loomed in the doorway, a tall dark shape swathed in a long black cloak that fell to his ankles.

Clutching the blankets to her chest, she cringed against the headboard as he walked into the room. There was a ruddy glow to his skin that had not been there before.

"And so," he said quietly. "You are still here."

She glared at him. "I would not be here if you had not locked the gate against me."

He regarded her for a long moment. His steady gaze made her uncomfortable but she refused to look away. Silently defiant, she squared her shoulders and lifted her chin.

He grinned, his expression clearly telling her that he knew she was afraid.

"I want to go home," she said. "Back to my own time." It annoyed her that she sounded like a little girl frightened of the dark.

"Is that right? Anxious to go back to the stake, are you?"

She shuddered at the memory she had been visualizing only moments earlier. "Of course not. I shall go somewhere else, to another town, someplace where no one knows who I am." She didn't want to stay here, where everything was strange. Didn't want to stay here, with him. He frightened her in ways she did not understand.

She recoiled when he sat down on the foot of the bed.

"Dammit, stop that," he said irritably. "I'm not going to hurt you."

"I do not believe you. Why did you seek me out? Why did you bring me here?"

"Because I want you."

A maiden she might be, but she recognized the heat in his eyes, the longing in his voice. Ah, his voice, as dark as midnight, as deep as eternity. It reminded her of Granny O'Connell's homemade whiskey, warming her from the inside out.

"You saved my life," he said in that same whiskey smooth voice.

His words startled her so that, for a moment, she forgot to be afraid. "How did I do that?"

"I was on the verge of ending my existence," he said. "I felt I had nothing to live for, no reason to go on. And then I saw your picture . . ."

"In that book you told me about?"

He nodded, thinking he would have to find that book and see what it said about Brenna now. "I saw your picture and I wanted to know more about you. Learning about you gave me something to look forward to when I rose. And then I began to wonder if there wasn't a way for me to find you. I read dozens of books about traveling through time. I wondered if it was possible and then I decided to try it." He shook his head. "I wasn't really sure it would work, but I pictured you in my mind and"—he shrugged—"suddenly I was in that field watching you dance."

She felt a rush of warmth flood her cheeks. He had seen her dancing under the full moon, naked.

"Oh!" She blushed hotter as she remembered the

words she had been chanting at the time. *Light of night, hear my song, bring to me my love, ere long.*

She had dreamed of this man, had been thinking of him that night as she cast her spell. *Bring to me my love, ere long.* Oh, my. Was it possible that her spell had conjured him, that he was, indeed, her true love?

She shook her head. It couldn't be, yet how else to explain it? Somehow, across time and space, her magick had connected with his to bring the two of them together.

CHAPTER 5

"Who are you?" she asked, her voice little more than a whisper.

Roshan leaned toward Brenna, his gaze holding hers. It was a question she had asked several times before, one he had refused to answer. "Do you really want to know?"

She nodded, her hands clutching the covers so tightly her knuckles were white. He could hear the rapid beat of her heart, smell her fear.

He took a deep breath. No mortal who had learned his secret had ever lived long enough to tell the tale to another. Dare he trust her? He considered it a moment longer and then said, matter-of-factly, "I'm a vampire."

She stared at him, all the color draining from her face. "Granny O'Connell was right," she murmured.

"Right about what?"

"Everything. She was a witch. It was she who taught me my craft. When I was very little, she told me fairy tales. And when I said there were no such things as werewolves or trolls, she told me that if there could be witches, there could be elves and fairies and all manner of fey folk, as well. I guess she was right."

He nodded.

"Are you going to . . . ?" She lifted a trembling hand to her neck.

He followed the movement of her hand, felt his hunger quicken at the sight of the pulse throbbing in the hollow of her throat. "I don't know." He lifted one brow. "Would you mind?"

It was a foolish question. Her eyes widened, and although he would have said it was impossible, she recoiled from him still farther, her back pressed tight against the headboard.

"Brenna, listen to me. I won't hurt you. I won't do anything you don't want me to do."

"You promise?"

"Yes." He grinned. "And now you're wondering if you can trust the word of a vampire."

She nodded, her deep green eyes filled with doubt and suspicion.

He shook his head. "If I wanted to kill you, why would I have bothered to save you from the flames? Or brought you here?"

"A midnight meal?"

He stared at her a moment, and then he laughed, genuinely amused.

"A fine idea," he agreed, "but as I said, I won't do anything you don't want me to do."

She considered that for several moments. Some of the fear faded from her eyes.

"Are you really a vampire?"

"Shall I prove it to you?"

Brenna shook her head vigorously. "I will take your word for it. How long have you been a vampire?"

"Two hundred and eighty-six years." It was not a vast age, for a vampire. He knew of others who were far older. Still, compared to the few years of a mortal life span, it was a great age indeed.

"How did it happen?"

He grinned faintly at the memory. "A woman, of course. She was beautiful and beguiling, and I was ripe for the taking." He had still been mourning the death of his wife and child at the time. Even though three years had passed since Atiyana had died delivering their son, he had mourned her as if she had been dead for three days instead of three years. But he was still a man, with a man's needs and a man's desires. "She seduced me late one night and then, before I knew what was happening, she worked the Dark Trick and when I woke the next night, I was a newly made vampire."

"Did it not frighten you, being a vampire?"

"At first. She didn't bother to tell me what to expect, she just brought me across and then left me. I didn't realize anything had happened until I woke that night and saw the world as I had never seen it before."

"What do you mean? How was it different?"

"Everything looked . . ." He paused, wondering how to explain it. "Colors were brighter, more vivid. I saw everything in great detail, each thread in my coat, each blade of grass, each leaf on a tree, each drop of water that flowed through the river. But it wasn't only my sight that was changed. I could hear people's thoughts and sounds that I'd never heard before." He licked his lips. "The beating of a thousand hearts calling to me."

He remembered that it had taken him months to learn how to shut out the unwanted noises, the cacophony of voices he did not want to hear.

"Daylight was forever lost to me," he went on, "and I

became a creature of darkness, prowling the night." Endlessly searching for prey, the sound of beating hearts a siren call he could neither resist nor ignore. In those early days, he had hunted relentlessly, certain he would never be able to drink enough to quench his awful thirst.

"And you drank . . . blood to survive?"

He nodded.

A look of revulsion flitted across her face. "How could you? Did it not make you sick?"

He blew out a heavy sigh. "I thought it would. But it didn't." To the contrary, the elixir of life was warm and sweet and rich. In the beginning, every time he drank, he craved it more. Even after he had just drunk his fill, he was already looking forward to the next hunt, the next victim, always afraid that the last taste was truly the last.

"Do you sleep here, in this bed?"

"No."

She shivered, as with a chill, and clutched the blanket closer. "It is true, then, that you sleep in your coffin?"

"I did, in the beginning." He had hated sleeping in that long square box, but he had done it to punish himself to atone for what he had become, for what he had to do to survive. After twenty years or so, he had dragged the damn thing outside and set it on fire, and then he'd bought a king-size bed with a firm mattress, silk sheets, and a feather pillow. If he had to spend the daylight hours sleeping the sleep of the undead, at least he would do so in comfort!

"And now?" she asked curiously.

"I think a bed is far more comfortable."

"But not this bed?" She frowned. "Where do you sleep, then?"

"There is no need for you to know." He had already told her far too much, he thought. Years ago, he had foolishly told a woman where he slept. She had claimed to love him, promised she would never betray him, and though he had not truly loved her, he had been desperate for companionship, so desperate that when she insisted it would prove he loved her in return if he told her where he slept, he had done so. The next day she had come with her father and her two brothers to destroy him, unaware of the fact that he could emerge from the Dark Sleep when his preternatural senses warned him that his life was in danger. He had killed them all and fled the town. Never again had he told another where he took his rest.

"Are you truly immortal?"

"No. Those who are immortal can't be killed."

He watched her absorb that bit of information, saw the questions rise in her eyes.

"Yes," he said, "vampires can be killed in a number of ways."

"Truly? There are other ways, then, besides a stake through the heart?"

"Several."

She shuddered and drew the covers up to her chin. "I do not want to know what they are."

"I wasn't going to tell you," he said with a wry grin.

"So," she said, nettled by his admission, "now it is *you* who do not trust *me*."

He smiled and she smiled back. Warmth flowed between them, the first flowering of friendship mixed with a wave of unmistakable attraction and desire.

He recalled the night he had first seen her, dancing naked in the moonlight. He had wanted her then; he wanted her now. But he would have to go slow. She was young and innocent, and there was no need to hurry.

Her cheeks turned pink with awareness and her gaze slid away from his.

He settled back, resting his shoulder against one of the bedposts. "How did you come to be a witch?"

She shrugged. "All the women in my family are witches."

"So," he said with a grin, "are you a good witch or a bad witch?"

"A good one, of course." She fixed him with a steady look. "And you?" she asked. "Are you a good vampire or a bad one?"

He considered her question for a moment, then shook his head. "I'm not sure there are any good ones."

That was not the answer she had been hoping for. A shadow of doubt rose in her eyes and she stirred restlessly on the bed, her gaze darting toward the door, and the hope of freedom.

"I will not hurt you, Brenna."

"But you won't let me go."

"No. The world is greatly changed from the one you knew. You are safer here than out there, believe me."

She plucked at a fold in the covers. "I tried two spells on your gate," she remarked candidly. "Neither one of them worked. I fear my magick is of little use here."

"There's nothing wrong with your magick. There are already a couple of . . . I guess you could call them spells of a sort, on the lock," he said. "You would have had to reverse the first and remove the second to open the gates."

"Are you a witch then, as well as a vampire?" she asked.

"No, but I have certain supernatural powers. There are wards on my house, and on the lock on the gate."

"To keep me in?" she asked with a touch of bitterness.

"No, darlin', to keep trespassers out."

"Oh. Because you're vulnerable when you sleep."

"Yes." Being cautious had become an ingrained habit over the years. There were few people these days who believed in vampires, but there were still a few determined hunters out there, men like Edward Ramsey and Tom Duncan, who had spent the best part of their adult lives pursuing and destroying the undead throughout the world. Roshan had come in contact with one or two vampire hunters in his time. They were a breed apart, dedicated to the hunt and little else.

"Are there other vampires here?" Brenna asked.

"A few."

"Are they friends of yours?"

He snorted softly. "No."

She tilted her head to one side in a gesture he was coming to recognize. "Why not? I should think you would seek each other out."

"Vampires are territorial predators, not social creatures."

"Oh."

Silence fell between them. It occurred to Roshan that Brenna might wish to bathe in the morning, and that she would no doubt need to use the bathroom facilities long before he rose again the next night.

"Come," he said. "There are a few things I need to show you."

She looked at him suspiciously. "What kinds of things?"

With a sigh of exasperation, he took her by the hand

and pulled her, gently, off the bed. She followed him hesitantly as he led her into the bathroom.

She glanced at her surroundings, frowning at what appeared to be a large trough across from the door. Surely he didn't keep a horse in the house!

"This is the bathroom," Roshan said. "This is a sink." He showed her how to turn the faucet on and off, how to use the stopper, how to adjust the temperature.

Brenna stared at the running water for several seconds, her eyes widening as the water grew steamy. Was it a pump of some kind? She had never seen a pump inside the house, or heard of one that spewed hot water. Wonder of wonders, she realized that this room was similar to one she had seen downstairs. What luxury, to have two such rooms that dispensed hot running water.

"Where does it go?" she asked, watching the water disappear down a small hole in the bottom of the sink.

"Down a drainpipe and out to the ocean. This is a tub, for bathing." Again, he showed her how to turn the water on and off and how to adjust the temperature, as well as how to turn the shower on and off.

"You can deny it all you wish," she muttered, "but I still think you are a sorcerer, and a powerful one at that."

"You ain't seen nothing yet," he replied, thinking of all the modern wonders she had yet to see.

"And what is this?" she asked, pointing to an odd-looking contraption that vaguely resembled a chair.

He lifted the lid, revealing a bowl of clear water. "It's a toilet."

"Toi-let? What does it do?"

To his amusement, she blushed when he explained, as delicately as he could, what a toilet was used for and the function of toilet paper.

He pointed out the towels and the soap, showed her where he kept his shampoo.

She nodded, then yawned behind her hand.

"It's late," he said. "You should get some sleep."

"Will I wake up again?"

He shook his head in exasperation as he walked her back to the bedroom. She watched him warily as she slipped under the covers, her trepidation evident in every taut line of her body, the wary expression in her eyes.

"Go to sleep, Brenna." He spoke quietly, his gaze holding hers, his voice winding around her like silken threads, stealing her will.

With a soft sigh, her body went limp, her head falling back on the pillow. Moments later, she was sleeping soundly.

"Forgive me, Brenna," he murmured. "But you need the rest."

He stared down at her. How like his Atiyana she was, with her long red hair and deep green eyes. She possessed an innocence that had nothing to do with her age and everything to do with the purity of her heart and her soul. Impulsively, he smoothed a lock of hair from her brow, then bent down and brushed his lips across her cheek. Her skin was warm and smooth. His gaze moved to her throat.

Muttering an oath, he dragged his gaze away and left the room.

She would be hungry when she woke in the morning. He would have to stock the shelves before he sought his rest.

With that thought in mind, he headed for the nearest grocery store, surprised by the number of people shopping at such a late hour. Mostly women alone, most of them in their twenties or thirties, though there were a few older women, as well. He filed the knowledge away, thinking that he had stumbled upon another hunting ground, one where he could prowl the aisles like a lion stalking the jungle for prey.

Thrusting the thought aside, he perused his surroundings. He had never been in a grocery store before. He usually picked up the few items he needed for his own personal use at the local drug store.

He glanced at the bounty spread before him—shiny red apples, bunches of bananas, fragrant oranges, grapefruit, lettuce, celery, carrots, potatoes, and onions. When he had been a mortal man, his family had raised or grown everything they needed. He had loved working in the fields. He remembered the scent of freshly turned earth, the feel of it in his hands, the satisfaction he had felt when he saw the first green shoots push their way through the earth. Though it was no longer necessary for him to grow food, he had never lost his love of the land. Save for a few ancient oaks, he had planted all the trees and shrubs that grew in such abundance around his house.

He moved down the next aisle, shaking his head at what he saw. Frozen foods and prepackaged meals were unheard of in the days when he had walked the earth as a mortal man, as were cuts of meat in neat little packages, milk in plastic containers, and eggs in cartons.

The glaring lights in the supermarket hurt his eyes as he wheeled a wobbly cart up and down the aisles. Though he had never tasted any of the foodstuffs he tossed into the basket, he had seen a good number of them advertised on television. He grinned as he plucked a box of Rice Krispies from the shelf, wondering if they really did go *snap, crackle, pop*. Dry cereal was as foreign to him as it would be to his houseguest. With that in mind, he bought a box of oatmeal, thinking that Brenna might find it more familiar. He bought buttermilk and bread and cheese, thinking that, although they were not exactly like what she had known, they, too, would at least be familiar.

He bought sugar and flour, salt and pepper, cans of corn and carrots, peaches and soup, a bag of rice, a variety of drinks. Though he had soap at home, he bought some pretty little scented bars, thinking she might fancy them. He bought everything he thought she might like, including four flavors of ice cream and several candy bars.

He grimaced when he came upon a display of Halloween items for sale at half price. Aside from numerous bags of candy and fake pumpkins, there were several talking dolls dressed as Frankenstein and the Mummy. And, of course, Dracula, complete with bloodied fangs. Unable to resist, he pulled the string on the vampire doll, grinned when a faintly accented voice trilled "The Monster Mash."

Leaving the food aisles, he picked up several pots and pans, some paper plates and plastic cups, plastic knives, forks, and spoons, a coffee cup, napkins, a roll of paper towels, and soap for the dishwasher. He paused in the pet food department and then, with a shake of his head, he tossed a bag of cat food into the cart. Passing a display of cookbooks on his way to the checkout line, he picked one up, thinking Brenna might find it useful.

By the time he had finished shopping, he had spent a small fortune. With a shake of his head, he wheeled the cart out to his car. After loading the bags into the trunk and the backseat of the Ferrari, he slid behind the wheel and drove home.

It was near dawn by the time he put everything away.

All the appliances in the kitchen were recent additions, purchased a few months back when he had been thinking of selling the house and finding a new dwelling place.

He smiled faintly as he left the kitchen and headed toward his lair. Tomorrow night he would take Brenna Flanagan shopping for a new wardrobe, and then he would take her out and show her a world she had never seen before.

He paused in the hallway, then turned right and went into his library. Pulling the book on ancient myths and legends from the shelf, he thumbed through the pages.

He had indeed changed history, he mused as he replaced the book on the shelf and walked toward his lair.

There was no longer any mention of Brenna Flanagan being burned at the stake. There was on longer any mention of her at all.

CHAPTER 6

Brenna woke with a start. She stared around the room, forgetting for the moment where she was. And then she remembered. She was in Roshan DeLongpre's house. In his bedroom. In his bed. Even though he said he didn't sleep in it, it was still his bed.

Vampire. The word whispered through her mind. Growing up, she had been taught that vampires were soulless monsters, merciless creatures who preyed on the living, draining them of blood or, worse, turned them into creatures like themselves. Granny O'Connell had said they were fiends of the worst kind.

Brenna had never met one, of course, nor had she truly believed they existed, any more than she had believed in werewolves or elves or any of the other fey folk of ancient legend and myth until she met Roshan. He was very real, though he didn't seem like a ravening monster. He had saved her from an agonizing death, and she would be forever grateful for that. Less grateful that he had brought her here, to this time and place.

Why hadn't he just taken her to another village, some-place where no one knew her? How was she to find her way in this new world where everything was strange and everyone was a stranger?

Pressure on her bladder sent her into the bathroom. She regarded the toilet for several moments before finding the courage to hike up her skirts, lower her drawers, and sit on the cold slippery seat. Did everyone in this century have an indoor privy? Who had ever thought of such a thing? It seemed rather indecent, somehow, having it right inside the house, but then she thought of all the cold winter nights when she'd had to bundle up and go outside. Perhaps an indoor privy wasn't such a bad idea after all.

Rising, she put her clothing in order, then turned and flushed the toilet. She jumped a little at the noise it made, then stood there, staring at the water as it swirled in the bowl and then disappeared, carrying the scrap of toilet paper with it. A moment later, the bowl was full of clean water.

Amazing!

A loud rumbling in her stomach reminded her that she hadn't eaten since yesterday, and that yesterday had been three hundred and thirteen years ago. No wonder she was hungry!

She ran her fingers through her hair, which was badly tangled, and then tried to smooth the wrinkles from her dress. A glance out the window showed that the sun was high in the sky. Impossible as it seemed, she had slept the morning away, she who had always risen with the sun.

With a shake of her head, Brenna unlocked the door and padded down the stairs. There was no reason to be cautious or quiet, she decided. Since the sun was up,

Roshan DeLongpre was undoubtedly sleeping the sleep of the dead.

She thrust the grisly thought from her mind as her stomach again sounded its displeasure.

She paused at the bottom of the staircase, her nostrils filling with a wonderful aroma. Following the scent, she went into the room with all the cupboards. An odd-looking contraption sat on a long counter. A large cup and a spoon sat beside it. She picked up the spoon and turned it over in her hands. Shiny and white, it was unlike any spoon she had ever seen before.

Lifting the glass pot, she filled the cup. Thinking it was tea, she took a sip.

It definitely wasn't tea. It was too strong, and too bitter. Grimacing, she set it aside, wondering how something that smelled so good could taste so bad.

Glancing around the room, she noticed one of the cupboard doors was open. When she went to close it, she saw to her surprise that the shelves, which had been empty the day before, were now stocked with an odd-looking assortment of boxes and bags.

She pulled them out, examining each one. Corn Flakes. Rice Krispies. Oatmeal.

Bread. Salt and pepper. Spaghetti. Spaghetti sauce. Pure Cane Sugar. 100% Grated Romano Cheese. Boysenberry Jam. Bisquick. Gold Medal Flour. Skippy Creamy Peanut Butter. Some of the words were peculiar and made no sense to her. Others she recognized.

She studied the boxes for several minutes, her stomach growling all the while. She wasn't sure what most of the items were, but she figured Roshan must have bought them for her, since he didn't eat.

Secure in the knowledge that he wouldn't be rising for several hours, she poked around in the kitchen, touching everything. There was a sink similar to the one in the bathroom upstairs, and beside the sink was a bag with a picture of a smiling cat and the words Tabby Cat Food.

She smiled at Roshan's thoughtfulness even as she wondered what Morgana would think of food that came out of a sack.

When Brenna came to a pair of large double doors, she opened one, gasped with surprise when she felt a breath of cool air against her face. Peering inside, she saw more odd-shaped boxes. One said milk, one said eggs, another said butter. She placed her hand against the one that said milk, surprised at how cold it was. She opened a drawer in the bottom and saw apples and lettuce, potatoes, onions, tomatoes, and cucumbers.

Closing that door, she opened the other one. More cold air brushed against her cheek. This cold cupboard held chocolate ice cream and funny-looking little packages. She picked one up. It was as hard as ice. The label said chicken breasts. Another one said New York steak. Another said center-cut pork chops.

Brenna frowned. She had never seen meat quite like this before.

With a shake of her head, she closed the door and continued exploring. She discovered a package that said "paper plates" in one of the cupboards, along with paper towels and small containers that read "plastic knives," "plastic spoons," and "plastic forks." They were made of the same strange material as the spoon beside the cup. She found pots and pans in one of the bottom cupboards.

Growing hungrier by the minute, she opened the package of bread, spread butter on two slices, then looked at the container of jam. After several tries, she managed to get it open and she spread a thick coat of jam on the bread. She poured the contents of the cup down the sink, then filled the cup with milk.

She quickly wolfed down both slices and drank the milk, which didn't taste anything like the milk she was used to.

With her hunger appeased, she wandered through the house again, running her hands over the sofa and chair, marveling at the fine material, at the thick dark green carpet that stretched from wall to wall. She dug her toes into the softness, thinking how much better it felt than the raw plank floor of her cottage back home.

Going upstairs, she went into the bathroom and turned on the water in the bathing tub. She watched the tub fill with hot water, thinking again what a miracle it was.

Smiling with anticipation, she removed her apron, stepped out of her dress, shift, and drawers. Taking the shampoo from the cabinet, she put it within easy reach and then stepped into the tub, sighing as warm water swirled around her ankles. Sitting down, she let the tub fill with water, turned off the faucet, then lay back and closed her eyes.

She woke, shivering, to find that the water had grown cool. She quickly washed her hair and then her body, rinsed the soap away, and stepped carefully out of the tub, which was quite slippery.

Grabbing a towel from the shelf, she wrapped it around her hair. When that was done, she wrapped a second towel around her body; then, kneeling beside the bathtub, she washed her clothes. She drained the water, then filled it again to rinse her clothes. Frowning, she looked around for a place to hang them. In the end, she draped them over the rod above the tub. Removing the towel from her head, she shook out her hair, then ran her fingers through it as best she could.

Going back into the bedroom, she stood in the middle of the floor. Until her clothes were dry, she had nothing to wear unless . . . Did she dare?

Worrying her lower lip between her teeth, she went to the chest across from the bed and rummaged through the drawers until she found a large white garment with a round neck and short sleeves. When she held it up, the hem fell almost to midcalf. Still, it was better than wearing a towel. She slipped it over her head, her nostrils filling with a fresh, clean smell, and a faint masculine scent she recognized as DeLongpre's. The material was soft and warm against her bare skin.

Going downstairs, she went into the room with all the books, browsing through them until she found a Bible that looked similar to the one she was used to. Carrying it to the chair, she sat down and began to read, grateful once again that Granny O'Connell had known how to read and had insisted that Brenna learn, too.

She read for a while, then went into the kitchen. Taking an apple from the cold cupboard, she poured milk into the cup, and then carried both outside. Sitting on a stone bench, she admired the shrubs, the changing leaves on the trees, the smooth, green grass. She wondered if Roshan cared for the grounds himself, though she could not visualize him cutting the grass in the middle of the night. It seemed out of character for a vampire to have such a well-tended yard. It was easier to imagine him living in a run-down house surrounded by gaunt trees and dying shrubs.

Birds flitted from branch to branch, their songs lifting her spirits. She nibbled at the apple, which was crisp and sweet. Lifting the cup, she took a drink, thinking again that it tasted far different from the milk at home. But then, here in this strange world, everything was different.

She took a leisurely stroll through the gardens, then went back into the book room. After opening the curtains, she sat down in the chair and began to read again, soothed by the lyrical passages of the Psalms. Sometime later, Morgana padded into the room.

"Morgana, where have you been?" Brenna asked as the cat leaped onto her lap.

The cat blinked at her, arched her back, then curled up and went to sleep.

From somewhere outside, a clock chimed the hour. Four o'clock. Putting the Bible aside, Brenna stroked the cat's fur and then, feeling suddenly sleepy herself, she rested her head against the back of the chair and closed her eyes.

And that was how Roshan found them when he rose an hour later.

He gazed down at Brenna, amazed again by her resemblance to Atiyana, at the pale beauty of her skin, the way her hair spread out over his T-shirt, like a splash of bright red blood. She looked incredibly warm and sexy curled up in the chair, and yet she looked innocent and vulnerable at the same time. It was a potent combination, arousing his desire, his hellish thirst, and a strong urge to protect her all at the same time.

She stirred, a sleepy sound emerging from her throat. He groaned softly as his nostrils filled with the scent of soap and the warm musky scent of woman.

Of prey.

He imagined himself bending over her, sweeping her hair away from her slender neck, burying his fangs in the soft, sweet flesh just below her ear.

He was so intent on fighting his hunger that it took him a moment to realize that she was awake and staring up at him, her face suddenly pale, her eyes wide with horror.

He turned away from her, his hands clenched as he fought his hunger and his desire. It took all his considerable self-control to keep from drawing her into his embrace, from slowly seducing her until she was under his spell, her will subjugated to his. Only his fear of incurring her hatred, and the even stronger fear that, once he had satisfied his desire for her flesh he would be unable to resist giving in to his desire for her blood, kept him from making his fantasy a reality.

When he turned to face her, all his hungers were again under control.

She was still staring up at him.

He took a step toward her

She lifted one hand. "Stay away from me," she warned.

Roshan shook his head. "Let's not go through this again. How many times do I have to tell you that I won't hurt you before you believe me?"

"I know not. Perhaps when I look at you and I do not see your fangs, or see the hunger in your eyes."

He lifted both hands in a gesture of surrender. "You're perfectly safe."

She looked skeptical.

"Why don't you go upstairs and get dressed? We need to go shopping."

"Shopping?"

"For clothes. Fashions have changed in the last three hundred years or so."

She glanced around the room. "So have dwellings."

He grinned at her. "Yes. I guess I'd better show you how things work."

She studied him a moment, then nodded.

He watched her walk out of the room, noting the gentle sway of her hips, the way his T-shirt seemed to cling to her body even though it was many sizes too large.

Going into the living room, he paced the floor, her image strong in his mind. She had courage, his little witch. Her fear of him was a palpable thing, yet she had been ready to take him on.

He heard her footsteps on the stairs a few minutes later, and then she was there, walking toward him, her hair falling over her shoulders in glorious disarray. It occurred to him that he had forgotten to buy her a hairbrush and a comb, as well as a toothbrush. He would remedy that tonight.

He frowned when he saw she was wearing her boots, but carrying her dress over one arm.

"I washed my clothes earlier," she said. "They are still damp."

A wave of his hand brought the fire in the hearth to life. Bringing two of the kitchen chairs into the living room, he draped her dress over the back of one, her underwear over the other.

"I'll show you around the house while we wait for your clothes to dry. So," he mused, "where to start?" He glanced around the room. "Here," he said. "This is a television set."

She regarded him warily.

Roshan picked up the remote. "You turn it on like this," he said, showing her which button to push.

Her eyes widened as the screen flickered to life and an old *I Love Lucy* rerun appeared.

"What sorcery is this?" she asked softly. "How did you capture all those people in that little box?" She took a step closer. "Have you captured their souls? Why is everything in black and white?"

"And you change the channels like this."

Her eyes grew even wider as he flipped through the channels, the black and white images giving way to color. Cowboys and Indians, old sitcoms, country music videos, news, weather, and sports. He tried to explain what she was seeing, the difference between news programs, which informed watchers of the day's events, and movies, which were like stage plays and had little basis in fact.

She looked up at him, speechless.

"I know, it's pretty amazing," he said. "But it isn't magic, at least not the way you know it. It's just technology . . ." He shrugged, not knowing how to explain it to her in terms she would understand. "Anyway, it's a form of amusement, something to while away the hours if you've got nothing else to do. Practically every household in America has at least one." Most had two or more.

He showed her how to turn the lights on and off, stood there, grinning, while she played with the light switch.

He took her into the kitchen and explained what frozen foods were, then showed her how to work the stove and the built-in microwave, then the dishwasher. He opened the silverware drawer and showed her the plastic utensils.

She picked up one of the forks. "I have never seen anything like this," she remarked. "'Tis made of an odd substance." She bent the handle of the fork and it broke in her hand. "Oh! I am sorry."

"It doesn't matter," he said, taking the broken pieces from her hand and tossing them in the trash. "They're disposable. Only meant to be used once."

"'Tis wasteful. Of what are these made?"

"Plastic," he said. "It's quite common."

He took her through the rest of the house, assuring her that she was to make herself at home.

When they came to his office, she pointed at his computer. "What is that?"

"It's a computer." He booted it up, then turned on the screen.

"It looks much like the television in the other room," she observed, "only smaller."

"Yes, it does."

"I saw it, in my scrying mirror, when I saw you."

He nodded. He had read about the ancient art of scrying when he'd been doing his research on witches. Mirrors were the preferred method, but countless other objects had been used throughout the centuries. The Egyptians used ink, blood, or other dark liquids. The Romans used shiny objects and stones. Water was also used. Scrying was derived from the English word "descry" meaning "to make out dimly" or "to reveal." Witches used it to see into the future, or to find lost objects or people.

"This is where I found your picture." Sitting down, he signed on, then went to the Internet and pulled up the Web page where he had seen her photo.

Brenna stared at her image, wondering how John Linder's painting had found its way to this time and place.

"Listen to this," Roshan said, reading the words beneath the image. "*Woman in White*, painted by renowned seventeenth-century artist John Linder. This painting is one of Linder's first works. There is speculation as to the model's identity. Some claim she was a local witch; others opine that she was Linder's first love, Brenna

Flanagan, who disappeared under mysterious circumstances." He glanced over his shoulder at Brenna. "I guess he didn't jump to his death after all."

"You saved two lives that night," Brenna murmured. "Mine and his."

Roshan grunted softly. "So it would seem."

"I owe you my thanks for his life, as well as my own."

"Were you in love with him?"

"No."

He regarded her a moment, as if searching for the truth, then turned back to the matter at hand. "This is a printer," he said, indicating the gray object beside the computer.

He hit *"print."* Brenna jumped a little when the machine made a soft whirring sound and started printing the photograph.

"Here." He handed the picture to her.

She stared at her likeness, hardly able to comprehend such magic. "'Tis all so . . . unbelievable."

He nodded, wondering how he would have done had he been thrust into the present from the past. "There's a lot more for you to learn. For instance—"

She grinned sheepishly when her stomach growled loudly.

"I think I'd better take you out and get you something to eat. Why don't you go and see if your clothes are dry," he suggested. "I'll wait in here."

Her undergarments were dry; the hem of her skirt was still a little damp, but she put the dress on anyway. She had nothing else.

"Ready?" he called.

"Yes."

She was frowning when he entered the living room again.

"What's wrong?"

"My dress," she said, smoothing her hands over her skirt, "'tis badly wrinkled."

He grunted softly, but there was no help for it. Mentally, he added an iron to the list of things he had forgotten.

"Don't worry about it," he said. "We'll buy you something new." He held out his hand, waited patiently while she decided whether to trust him or not. He felt as if he had accomplished a major feat when she finally placed her hand in his. It was small and warm, vibrant with young life.

Roshan turned off the lights as they walked toward the entryway. He opened the front door for her, then took her hand again and led her around the side of the house to the garage. Morgana trailed at Brenna's heels, then bounded off, no doubt in search of prey.

Roshan squeezed Brenna's hand. "Wait here."

Going into the garage, he slid behind the wheel of the Ferrari, started the engine, and backed the car out of the garage.

Putting the car in park, he opened the door and got out, only to find that Brenna had retreated to the front porch. He laughed softly. "Come here."

She shook her head. "What is that thing?"

"It's an automobile. A car. You've seen them on television, remember?"

"They were not that big. Nor did they make such a dreadful noise."

Walking over to the porch, Roshan climbed the steps and took her hand once again. "Come on, there's nothing to be afraid of."

It was with great trepidation that she followed him down the stairs.

He opened the car door for her, waited patiently while she peered inside, apprehension visible in every taut line of her body.

"Brenna, you're going to have to trust me here. I swear I won't hurt you, and I won't let anything else hurt you, either."

She glanced at him over her shoulder and he realized again how young she was, how vulnerable and innocent. He had saved her from a horrible death, and in so doing, had catapulted her into a world beyond anything she could have imagined, a world she had not been prepared for.

Apparently deciding to take him at his word, she slid into the passenger seat. He shut the door, rounded the front of the car, and slid behind the wheel.

"This is a seat belt." Reaching in front of her, he snapped it into place. He let the car idle for a few minutes, giving her a chance to get used to the noise.

Putting the car in gear, he drove down the long curved driveway and pulled up at the gate. "You all right?" he asked.

She nodded, her eyes wide, her hands clenched in her lap.

Roshan grinned as he disabled the wards on the gate and pulled onto the road. Though it had been years ago, he could remember his apprehension the first time he got behind the wheel, the sudden rush of power as the engine roared to life. Though he could will himself anywhere he wished to be, driving a fast car was an exhilarating experience that could be had no other way.

Brenna stared out the window as houses and buildings rushed by in a blur. Time and again, she looked over at Roshan, seeking reassurance, listening to the calming sound of his voice as he explained what he was doing, telling her the names for the various parts of the car—steering wheel, radio, dashboard, gearshift, gas pedal, brake pedal. He showed her how to turn on the radio and the inside of the car was suddenly filled with music, though it was music such as she had never heard before.

A short time later, she saw a building that looked big enough to hold her entire village and everyone in it.

"That's the mall," he told her as he pulled around the corner and into the parking lot.

They stopped moments later. He showed her how to unfasten her seat belt and open the door, then helped her out of the car.

Taking her by the hand, he led her across an expanse of black ground, though it was like no ground she had ever seen. They entered the building through a large door made of steel and glass.

Brenna glanced around. There were lights everywhere, and, to her amazement, trees. There was also a fountain. And noise! So much noise. Music that seemed to come from the walls, the sound of people talking and laughing, babies crying. The air was filled with a myriad of scents she could not identify.

"This is a place to shop," Roshan explained. "You can buy just about anything you want or need here."

She nodded, her gaze darting everywhere at once while Roshan read the names of the various stores aloud: Mrs. Field's Cookies; Robinson's-May; Mervyn's; the Disney Store; Sears; Bed, Bath and Beyond; Suncoast; Everything But Water; Waldenbooks.

She couldn't help staring at the people that rushed past them. Girls with pink curls, boys with hair rising from their heads in long spikes. And their clothing! It was scandalous. In her day, a woman was considered naked if she was caught wearing nothing but her shift, but these women! They wore clothing that revealed their arms and legs and, saints above, their stomachs!

She was staring at a boy wearing a shirt with no sleeves and breeches so low on his hips she wondered that they didn't fall off, when Roshan led her into one of the stores.

Again, she found herself staring, this time at shelves of shoes and boots in every style and color imaginable. He led her to a moving staircase. She balked when he tried to lead her onto it.

"Come on," he said. "There's nothing to be afraid of. This is an escalator. Quite safe. Step onto it when I do." He took a firm hold on her forearm. "Ready?"

She nodded uncertainly.

"Let's go."

She gasped as she put her foot on the bottom step, would have fallen if he hadn't been holding her arm. Before she could decide what to make of this new mode of transportation, they had reached another level, which was just as crowded and noisy as the last.

"That wasn't so bad, was it?" Roshan asked.

Moments later, he turned her over to a tall woman wearing a severe black dress. After giving the woman instructions to help Brenna pick out everything she needed, no matter the cost, he found a chair and sat down to wait.

Brenna felt a rush of embarrassment as the woman studied her appearance, taking in her wrinkled dress, her boots, her uncombed hair.

The next two hours were a little frightening at first. The woman took her from place to place, showing her all manner of clothes, asking which ones she liked. Brenna was embarrassed when the woman asked her her size and she didn't know the answer.

After a time, her arms laden with clothing, the woman took Brenna into a small room. Brenna was startled to see her reflection staring back at her. Somewhat timidly, she put her finger on the glass.

"It's all right, I assure you," the woman said. "No one is watching you from the other side."

"The other side?" Brenna took a step back, wondering if the mirror was a magical doorway to the hereafter.

"The other side of the mirror. I know some women feel uncomfortable ever since that story came out on the Web about dressing rooms with two-way mirrors, but I can assure you that you don't have to worry about that here."

Not wanting to show her ignorance, Brenna kept silent. A story on the web? What did spiders have to do with mirrors?

While Brenna was still pondering this new mystery, the woman began unfastening Brenna's dress. It was a new experience, having a woman assist her while she tried on intimate apparel. New but necessary, she thought as the woman helped her into something called a bra, then handed her something called panties. Brenna marveled not only at the bright blue color, but at their silky texture, as well.

"They are nice, aren't they?" the woman said, smiling.

"Yes, indeed, but . . . is this all there is to them?" Brenna held them up. "I mean, they do not cover very much."

She blushed when the woman laughed and assured her that the briefs, however brief, covered all that was necessary.

Brenna tried on slacks and blouses and nightgowns, dresses and skirts, slips both long and short, marveling at the variety of colors, the rich texture and needlework of each garment. Her own clothes seemed drab indeed when compared with such finery!

Roshan was waiting for her when she stepped out of the trying-on place. She stood there, wearing a pair of jeans and a pretty dark green sweater, waiting for his re-action, surprised to find that she cared what he thought. She had never worn pants before. Though they were very snug and felt very odd, she had liked them imme-diately. Still, she couldn't help glancing around, won-dering if people were staring at her, scandalized that the shape of her legs and her buttocks were clearly out-lined for all to see, but no one seemed to be paying any attention to her at all, no one but Roshan. Embarrassed by his frank gaze, she looked down at her feet. Never before had she worn shoes that felt so light, almost as if she were barefoot.

When she looked up again, Roshan smiled at her. "You look terrific," he said, his voice husky. "Beautiful."

His words filled her with pleasure. "I feel very strange."

"Did you get everything you need?"

She glanced over her shoulder to where the saleslady stood, her arms laden with clothing. "I think I have far more than I need."

"Just let me pay for all this," he said, laughing.

"With what will you pay her?"

"Money, of course." He held up what looked like a piece of small, hard paper. "This is a credit card. I give them this card and they send me a bill for the amount due."

She nodded. She had rarely seen money. A few shillings now and then, a Spanish rial once. At home, she'd had little need for coin. She had bartered her potions for foodstuffs and other essentials.

Roshan followed the woman to a large desk and handed her his credit card. She gave him a piece of paper, which he signed, and then she returned his credit card.

Brenna watched the woman fold everything and place it in large sacks made of some strange material. Brenna looked at Roshan speculatively. "You must be very rich."

"I have enough to get by," he said, gathering up the bags. "Are you ready to go?"

She nodded.

"Is there anything else you want to see or do?" Roshan asked as they walked through the mall.

"I do not think so."

"Are you hungry?"

"Yes."

Roshan glanced around. If there was one thing of which he was completely ignorant, it was the kinds of food offered in places like McDonald's and Burger King. There was a place selling chicken, another selling pizza by the pie or the slice.

"What do you want to eat?" he asked, sickened by the myriad smells of so much food being prepared in such a small area.

She glanced around, obviously as confused as he. "I do not know."

"Well, come on," he said, and headed for a stand that sold hamburgers and hot dogs. He ordered her one of each, a side of fries, a chocolate shake, and a glass of water, then found an empty table.

Brenna stared at the food on the tray, then looked over at Roshan. "Do you expect me to eat all of this?"

"I didn't know what you would like, so . . ." He pointed to each item, telling her what it was. "Taste it all. Eat what you want and leave the rest. If you don't like any of it, we'll go somewhere else."

She picked up the hamburger and took a bite, chewed thoughtfully, swallowed, and took another bite.

She finished the hamburger, the malt, the fries, and half the hot dog, then sat back with a sigh.

"I guess you liked everything," Roshan mused dryly.

"It was very good, especially the malt."

He grunted softly. Chocolate. Most women seemed to like it, though he had no idea why.

They visited several other stores before leaving the mall. He let Brenna pick out a comb and a brush. He also bought her a toothbrush, a toaster, and an iron, explaining what each of them was used for. In addition, he bought a set of silverware, figuring that she would soon tire of using cheap plastic utensils

She clung to his arm as they took the escalator down to the first floor.

Brenna was a little less tense in the car on the ride back to his house. She asked numerous questions, mostly about the people and the customs of this time. When they reached the house, Morgana was waiting for them on the front porch.

Roshan carried the packages inside, then turned on the TV, thinking it was probably the best way for her to learn what life was like in this century.

As soon as Brenna sat down, Morgana jumped into her lap, meowing loudly.

Brenna stroked Morgana until the cat settled down, then turned her attention to the pictures on the TV screen. She watched avidly, her eyes wide, while Roshan went from channel to channel, explaining, as best he could, what she was seeing—airplanes and buses, trains and motorcycles, telephones, vacuum cleaners, washing machines and dryers, cell phones and pagers. After surfing the channels for a while, he settled on a recent movie, figuring that it would help her understand how people lived in this day and age.

After awhile, Brenna lost interest in the images she was watching. Instead, she found herself sliding glances at Roshan. He had a strong profile, rugged and masculine.

She wondered if he liked being a vampire. He had told her he had no vampire friends. It seemed unlikely that he would have mortal friends. Did he then spend all his time alone?

She knew little of what that was like, could not imagine living without friends or family for hundreds of years. Such a lonely existence. She wondered why anyone would want to live like that.

"Brenna?" His voice scattered her thoughts and she realized she had been staring at him. "Is something wrong?"

"Everything," she replied. "I do not belong in this time or this place." She stroked the cat's head. "I do not think I will ever belong."

"Sure you will. It might take a little while for you to get used to it, but you're young. You'll learn."

A single tear slid down her cheek and dripped onto the cat's head.

"Ah, Brenna." Reaching for her, he drew her into his arms. At first, she held herself away from him but then, with a sigh, she collapsed against his chest. With a low hiss, Morgana slipped out from between them and curled up in front of the hearth.

Brenna's tears dampened his shirt. Her scent filled his nostrils, not the scent of her blood, but the scent of her skin, and her sorrow. He stroked her hair, ran his hand down her spine, felt her shiver in response to his touch.

Placing one finger under her chin, he tilted her head back, his gaze meeting hers.

Though a maiden innocent in the ways of men, her eyes revealed that she recognized the heat in his.

She shook her head as he leaned toward her. "No."

"No?"

"Kissing," she said with a grimace. "I like it not."

"Indeed?" He cupped her head in his hands. "Perhaps I can change your mind," he murmured, and claimed her lips with his own.

Eyes wide open, Brenna braced her hands against his shoulders, prepared to push him away, but at the first touch of his mouth on hers, all thought of pushing him away fled her mind. His lips were cool yet heat flooded her being, arousing a fluttering in her stomach she had never felt before, making her press herself against him.

Closing her eyes, she wrapped her arms around his waist, wanting to hold him closer, tighter. She melted against him, hoping the kiss would never end, a distant part of her mind trying to determine why John Linder's kiss had not filled her with liquid fire the way Roshan's did. But it was only a vague thought, quickly gone, as Roshan deepened the kiss, his tongue sweeping over her lower lip. She gasped at the thrill of pleasure that engulfed her, moaned softly as he repeated the gesture.

She was breathless when he took his lips from her. Lost in a world of sensation, her head still reeling, she stared up at him.

"More," she whispered.

"I thought you didn't like kissing."

"I was never kissed like this." Feeling suddenly bold, she slid her hand around his nape. "Kiss me again."

He was only too happy to oblige. She was soft and sweet, eager to explore the sensual pleasures that were new to her. Without taking his mouth from hers, he stretched out on the sofa, drawing her down with him so that they lay side by side. He could almost feel her untapped passion coming to life as she moved against him, her body instinctively molding itself to his.

He ran his hands over her shoulders, down her back to her buttocks, drawing her closer against him, letting her feel the evidence of his rising desire.

She moaned softly, a husky sound of longing and trepidation all rolled into one.

He was moving too fast for her, he knew it, but couldn't seem to stop. He wanted her, here and now, with her eyes wide and a little afraid, her lips swollen from his kisses.

"Brenna . . . ?" He could have seduced her with his preternatural power, but he didn't want her that way. He wanted her warm and willing in his arms, in his bed.

She blinked up at him, her eyes cloudy with desire.

"Do you want me to stop?"

She considered for a moment, and then nodded.

He wasn't surprised, but he couldn't help feeling disgruntled. Though he was no longer mortal, he was still a man, still possessed of a man's needs. Living alone, unwilling to place his trust in anyone for fear of being betrayed, his encounters with women were usually one-night affairs. He had no trouble finding women. They were drawn to him without knowing why. Of course, there were always bars like the Nocturne that catered to those who fancied they were children of the night. The women wore long black dresses, black lipstick, and lots of dark eye shadow. Some of them sported fake fangs. The men wore black leather or long black capes and bristled with attitude. The Nocturne was one of his favorite haunts. It was one of the few places where he could be himself.

He kissed her one more time, then, taking a deep breath, he gained his feet.

"It's late," he said. "You should get some sleep."

She sat up, not quite meeting his eyes. "You are angry with me."

"No." He offered her his hand, felt a rush of heat flow up his arm when she placed her hand in his and let him draw her to her feet.

Still holding her hand, he walked her up the stairs to his bedroom. He kissed her again because he had no power to resist. She didn't move when he broke the kiss, only stood there, looking slightly confused. Grunting softly, he gave her a little push into the room, then closed the door behind her.

It was after midnight.

Time to dine.

CHAPTER 7

Roshan wandered the dark streets, listening to the muted sounds of the night—the hum of a white moth's wings, the whisper of a fat gray spider crawling up the side of a crumbling red brick wall, the distant barking of a dog.

He could have transported himself to his destination. He could have taken the Ferrari, but he enjoyed walking alone, late at night, while the rest of the city was asleep.

Moving on, he saw an old wino passed out in an alley; farther down the street, a young couple sat in a parked car, locked in each other's arms, the windows fogged up.

A patrol car slowed, keeping pace with him. The passenger officer gave him the once-over, then turned his head and spoke to his partner, and the car picked up speed again, disappearing around a corner.

Roshan grunted softly. He was used to being stopped and questioned by the police. They tended to be suspi-

cious of anyone walking the streets late at night. These
two officers knew him; they had stopped him a little
over a year ago, questioned him, checked his ID. When
asked about his peculiar hours, Roshan had told them
he had insomnia. They had warned him to be careful
and let him go. He was still stopped from time to time,
whenever there was a new cop on the beat.

He continued on, his senses alert to his surroundings, his thoughts drifting to Brenna as though drawn
by invisible cords. What was he going to do with her,
now that he had her here? She was totally dependent
on him; to his astonishment, he found he rather liked
the idea. But she had a quick intelligent mind; it wouldn't
take her long to get the hang of things in the twenty-
first century, and even though there wasn't much call
for witches these days, he was pretty sure she could find
a way to earn a living, if that was what she wanted,
though there was no need for her to work. He could
easily support her if she decided to stay with him. And if
she wanted to leave . . . what then?

He would not keep her in his house against her will,
though the idea was far more tempting than it should
have been. He could make her his creature, keep her at
his side, enchant her to do his bidding, drink of her
sweetness whenever he desired . . . oh yes, the idea was
tempting indeed. In days past, when women were little
more than chattel, he had done just that, not only to
satisfy his own cravings, but to save the life of a young
woman whose husband had abused her verbally and
physically until she was little more than a frightened
shell of a woman. Roshan had dispatched the husband,
then taken the girl under his wing. He had found her a
safe place to live, fed her and clothed her, cared for her
until she died.

"Bethany." He shared her name with the night. He had not thought of her in over a century.

He found his prey exiting a high-class nightclub in a wealthy part of the city. She was dark-haired and stat-uesque, with deep brown eyes and caramel-colored skin. Her clothes, a tight black sweater with a deep V neck, a pair of skintight white pants, and a white leather jacket, were expensive.

She smiled a knowing smile as he approached. "Sorry, honey," she purred, "but it's late and I'm on my way home."

"I'll walk you," he said, falling into step beside her.

"I'm not walking." Pulling a set of keys out of a small black handbag, she opened the door to a late-model luxury car.

Roshan glanced around. He could take her, here and now, in the car, but there was always the chance of being seen. Better to take her home where there was no chance of discovery.

"Then I'll be your chauffeur for the evening."

"That won't be necessary. I . . ." Her gaze met his, her voice trailing off as his mind captured hers. She smiled blankly. "Yes, of course."

"My pleasure." Taking the keys from her hand, he es-corted her around to the passenger side door, opened it, and handed her into the automobile. Returning to the driver's side, he slid behind the wheel and put the key in the ignition. The car started with a low growl.

"Where do you live?" he asked, pulling away from the curb.

She gave him her address, then sat back in her seat, her hands folded in her lap, her eyes slightly unfocused as he probed her mind.

On the way, he learned that she was a fashion model,

recently divorced from a high-profile movie star, that she was the sole support for her mother and her invalid grandmother.

A nice girl, Roshan mused as he parked the car.

She lived on the top floor of a high-rise condo. An elevator whisked them to her apartment. The walls were a stark white, the furniture black leather. Red accent pieces offered the only touch of color—a vase of blood red roses on the mantel, a couple of red throw pillows, a bird carved from a piece of red glass.

The woman—her name was Tiffany—turned on the lights, then shrugged out of her jacket and sat down on the sofa, waiting.

Roshan sat beside her, his arm slipping around her shoulders.

Confusion flickered in the woman's eyes. "You're not going to hurt me, are you?"

He glanced at the pulse throbbing in the hollow of her throat. A deep breath filled his nostrils with the scent of vibrant life. "No, Tiffany, not at all." He stroked her cheek. "Close your eyes, my sweet. You won't feel a thing."

The sound of his voice soothed her. She closed her eyes. Her head fell back across his arm, exposing the slender curve of her neck.

He ran his fingertips over her skin, then bent down, his tongue laving the sensitive skin below her ear.

She sighed as his teeth grazed her skin. She moaned with pleasure as he took what he needed, made a soft sound of protest when he lifted his head.

"Don't stop." She put her hand behind his head, drawing him toward her once again. "Don't stop."

He closed his eyes, fighting the urge to take what she offered, to drink her life, all of it. Past, present, and future. To drink and drink until he was replete, sated.

But she was the sole support of her family. To deprive her of her life would be to condemn her mother and grandmother to a life of poverty. He knew too well what that was like.

"Not tonight, my sweet," he murmured. "You will sleep now. You will forget me. You will forget any of this happened."

She looked up at him through eyes that were filled with sorrow. "I don't want to forget."

"I know." His gaze trapped hers, his mind sifting through her memories of the past half hour. "But you will forget," he said quietly.

A tear rolled down her cheek and then her expression went blank. A moment later, she was asleep.

Rising, he left the building. When the woman awoke, she would have no memory of him or of anything that had happened after she left the nightclub.

Whistling softly, he went home.

He paused on the front steps, his head tilted back to look up at the stars wheeling high overhead. Eternity dwelled there, beyond the white expanse of the Milky Way. How many times had he stood thus, contemplating the hereafter, wondering what awaited him should death find him? In the course of his existence, he had killed countless times, sometimes in self-defense, sometimes because the temptation to drink his fill was more than he could withstand. Would he be called to answer for all the lives he had taken, or just those he had taken because he was too weak to resist? Would he writhe in the flames of an unforgiving hell forever, or was there redemption even for one such as he? He had not asked for the Dark Gift. Would he be punished for what he had done to survive?

He blew out a sigh. He regretted the lives he had

taken. Not long ago, he had considered ending his own existence, but then he had found Brenna. She had added meaning and luster to his life, given him something to look forward to when the moon chased the sun from the sky.

A shift in the wind carried her scent to him. He turned toward her window. An errant breeze carried the fragrance of her hair, her skin, her very being.

A thought carried him to her bedside. She slept on her back, her face turned away from him. Moonlight filtered through the window, casting her face in light and shadow. She was quite the loveliest creature he had seen in centuries. And she was here, in his house. In his bed. His for the taking . . .

Though he had just fed, the beast stirred deep within him. Leaning down, he gently brushed a lock of hair away from the side of her neck. He could see her pulse beating there, slow and steady. He stroked it with his fingertip, felt his own heart begin to beat in time with hers.

His mouth watered.

His fangs lengthened in response to the turn of his thoughts.

One taste.

What could it hurt?

He ran his tongue across the silky warmth of her skin, closed his eyes in sensual pleasure, and then, quietly cursing himself, he pierced her tender flesh. It was the tiniest of bites, hardly more than a scratch, yielding only a few drops of blood. But it was enough. Enough to tell him that he could never let her go.

He closed the wound with a stroke of his tongue and then, muttering a vile oath, he turned and fled the room before he surrendered to the demon within him.

* * *

She dreamed, a dark, sensual dream, and in her dream she saw a man standing in the shadows, a tall, broad-shouldered man clad in a long black cloak. He blended into the darkness as though he were darkness itself. She couldn't see his face but she knew it was him, the stranger, Roshan DeLongpre. She could feel his supernatural power crawling over her skin, sense his gaze upon her face. His loneliness whispered to her, a wordless cry of desolation and pain that sank deep into her heart. She reached for him and he backed away, stepping into a pool of moonlight that cast silver shadows in his long black hair. She saw the sadness in his dark eyes, yearned to comfort him. She reached for him again, felt a sudden rush of motion, a subtle shift in the fabric of the night, and she was no longer standing outside but lying in her bed overshadowed by a dark presence. Fear roiled deep in the pit of her stomach. She saw a flash of sharp white teeth, opened her mouth in a silent scream as she felt the prick of fangs at her throat . . .

Brenna woke to the sound of her own screams. Sitting up, she turned on the light beside her bed, her gaze darting around the room. A faint breeze ruffled the curtains at the window. She frowned, certain that she had closed the windows before she went to bed.

Rising, she went into the bathroom and turned on the light, then looked into the mirror on the medicine cabinet. It was, she realized, the only mirror in the house. Holding her hair back, she turned her head from side to side. There! Was that a bite? Fear congealed in the pit of her stomach. She leaned closer to the mirror, her eyes narrowed in concentration, and then she frowned. She would have sworn there was a bite there a moment ago but now it was gone. Had she imagined it?

With a sigh, she turned off the light and went back to bed, one arm curling around Morgana, grateful for the cat's presence. And then she noticed the cat was staring at the window, a low growl rumbling in her throat.

Fear clutched at Brenna's heart once more. "Who's there? Roshan, is that you?"

He materialized in a swirl of sparkling silver motes to stand before her. Even in the unfamiliar light cast by the strange lamp beside her bed, he seemed to be a part of the night.

"What are you doing here?" she asked.

He glanced at her neck. "I heard your scream."

The skin beneath her ear felt suddenly hot and she covered it with her hand. "What have you done to me?" she asked, her voice hushed. "Have you made me what you are?"

"No, my sweet Brenna, I have not cursed you with the Dark Trick."

"But you bit me? You took my blood while I slept."

He nodded.

"You promised I would be safe here!"

Upset at the anger in her mistress's voice, Morgana sprang to her feet, hissing.

"And safe you shall be," Roshan said.

She glared at him. "Safe? Hah!"

"Forgive me, Brenna. I took but a small taste, hardly more than a drop."

"You are no more trustworthy than the fox who promised safety to the goose if she would carry him across the lake."

He lifted one brow, waiting for her to explain.

"When the fox reached the safety of the other side, he attacked the goose. As the goose lay dying, she asked him why he had betrayed her. 'It is my nature,' replied the fox.'" She stared at him, her eyes filled with accusation. "Like the fox, sir, I fear you cannot change your nature. Like the goose, I fear I have sorely misplaced my trust."

Roshan grunted softly. "Think what you will, Brenna Flanagan," he said quietly, and vanished from her sight.

She stared after him. She could not stay here. All too clearly, she remembered the dream she'd had before he came to her cottage, the cold certainty she'd had upon waking that she would die by his hand.

Things seemed less ominous in the clear light of day. Rising, Brenna stepped into the shower and closed the curtain. What a marvel, to have hot water anytime one wished without having to heat it on the fire or cast a spell. She stood under the spray, luxuriating in the warmth.

Exiting the bathroom, she noticed the boxes and bags containing the clothing she had chosen the night before sitting on the floor beside the bed. Roshan must have brought the packages up sometime last night, while she was asleep. The thought of him being in the room, watching her while she slept, drinking her blood, sent a shiver down her spine.

She rummaged through the packages for a change of clothing, taking out what she needed for the day, leaving the rest of the items in the bags and boxes since there was no room in the closet or the chest of drawers.

She dressed quickly, ran the brush through her hair, then, her feet bare, she went downstairs to break her fast. Entering the kitchen, she glanced around, trying to remember all the things he had told her, quietly whispering the name of each object—stove, refrigerator, sink, garbage disposal, dishwasher. Such wondrous inventions. Truly, this was a magical age.

She opened the refrigerator, marveling anew that the big box kept food cold with no visible means. Electricity kept it cold, Roshan had told her. Electricity. To Brenna, it was just another name for modern magick. She had learned that it was electricity that powered the television, cooled the house in summer, and caused the lamps to glow with light. How was it possible for the same source to provide both heat and cold, as well as light?

She withdrew two eggs and the bacon from the refrigerator and set them on the counter. She found a frying pan and placed it on the stove. And then she stood there, wondering if she dared turn on the stove. What if she did it wrong? Chiding herself for her fears, she turned on the front burner the way Roshan had showed her. If she was going to live in this century, she needed to learn how to do these things. She cracked the eggs in the pan, added two strips of bacon.

While she waited for the food to cook, she buttered two pieces of bread, noting that each slice in the package was exactly the same size as the other. She turned the eggs and the bacon, jumping a little when grease splattered on her hand. After filling a glass with buttermilk, she poured some into a small bowl for Morgana. Turning off the stove, she dished up the eggs and bacon and sat down at the table.

She glanced out the window while she ate, wondering where Roshan passed the hours of daylight, wondering what vampire sleep was like. Was it truly like death, or did he dream? She had heard that vampires were vulnerable when the sun commanded the sky, that they could be destroyed while taking their rest. Did he sleep somewhere here, in the house?

Closing her eyes, she reached out to him with her mind, but she had no sense of his presence, no inkling that he was anywhere nearby. She was mystified by her overwhelming urge to see him while he slept. Was it the same sort of curiosity that had brought him to her room last night?

After finishing her meal, she put her plate and glass in the dishwasher and closed the door. A wave of her hand and a small incantation quickly washed and dried the frying pan and put it away. She could have washed and dried her dishes in the same manner but she was curious to see how the dishwasher worked.

Leaving the kitchen, she went into the living room and sat down, Morgana at her side. Settling back on the sofa, Brenna turned on the television. For a time, she was content to sit there, occasionally switching the channels. She did not understand everything she saw. Sometimes the screen was filled with horses and cattle and men in big hats, sometimes there were cars and airplanes, sometimes there were dragons and knights. Did all these people and creatures exist in this time and place? If so, how was it possible? She would have to ask Roshan when next she saw him.

Rising, she began a deeper exploration of the house than she had done before. She peeked into closets and cupboards, peered behind doors, checked in the basement and the attic. The basement was empty; the attic held several pieces of furniture and two large trunks, both of which were locked.

Returning to the parlor, she sank down on the sofa, wondering where to look next. She refused to admit that she was searching for his resting place, but she was sorely disappointed that she had failed to find it. And yet, had she found his resting place, what would she have done, assuming she would have been able to get in? And had she gained entrance, would she really want to see him sleeping the sleep of the dead? She grimaced at the thought, though it did little to diminish her curiosity.

With a little huff of irritation, she admitted that she was probably wasting her time. For all she knew, he passed the hours of daylight in some place far from this house.

She sat there for several minutes and then, tired of watching the images on the screen, she went back to the attic.

A simple spell unlocked the first trunk. Smiling with pleasure, she lifted the lid, and then frowned as she pulled out several dresses, petticoats, and three pairs of long wool stockings. Examining the clothes, she noted that they were far more similar to the clothing she was used to than the styles women wore today. Why would Roshan keep a trunk filled with old clothes.? Had they belonged to his mother? A sister? A wife?

Delving further into the trunk, she found a hairbrush and comb, more stockings, a handful of colorful ribbons, a pair of tortoiseshell combs, as well as a little pewter cup. There was an oval mirror wrapped in newspaper, a small glass jar, a dried flower in a box, a small white blanket, a baby-sized sacque, a pair of booties, a tiny white cap, a rag doll.

She carefully replaced everything in the trunk and then opened the second chest. This one held an assortment of odds and ends—a box filled with a variety of coins, a small curved dagger with a jeweled hilt, a silver watch and chain, a pair of dun-colored trousers and a white linen shirt. There was a straight razor, the blade still sharp, and a shaving mug. She knew somehow that these things belonged to Roshan, that they had been a part of his life before he became a vampire.

She replaced everything, then closed the lid. After

locking both trunks, she gained her feet and examined the furniture. There was a curved settee covered in dark red velvet, a rocking chair, a three-drawer chest, a clock. A small table with an elaborately carved top contained a compartment lined with copper. It smelled faintly of tobacco.

Feeling hungry again, she went into the kitchen and made a peanut butter and jelly sandwich the way she had seen a woman make it on television. She took a bite, chewed it carefully, and smiled. Carrying the sandwich with her, she went outside and walked the grounds. Morgana paced at her heels, running off now and then to investigate a corner of the yard.

Brenna sat on a bench, admiring the changing leaves on the trees and the late blooming flowers while Morgana stalked a sparrow.

Returning to the house sometime later, Brenna found the remote control device and turned on the television. There was something fascinating about skipping through the channels, and she did so several times before she stopped, her gaze riveted to the screen as she watched a large black wolf transform into a man. He stared at a woman for several moments and then she transformed into a bird and flew away. A horrible cry of anguish rose in the man's throat. Intrigued, Brenna settled back on the sofa, her head pillowed on her hand, as she watched the story unfold, pleased when, in the end, good triumphed over evil and the wolf/man and the bird/woman were freed from the power of the evil clergyman who had cursed them.

A short time later, a new story began to unfold. Yawning, she turned off the television and went upstairs to Roshan's room. Folding back the bedspread, she slipped underneath the covers and closed her eyes.

She woke to the sound of Morgana growling in her ear.

Opening her eyes, Brenna saw that night had fallen. Roshan sat in the chair across from the bed, watching her through fathomless midnight blue eyes.

CHAPTER 8

"Did no one teach you that it is rude to stare at other people?" Brenna exclaimed, discomfited to wake and find him watching her so intently. She thought it unfair that he had access to her sleeping chamber but kept his so carefully hidden.

"Did no one teach you that it's rude to go through other people's belongings?"

How had he known? She lifted her chin defiantly. "I got tired of watching the television. I do not understand it."

"I thought I explained it to you."

"I still do not know what is real and what is, what was the word? Fiction?"

"I'll explain it to you again later tonight, if you like."

She sat up, the bedspread drawn up to her chin even though she was fully clothed. "What are you doing in here?"

He lifted one dark brow. "This is my room, remember? My clothes are in here."

Her gaze swept over him, noting that he was wearing the same shirt and breeches he had worn the night before.

Rising, he went to the dresser and pulled out a change of underwear, then went to the closet and selected a shirt and a pair of trousers. She noted that he favored black.

"I'm going to take a shower," he said, moving toward the bathroom. "I won't be long. Later tonight I'll move my things into another room."

She nodded, thinking she should probably feel guilty for making him move out of his bedroom, but she didn't. After all, she hadn't asked to come here.

She watched him go into the bathroom and close the door. A moment later she heard the sound of running water. To her consternation, she found herself imagining Roshan standing under the spray, the water coursing down his shoulders and arms, his broad chest, his stomach, his—

With a gasp, she jerked her thoughts away, horrified at the path her mind was wandering. No matter that she was attracted to Roshan DeLongpre, no matter that he walked in her dreams by night and occupied her every waking thought by day. Even though he was the most handsome of men, she had to remember that he was not truly a man at all. To love a vampire . . . ah, 'twould be folly indeed.

She glanced around the room, trying to find something else—anything else—to think of besides Roshan standing in the shower, but to no avail. The more she tried not to think about him, the more vivid her fantasies became. She had felt the strength in his arms. Was the rest of his body as hard and well-muscled? She licked her lips, remembering the excitement of his kisses, the way her very being had tingled at his touch. To her shame, she wished he would kiss her again so that she could feel his arms around her, feel her breasts crushed against his chest. Such unseemly thoughts for a maiden, she scolded. Until she met Roshan, she had never known such wicked imaginings.

Heat flooded her cheeks when the bathroom door opened. She stared at him, fervently praying that he could not read her mind.

He didn't say a word, but she knew from the amused look in his eyes that he was aware of her wayward thoughts. Whistling softly, he left the room.

Scrambling out from under the covers, Brenna closed and locked the door. Going into the bathroom, she locked that door, as well, then took a quick shower, all too aware that Roshan was in the house and that, should he wish to enter the room, the lock would not keep him out.

Stepping out of the shower, she grabbed a towel, marveling at its softness as she used it to dry off and then wrapped it around her.

Going into the bedroom, she pulled a vibrant green silk blouse from one of the bags, a long white skirt from another, undergarments from a third. She pulled on a pair of panties, loving the silky feel of the material against her skin.

So many changes in fashion, both in fabric and style, so many varieties to choose from in this new world. At home, she'd had but three dresses, two for everyday wear and one she kept for special occasions and holidays. No woman in her village had ever worn breeches. It simply wasn't done, nor, she was certain, had it ever been considered.

She brushed her hair and then her teeth, marveling

again at the wonders of Roshan's time. Imagine, a brush just for keeping her teeth clean. An oven that cooked things in seconds instead of hours, machines that washed dishes and clothes, cooking on a stove instead of on a tripod. She couldn't count the number of women she had treated for burns because their skirts had caught fire when they reached into the hearth to stir a pot or retrieve one from the coals.

She glanced around the room, wishing for a looking glass so that she might see how she looked, only then remembering that there were no mirrors in the house save for the small one on the medicine cabinet. Of course, she thought with a sheepish grin. Roshan had no need of mirrors, since vampires cast no reflection.

Taking a deep breath, she unlocked the door and made her way down the stairs. Morgana trailed at her heels, meowing softly. Going into the kitchen, Brenna opened the back door so the cat could go outside.

Brenna found Roshan sitting at his computer. Coming up behind him, she watched his fingers fly over the keyboard.

"What are you doing?" she asked, peering over his shoulder.

"Writing."

"Writing what?" She looked closer, frowning when she saw her name appear on the screen.

"My journal," he replied.

"Oh?"

"I've kept a record of my life since I became a vampire," he explained. At first, he had jotted his thoughts on scraps of paper; later, he had typed them up on a manual typewriter. With the advent of modern technology, he had transferred everything to his computer with the vague idea that someday in the future he might take a go at writing a novel based on his life story. He would have to sell it as fiction, of course. No one would ever believe any of it was true.

"I should like to read it," Brenna said.

"Indeed?" He closed the file, then swiveled his chair around to face her.

"Very much, especially since my name is in it."

"Perhaps one day," he replied. "What would you like to do this evening?"

"What did you say about me?"

"I wrote about how I found your name in a book and then how I traveled through time to find you, and what has happened between us since. Now, what would you like to do this evening?"

She stared at him, trying to imagine what it would be like to live as long as he had, to have seen all the wondrous things he must have seen in his long life.

"Brenna?"

"What? Oh, I should like to see more of the city."

"Let's go."

He showed her the city from one end to the other. When she expressed an interest in driving the car, he explained about turn signals and hand signals and then he drove to the outskirts of town and let her drive along a long stretch of quiet road.

She was a quick study. It was one of the things he liked best about her.

In the weeks that followed, he let her drive along quiet streets until he felt she was ready to handle heavier traffic, and then he let her drive in the city and finally on the freeway. He showed her how to put gas in the Ferrari and how to pay for it with his credit card. He found a copy of the Department of Motor Vehicles handbook and went over it with her until he was confident that she knew all the rules and traffic signals.

Late one night, he made a visit to the seedy side of town, and for a couple hundred dollars he obtained a birth certificate certifying that Brenna Flanagan had been born in a small town in Ireland in 1989. Another hundred dollars procured a driver's license from the same country.

He bought a washing machine and a dryer and together they learned how they worked. When she asked how he had washed his clothes before, he explained about dry cleaners and told her that some clothes could be washed at home but some had to be sent out. Not wanting to be bothered with laundry, he sent everything out, including his socks and underwear.

She learned how to run the vacuum and the DVD player, how to order takeout food over the phone.

Late one night, he spread a handful of currency and coins on the kitchen table and explained to her the value of each one.

Brenna spent part of her days watching television, trying to absorb what she was seeing. She understood now which programs were real and which weren't. For a time, she watched nothing but the news, completely astounded that she could watch things happening as they happened, not only in this place but on the other side of the world. She had never realized just how big the world was, or what a frightening place it could be. Sitting on the sofa in Roshan's house, she saw the grim faces of war and hunger and poverty. How blessed she was, she thought, to live in this country, in this time of peace and prosperity, a time when women were no longer considered chattel. No longer were they compelled to obey their husbands or marry for land or titles. Women were allowed to be independent now. They lived alone if they wished. They worked. They voted. They held public office. Truly, it was a wondrous age!

She spent hours experimenting in the kitchen. Once she got over her initial uneasiness at using the stove and the oven, she immersed herself in learning how to cook. Eating was, after all, a pleasurable experience, more so in this century than her own. There were so many foodstuffs she had never encountered before, so many ways of preparing various dishes.

One night, Roshan took her grocery shopping. She was aware of his wry amusement as she examined practically every item on the shelves. She was amazed at the way food was packaged, surprised to learn that you could buy milk when there wasn't a cow in sight, astonished that she could buy dinners that were already cooked and ready to eat. She discovered that bread came in a number of varieties. There was white bread and wheat bread, potato bread and egg bread, pumpernickel, dill, and rye. She was eager to try all of them, not to mention rolls and biscuits, croissants and cupcakes.

"I shall soon be as fat as old Mrs. McKenna," Brenna remarked as she placed several loaves of bread in the cart. "Do you not miss eating?"

He shook his head. "I can scarcely remember what solid food was like."

"How can you drink blood?" she asked with a shudder.

"It's normal for me." At first, he had been certain that he would rather die than do what was necessary for him to survive in his new lifestyle. He had gone for several nights without feeding, refusing to succumb to the hellish thirst that had plagued him. In the end, it had been the pain that drove him to it, pain so bad he would have done anything to end it. All it had taken was one taste, one drop, and all his revulsion had been swept away.

Brenna added a bunch of carrots to the basket. "But to drink nothing but . . . but that for such a long time. Do you never tire of it?"

He laughed softly, amused by the question and the expression on her face. "No," he said, "I never tire of it." Nor did he ever get enough. It was a thirst that could not be quenched, a hunger that was ever present, lingering in the back of his mind, always a remembered taste on his tongue.

"Do you like being a vampire?" she asked when they were finally on their way home.

He slid a glance at her, his gaze drawn to the pulse throbbing in her throat. Like it? Right now, with the low thrum of her heartbeat whispering in his ears and her scent filling his nostrils, he couldn't think of anything else.

"Roshan?" She glanced at him, her hands tightening on the wheel when she saw the direction of his gaze.

Knowing his eyes were probably glowing and red, he jerked his gaze away. A moment later, he grabbed control of the wheel as the car started drifting toward the ditch along the side of the road.

"Dammit, girl, if you want to drive, you have to watch where you're going!"

Pulling the car to a stop, he switched off the ignition. "I'm sorry. I didn't mean to shout at you."

"Your eyes," she whispered. "They were red . . . and . . . and glowing."

He nodded, his hands clenching at his sides, his

whole body tense, reminding her of the way Morgana looked before she pounced on an unwary bird.

"You were thinking of . . . of drinking from me."

He didn't deny it.

Without moving, she seemed to recoil from him.

He could hear the fierce beating of her heart, smell the fear rising from her in waves as the realization that she was alone on a dark road with a vampire struck her anew. In spite of all his assurances that she had nothing to fear, she was still afraid of him. Well, who could blame her? In spite of all his assurances to the contrary, she was right to be afraid.

He blew out a deep breath, tamping down the urge to draw her into his arms, to run his tongue over her skin, to taste of her sweetness. Just one drink to turn away the hunger . . .

As if sensing his thoughts, she pressed herself against the car door, her eyes wide and frightened.

"Can you find your way home?" he asked.

She nodded, her expression wary. "I think so."

"Good. I'll meet you there." In a single fluid movement, he was out of the car and striding away into the darkness.

Brenna stared after him. How long would he be able to resist the urge to drink her blood? How long before he gave in to the hunger that simmered below the surface?

She sat there for several minutes before she felt calm enough to drive home.

Roshan stormed through the night, his anger trailing behind him like thick black smoke. He should let her go. Send her away. Now, before it was too late.

Before he took what he wanted so desperately, needed so badly. He knew, deep inside, that the one small taste he'd had would never be enough. If he drained every mortal he hunted from now until the end of eternity, he would still hunger for one more taste of Brenna's sweetness. And yet, right or wrong, he couldn't help feeling that this woman had been destined to be his since the beginning of time, that the only reason he had been able to travel through time to find her was because she was meant to be his.

He was waiting at the open gate when she drove up. She slowed, her gaze meeting his through the windshield, and then she continued up the driveway.

A thought took him to the front of the house.

He was there to open the car door for her when she switched off the ignition.

She stared at him a moment, then took his hand and let him help her out of the car.

Wordlessly, he took the keys from her hand. Unlocking the trunk, he picked up the grocery bags and carried them into the house.

Brenna followed a few moments later, carrying the bag that had been in the backseat.

"Is that everything?" he asked.

She nodded as she set the bag on the counter.

Roshan stood in the doorway, his arms crossed over his chest while he watched her put away the groceries and paper goods. To his surprise, she moved around the kitchen as though she had lived in the house for months instead of a few weeks. Morgana sat on one of the kitchen chairs, regarding him warily, as always.

Brenna spared him hardly a glance as she moved around the kitchen but he knew she was as aware of his presence as he was of hers.

Finally, she whirled around, her eyes narrowed, her hands fisted on her hips. "Do you have to stare at me like that?"

She grimaced when he murmured an apology that he didn't mean.

Desire pulsed between them, charging the air, bringing a flush to her cheeks. She knew he wanted her. His need was almost tangible. He stood there, his hands tightly clenched at his sides, his eyes dark, burning with hunger. But hunger for what? Her blood? Or something equally dear? She didn't know which prospect was more frightening, the thought of satisfying his dark hunger or sharing his bed.

Crossing her arms over her breasts, she cast about for something to say, anything that would break the tension in the air.

"I want to know how to open the gates." She blurted the words, felt the back of her neck grow hot at the knowing look in his eyes.

He lifted one brow. "Going somewhere?"

"What if I said yes? Would you let me go?"

"Is that what you want? To leave here?" The words, *to leave me*, hung unspoken in the air between them.

"Yes. No. I don't know. All I know is that I'm tired of being locked behind these walls day in and day out like some kind of cloistered nun."

He grinned. She was the most unlikely-looking nun he had ever seen, with her long red hair falling over her shoulders like a crimson waterfall and her eyes blazing with righteous anger.

Her eyes narrowed. "Do you ever intend to let me go?"

He didn't want to, even though he knew it was for the best. Better to end it now before he did something they would both regret. All that aside, he realized it was unfair of him to keep her imprisoned here against her will. He had taught her what she needed to know to survive in her new environment. The rest was up to her. Even if she decided to leave here, leave him, he would always be able to find her. The tiny bit of blood he had taken would guide him to her no matter where she might be.

Reaching into his pants pocket, he withdrew the keys to the Ferrari and placed them in her hand. "I'll remove the wards from the gate before I take my rest."

Rising on tiptoe, she kissed his cheek. "Thank you."

He nodded, wondering if, once she was away from here, from him, she would ever come back.

CHAPTER 9

The atmosphere between the two of them was strained the rest of the evening.

Roshan went into the living room and turned on the television. He lit a fire in the hearth, then sank back in his favorite chair, his gaze fixed on the flames, oddly discomfited by the thought that she would leave and not return, even though he knew it would be for the best. He had nothing to offer her; he couldn't even guarantee her safety.

He drummed his fingers on the arm of the chair. He had accomplished his goal. He had found Brenna Flanagan and saved her from death at the stake. And now, to his astonishment, he found that he was in danger of falling in love with the lady. He had already grown accustomed to her presence in his house, to knowing she would be there when he woke. Lately, lying in his lair as the rising sun edged over the horizon to sweep night's dark cloak from the sky, the last thing he was aware of before he tumbled into the Dark Sleep was the soothing sound of Brenna's heartbeat.

He snorted softly, amused by the turn of his thoughts. Falling in love, indeed. Should he be foolish enough to do so, he would only be asking for heartache. Surely no woman in her right mind would knowingly get involved with a vampire.

She entered the room a few minutes later, her footsteps little more than a whisper on the plush carpet, the cat at her heels.

Brenna hesitated when she saw him there, then she sat down on the sofa, her arms folded across her breasts, her gaze fixed on the television as if she hoped to discover all the unanswered questions of the universe on the screen.

Morgana stared from one to the other, then curled up in front of the fireplace, staring at the two of them through unblinking yellow eyes.

Roshan grinned in wry amusement as the commercial ended and the football game resumed. He watched Brenna for several minutes, aware that his scrutiny was making her increasingly nervous.

"Feel free to change the channel," he said, tossing her the remote.

She rewarded him with a tentative smile, then flipped through the channels until she found a movie. It was one he had seen numerous times, starring Meg Ryan and Billy Crystal.

Brenna settled back on the sofa, her hands clasped in her lap, one leg folded beneath her.

Tension flowed between them.

He pretended to watch the fire.

She pretended to watch the movie.

He swore under his breath.

She fidgeted with a lock of her hair.

When he couldn't stand it any longer, he turned to

look at her, admiring the soft curve of her cheek, the way the light from the fire played over her face. He never tired of looking at her. An in-drawn breath carried the scent of lilacs and warm womanly flesh to his nostrils. His hunger quickened, not for her blood, but for the taste of her lips, the touch of her skin beneath his hand.

As though sensing his heated gaze, she turned to face him.

Desire arced between them, sizzling with electricity, like the air before a summer thunderstorm.

Without conscious thought, he was on his feet and moving toward her.

She stared up at him, her eyes wide, her lips slightly parted. He could hear her heart beating wildly in her breast.

"Brenna."

She didn't say anything, only continued to stare at him.

Kneeling before her, he stroked her cheek, reveling in the warmth of her skin beneath his palm. His own skin was always cool to the touch unless he had just fed.

"Kiss me, Brenna," he whispered. "One kiss, to chase away the shadows and keep me warm when I take my rest."

She stared at him, her heart racing, and then she leaned toward him.

His hand slid behind her nape as his mouth covered hers. Her lips were as soft and sweet as he remembered and he knew one kiss wouldn't be enough. Would never be enough.

Taking hold of her waist, he drew her down onto his lap, his mouth never leaving hers. He deepened the kiss, his tongue teasing hers, his preternatural senses filling with her nearness until he could think of nothing else, wanted nothing else. Her body molded to his, her lush curves soft against the hardness of his chest.

He scattered kisses on her eyelids, her cheeks, her brow, then slid to her neck. Unable to resist, he ran his tongue over the skin behind her ear, kissed the hollow of her throat.

The seductive sound of her heartbeat resonated in his ears; the call of her life's blood like a siren's song, overshadowing the ache in his body. His teeth grazed her skin.

With a cry, he quickly turned his head away lest she see his fangs and the hunger that was surely blazing like red death in his eyes.

Moaning softly, she reached for him.

Roshan drew back before she could touch him. Rising, he took a few steps away, careful to keep his back toward her. He knew how he looked, his eyes wild, blazing with the lust for blood. He ran his tongue over his teeth, felt the sharp prick of his fangs. Oh, yes, he knew how he looked—he had seen the face of the vampire before, the night Zerena had seduced him . . .

He had been on his way home from the local tavern when he realized he was being followed. Glancing over his shoulder, he had seen a woman trailing a few yards behind him. He had never seen her before, was, in fact, certain she was not from this part of the county. Her clothing was too fine, her skin too fair, her face unlined by the worry and hard work that marked the countenance of every other woman he knew.

Wondering who she was, he had focused on the road ahead once again.

And then she had called his name. Startled, he had come to an abrupt halt, surprised to find her standing at his elbow.

She had smiled up at him, revealing teeth whiter than any he had ever seen.

"Who are you?" he had asked, embarrassed by the tremor in his voice.

She tilted her head to one side, her deep brown eyes sparkling. "I am the Lady Zerena."

"Why are you following me?"

"Why, indeed?" She ran her fingertips down the length of his arm, her fingers caressing his biceps. And then her gaze trapped his and he was caught, unable to look away, unable to resist the promise he saw in her eyes.

Zerena led him to a small wooden house located far off the main road. From the outside, it looked like a hovel. Inside, it looked like a chamber fit for a queen. A large bed covered with soft furs and silken pillows occupied most of the room. Damask draperies covered the single window. Thick rugs were scattered across the floor.

She gave him a gentle push toward the bed. "Sit." She poured a glass of dark red wine and handed it to him. "Relax," she purred. "I'm not going to hurt you."

He was a big man. He could have crushed her with one hand, yet deep in his gut, he didn't doubt that she was the stronger. The thought sent a chill coursing down his spine.

"Drink," she urged. "It will relax you."

He had lacked the will to refuse. Lifting the glass, he drained the contents.

Still smiling, she took the glass from his hand and tossed it into the fireplace. It shattered against the bricks. Shards of sparkling crystal reflected all the colors of the rainbow before landing in the ashes.

Sitting beside him on the bed, she ran her hand

through his hair and down his neck, then slipped her fingers inside his shirt to caress his chest. He shivered at her touch.

She leaned against him, her body bearing him down until he was stretched out on the mattress, her body atop his, her hands boldly exploring his arms, his legs, the width of his shoulders.

When he started to protest, she covered his mouth with her own. At the touch of her lips, all thought fled his mind until he felt her teeth at his throat.

Awareness flooded through him and he opened his eyes to find himself staring up at a monster with blazing red eyes and fangs stained with his blood.

Too late, he had tried to fight her off, but he was no match for her preternatural strength. He cried out, a mingled protest born of fear and outrage as her fangs pierced his throat again. And then, to his amazement, he lost the will to fight. Instead, he was overcome with such a sense of euphoria that he placed his hand at the back of her head, pressing her mouth closer, wanting her to take more, wanting her to take it all.

And she had. His memory of what had followed was hazy. He remembered her voice calling to him, remembered her wrist pressed to his mouth, her voice commanding him to drink before it was too late.

He had been too weak, too weary, to resist the power in her voice. He had closed his mouth over her wrist and drank and drank until she jerked her arm away.

"Sleep now," she had told him, a wicked gleam in her eyes. "Sleep your last night as a man."

He had stared up at her, confused by her words, alarmed by the expression on her face, but before he could demand an explanation, mortal sleep had claimed him for the last time . . .

"Roshan?"

With a shake of his head, he realized that Brenna had asked him a question.

Taking a deep breath, he stilled the hunger within him, then turned to face her.

"Are you all right?" she asked again. "Have I done something wrong?"

"No."

"Then why . . . ?" A rosy flush colored her cheeks. "Why did you stop?"

"Because I don't want to hurt you."

"Hurt me?" She looked confused for a moment, and then, as comprehension dawned in her eyes, she lifted a hand to her throat.

"Just so," he said, his voice brittle. "The lust for flesh and the lust for blood are closely entwined. I can't always separate one from the other."

Still sitting on the floor, she blinked up at him, her expression thoughtful. "Do you like being a vampire?"

It was a question she had asked before, one he hadn't answered. She had a way of repeating herself until he told her what she wanted to know.

"Like it?" He pondered that for a moment. "I like living," he replied after a time. "I've enjoyed seeing the world change, experiencing the advances in civilization." Although some things, like war and poverty, never changed.

"Is there no cure?"

"None that I've heard of."

"Have you ever looked for one?"

He sat down on the far end of the sofa. "No."

"Why not?"

He grunted softly. "In the beginning, I didn't think of it. All I thought of was satisfying the hunger that possessed my every waking moment. Later, when I had learned to control the craving, I began to appreciate the supernatural powers the Dark Trick had given me. I explored the world, marveling at how very big it was, and how very little I knew. I spent years educating myself, learning all I could of the world and its people."

"It sounds like a very exciting life."

"Yes," he said quietly. "But a very lonely one."

"In all your long life, have you never found a woman who would accept you for what you are?"

"Would you?"

To his amazement, she answered without thought, without doubt. "Yes."

He shook his head. "You don't know what you're saying."

"I want you," she said, surprised by her own boldness. "No mortal man will ever fully accept me for what I am. Even John Linder, who professed to love me above all else, was not comfortable with my magick. But you . . ." She shrugged, a half-smile playing over her lips. "You understand."

"But you don't."

"What do you mean?"

"You've not seen what I truly am," he said, his voice almost a growl. "You have no idea of what I really am."

"Show me, then."

He lifted one brow. "Are you sure you want to know?"

She swallowed hard, and then nodded. "Show me."

Taking a deep breath, he let the hunger rise within him, felt his fangs lengthen in response to the scent of her blood, knew his eyes had taken on an unholy glow.

He clenched his hands at his sides to keep from reaching for her.

She stared up at him, her expression one of mingled horror and fascination.

"Is this what you wanted to see?" he asked, his voice harsh as he waited for her to run screaming from the room.

"'Tis quite a frightening sight," she admitted, a faint quiver in her voice.

"Then why aren't you afraid?"

"I am not sure."

With an effort, he fought down the beast within him. "You mystify me, Brenna Flanagan." He had seen fear in her eyes many times before with much less reason, and now, when he stood before her, his true self bared to her gaze, she claimed to be unafraid.

"'Tis hard to be afraid of the man who saved my life, someone who has shown me nothing but kindness. You may appear to be a monster, but I have seen the man beneath."

"I am not a man," he reminded her.

She waved a hand in a dismissive gesture. "You may not think of yourself as a man, but that is what I see when I look at you." Rising, she closed the distance between them. "Will you not kiss me again?"

"You're playing with fire, Brenna Flanagan," he warned. "Fire far more dangerous than the flames you escaped before."

"I am not afraid." Rising on her tiptoes, she wrapped her arms firmly around his neck. "Kiss me, my lord vampire."

How could he refuse? Her lips were warm and pink, her eyes alight with expectation, and her body . . . he could feel the heat of her breasts against his chest, the length of her thigh against his own. With a low growl, he slid his arm around her waist, bent his head, and claimed her lips with his.

It was just a kiss, yet fire burned through him, a bright white fire that burned away the everlasting darkness in his soul, made him believe, if only for that moment, that he didn't have to spend the rest of his existence alone.

She was breathless when he released her. He tried to take a step back, but her arms were still around his neck.

"Have you ever been with a man before?" he asked.

"Of course I . . ." Her voice trailed off, her eyes widening, as she perceived his meaning. "No."

Taking her hands in his, he took a step backward. On some deep inner level, he had known that she was still a maiden, her body untouched, innocent. With a sigh, he brushed a lock of hair behind her ear. "I think we'd better stop this, now."

A soft sound of protest rose in her throat as she leaned into him, her body again molding itself to his.

Damn! Didn't she realize the effect she was having on him? He murmured her name, a wealth of longing in his voice, in the depths of his eyes.

She made a soft sound low in her throat.

"Brenna, this isn't a good idea."

She looked up at him, mute.

"Your first time," Roshan said, his voice thick. "It should be with your husband."

He had lived in the modern world long enough to know how archaic and trite those words sounded. In this day and age, men and women lived together, openly and shamelessly, without the blessing of the church, yet he was still a product of his upbringing, taught since childhood that a man respected a woman, and that intimacy before marriage was a sin. In the years since he had been a vampire, it was not advice to which he had always adhered. He was a vampire, not a monk, but to his credit he had never considered bedding a virgin. On those occasions when he had sought out female companionship, he had made sure the woman knew the score, and then he had made certain she would remember nothing of what passed between them.

"I want no husband," Brenna retorted.

"No?"

She shook her head. "Marriage has brought nothing but misery to the women in my family."

He looked at her, waiting for an explanation.

With a sigh, she sat down on the sofa. "My great-grandfather betrayed my great-grandmother. She was burned at the stake. My grandfather vowed to love my grandmother as long as he lived, but after ten years of marriage, he left her, claiming she was in league with the devil. It was nonsense, of course. None of the women in my family has ever practiced black magick or invoked any of the dark arts. My own father abandoned my mother and me when he discovered that his daughter was a witch."

Roshan sat down at the other end of the sofa. "I take it there are no male witches in your family?"

"No. It passes from mother to daughter."

"So," he said slowly, "you don't want a husband, but you want me to make love to you?"

"Yes."

"I guess you're not as old-fashioned as I thought," he muttered.

"What?"

"Nothing."

"I may not want a husband," she said candidly. "But I do want a child. Your child."

Few things had taken him by surprise since the night Zerena had bestowed the Dark Gift upon him, but Brenna's words had caught him totally unprepared. For a moment, he pictured Atiyana in his mind's eye, her face pale, her eyes empty of life, the sheet beneath her stained with blood. He recalled picking up the tiny infant she had expelled from her womb moments before she died.

"I'm afraid that's impossible." He held up his hand, stilling the questions he saw rising in her eyes. "I can't create life, Brenna. I can only sustain my own, such as it is."

"I am sorry," she said quietly. "I did not know."

For a moment, he regretted telling her the truth. Had he been a less honorable man, he could have taken her to his bed, made sweet love to her night after night, let her believe that he could give her the child she yearned for.

"I'm sorry, too," he replied. There was hardly a day that went by that he didn't think of his son. Even after all these years, the memory of the infant's death was still painful. His son. Such a tiny scrap of humanity, dead before it had been born, and all Roshan's hopes and dreams with him.

He shook the memory from his mind.

Once again, tension flowed between them.

Brenna turned to stare at the television, all too aware that he was watching her. She tried to forget the taste of his kiss, the pleasure that flooded her whole being when his lips touched hers. She had heard that vampires possessed an aura, a charm that mortals found irresistible. Was that all it was? Or was her attraction to him real?

She glanced at him surreptitiously, trying to see his aura. Granny O'Connell's aura had been green, which was associated with nurturing. John Linder's had been a dingy orange. Brenna's own aura was blue, an indication of psychic energy.

Roshan DeLongpre's aura was gray. She frowned, trying to remember what that represented. Gray . . . ah, of course, it implied a closeness to otherworldly things and the ability to influence the wind and the rain.

"Something wrong?" he asked.

"No. I was just wondering . . . can you make it storm when you wish?"

He nodded. "Why?"

"I was studying your aura."

"Indeed?"

"It's gray. A rather dark gray."

"I always thought that was a lot of hocus-pocus."

"Oh, no. My mother's was pink."

"And that means . . . what?"

"Those with pink auras are very loving and affectionate," Brenna said wistfully. "As was my mother. There was no kinder woman in all our village. Everyone loved her."

"What happened when your father left?"

"My mother never got over it. She died a year later. Granny O'Connell raised me."

"How old were you when your mother died?"

"Eleven."

"And how old are you now?"

"Nineteen."

He muttered an oath. Nineteen! "Did you ever see your father again?"

"No." She crossed her arms over her breasts, the gesture blatantly defensive. "I do not want to talk about it anymore."

He glanced at the window. It was late, after midnight. He shifted restlessly as the hunger stirred within him, reminding him that he had not yet fed.

Brenna followed his gaze to the window, then looked back at him. "I guess you will be going out soon." It wasn't a question.

He nodded curtly, the beating of countless hearts calling to him like distant thunder.

Brenna lifted a hand to her throat. He had bitten her once, tasted her blood. What would it be like if he did it again, while she was awake? Would it hurt? She shook her head, stunned by the turn of her thoughts yet unable to put it from her mind.

He was watching her, his eyes narrowed. It reminded her of the way Morgana sometimes watched a mouse before she pounced on it. Morgana was a fearsome predator, but sometimes the mouse got lucky and escaped the cat's claws and teeth.

Roshan was a far more fearsome predator than Morgana, Brenna mused. If she lingered here, in the lion's den, how long would she be safe from his bite?

CHAPTER 10

Searching for prey, Roshan had moved swiftly through the darkness, enjoying the feel of the night's cool breath against his skin, the whisper of an errant breeze in his hair. He had fed quickly, savoring the rush of energy that flowed over his tongue and slid down this throat like the sweetest nectar.

Now, after sending the woman on her way, he walked the dark streets of the city. As always these nights, his thoughts turned to Brenna. She was unlike any woman he had ever known, and not just because she was a witch. She was afraid of him, yet she stayed in his house. He admired her courage in coming to terms with life in a world so vastly different from the one she left behind. He loved the fact that she wasn't afraid to give him the rough side of her tongue. If he had one complaint, it was that she was so young. Nineteen. He could scarcely remember what it was like to be that young, and even though his physical body appeared to be that of a twenty-seven-year-old man, in reality he was three hundred and thirteen years old. Far too old for a sweet young thing like Brenna Flanagan.

Returning home, he went upstairs to Brenna's room. He stood beside her bed for twenty minutes, watching her sleep. He listened to the slow, steady sound of her breathing, admired the soft golden glow of her skin, the way her eyelashes made perfect crescents lying against her cheeks. Moonlight filtered through the window, casting silver highlights in her hair. A soft sigh escaped her lips, followed by a faint smile. He wondered what she was dreaming about, wondered if he dared hope she was dreaming of him. Grunting softly, he turned away from the bed. Any dreams she had about him would no doubt be nightmares from which she would awake screaming.

Going downstairs, he went into his den and sat at his computer. Bringing up his journal, he opened the file titled 2005. Before Brenna entered his life, he had written in his journal every night. Ah, Brenna. What a welcome distraction she was in his existence! He smiled, thinking of her. How pale and empty his nights had been without her.

He stared at the last entry in his journal and blew out a sigh. He had a lot of catching up to do. His fingers flew over the keys as he recorded his thoughts, starting with the night he had decided to end his existence. He had written a few notes soon after rescuing Brenna; now he expanded on them, writing his memories of what it had been like to travel through time, the exhilaration of speeding backward through the centuries, catching glimpses of people long dead and places long gone from the earth. He described his surprise at actually arriving at his destination, the sheer delight of watching Brenna Flanagan dance in the light of the moon, his horror when he saw her bound to the stake, his apprehension as he reached through the flames to free her.

He wrote of her reaction to the twenty-first century, of teaching her how to drive and taking her shopping. He described, in great detail, her wary acceptance of what he was, the attraction that burned between them whenever their eyes met, the first time he had kissed her.

Grinning, he went back and added a few sentences about his feelings when she had tried to turn him into a frog. He had been highly amused at the time. The memory made him laugh now, and it felt good. Laughter had been sorely missing from his life until now. He had Brenna to thank for making him laugh again, among other things.

Two hours later, his journal was up-to-date. He wondered what she would think, should he let her read the story of his existence. Would she find it fascinating, or would she be repulsed by his thoughts and deeds as he adjusted to life as a vampire?

Sitting there, with hours yet until dawn, he pulled up some of his older files. He skimmed through the years, reliving the confusion he had felt in the beginning, when every sunrise had filled him with dread and the niggling fear that he might not rise again. Vampire hunters had been everywhere in those dark times. Vampires had been more numerous in those days, and though he had called none of them friend, he had met with others of his kind to exchange information. In those days, every night brought reports of new deaths. The most fearsome hunter of them all had been Stuart Ramsey. He had destroyed more than fifty vampires before he died sometime in the seventeenth century. The name Ramsey had been feared through the ages as the descendents of Stuart Ramsey followed in his bloody footsteps. Today, the name Edward Ramsey was enough to send vampires scurrying for cover, though Roshan had recently heard a rumor that Ramsey was no longer a hunter but had become one of the hunted. An amusing irony, if it was true.

In the early 1800s, Roshan had taken a ship to America. It had been the worst journey of his entire existence. He had been trapped inside a coffin down in the hold of the ship by day and had prowled the deck by night, feeding off rats and an occasional crew member.

He had loved America at first sight. The crowded cities, the diversity of its people. A veritable smorgasbord. Italians and Mexicans, Russians and Slavs, Poles and Germans, Danes and Swedes. And Indians. He had spent some time in the West, intrigued by the way the Indians lived. He had moved among the tribes, Sioux and Cheyenne, Crow and Arapaho, Apache and Comanche, studying their ways and their religions.

He had found it interesting that no matter the culture, whether the people were red, white, brown, or yellow, the mythology of every civilization included vampires, from the _vampir_ of Hungary and the _upior_ of Poland to the _vyrkolakas_ of Greece. He supposed that accounted for the fact that vampires were the most popular monsters of all, and that vampire tales had been told and retold for thousands of years. He remembered reading his first vampire novel, _Varney the Vampyre,_ which had been published back in 1847. Hundreds of books and movies had been made about the undead since then. He had read all the books, seen all the movies.

But none of those fictionalized works came close to the reality that he had lived for the last two hundred and eighty-six years.

Never, in all that time, had he felt the way he did now. For the first time in his long existence, he had hope, and that hope was embodied in the red-haired woman sleeping in his bed.

CHAPTER 11

Brenna slept late the following morning. Lying in bed, the blankets pulled up to her chin, she stared at the ceiling, thinking about her life and how drastically it had changed in such a very short time. Who would ever have thought that poor Brenna Flanagan, who had barely had the means to keep body and soul together, would ever be living in a house as grand as this one? She had more than enough food to eat, not to mention enough raiment to clothe a dozen women. She had seen wonders and inventions that no one in her time had ever imagined and would never believe possible. If she was dreaming, she wasn't sure she wanted to wake up.

She smiled as Morgana slid under her arm, begging for her attention.

"Good morrow," Brenna said. Rolling onto her side, she scratched the cat's ears, smiling as the cat began to purr.

Brenna's eyes widened suddenly. Roshan had promised

to unlock the gates before he went to bed. Today, for the first time, she would be on her own, able to go anywhere she wished. Independent, she thought, just like the women of the time.

Rising, she went into the bathroom and filled the bathtub with water. Pinning her hair on top of her head, she stepped into the tub. Morgana sat on the lid of the toilet, tidily washing her paws while her mistress luxuriated in a hot bubble bath.

Lying there, Brenna marveled anew at how wonderful it was to have hot and cold running water inside the house. The soap she used to wash with smelled like lavender.

Thirty minutes later she stepped out of the tub and dried off with a large fluffy blue towel. Dropping the towel into the hamper, she shook out her hair, then went into the bedroom. Opening the top drawer of the dresser, she pulled out a pair of pretty pink panties and a matching bra (a truly strange and slightly uncomfortable contraption). Clad in her underwear, she opened the closet, frowning while she tried to decide what to wear. Never, in all her life, had she had so many choices! Dresses, skirts, pants, blouses, sweaters, shirts, shoes, sandals, and boots, not to mention a wide variety of undergarments, nylons, and socks.

Finally, she slipped into a pair of blue jeans, a fluffy white sweater, and a pair of soft leather boots that laced up the side.

Going downstairs, she filled Morgana's dish with cat food, and then fixed herself a big breakfast—oatmeal smothered in brown sugar, scrambled eggs, buttered toast, and a glass of buttermilk.

She had never cared much for cooking, but here, with all the modern conveniences, it seemed less of a chore. She didn't have to make her own bread. She didn't have to milk a cow, or gather eggs. She didn't have to collect wood for the hearth, or worry that her skirts might catch fire when she reached into the hearth to stir a pot of soup. Of course, it had taken several days and a lot of trial and error to learn how to cook on the gas stove, but with the help of the cookbook Roshan had bought her, she was learning.

Of course, she had learned a lot of other things in the last few weeks, thanks to Roshan. He had patiently answered her endless questions, taken her into the city so she could get used to this strange new world, taught her to drive his car which, she now knew, cost a great deal of money. In spite of the fact that he was a vampire, she felt safe with him. Maybe he was right. Maybe she would get used to this time and this place.

After breakfast, she brushed her teeth, then ran a comb through her hair and pulled it back with a ribbon.

Roshan had left his car keys on the kitchen table, along with four hundred and fifty dollars. Feeling suddenly rich and carefree, she pocketed the cash, picked up the keys, and left the house. Moments later, she was driving toward the gates. Had Roshan remembered to remove the wards?

But yes, the gates swung open as she approached. Filled with excitement, she drove through the high arch, turned right, and headed for the city.

She drove up and down the streets, looking at the houses and the people. Until now, she had only seen her new world by night. Once again, she was struck by the noise of the city. The honking of horns, the rumble of trucks, the distant blast of a train's whistle, the quiet purr of the Ferrari's engine, the roar of an airplane overhead. She had never realized how quiet her own cottage had been until now. Roshan's home was never completely quiet. There was the hum of the refrigerator, the soft hiss of the forced air heating cycling on and off, the creak of the wood as the house settled.

Bypassing the mall, she parked on a narrow side street. Exiting the car, she locked the door, then strolled slowly down the street, pausing now and then to peer into one of the shop windows. The stores along the street were not so large or as crowded as the ones in the mall.

She passed a candy store, a video rental store, several dress shops, a shoe store, a toy store. There was an ice cream parlor on the corner. Seeing a picture of a malt in the window, she went inside, and after a moment's hesitation, she sat down at a small round table by the window.

She had no sooner taken her seat than a waitress came to take her order.

"Do you have chocolate malts?" Brenna asked, remembering the one Roshan had bought her at the mall.

"Sure thing," the girl said with a smile. "The best in town."

"May I have one, please?"

"Sure, honey. Anything else?"

"No, thank you."

When the waitress left the table, Brenna turned and looked out the window, watching the people pass by. Men in suits, women in shorts and halter tops, boys on skateboards, girls giggling together, they all seemed to be in a hurry to get somewhere.

Brenna smiled her thanks as the waitress placed the malt on the table. Brenna ate the whipped cream and the cherry, wishing she dared ask for more. As the waitress had promised, the malt was delicious. Brenna sipped it slowly, savoring the rich chocolate taste, thinking that this malt was even better than the one she'd had at the mall.

She felt quite proud of herself when she paid the check, even though it was Roshan's money. Although purchasing a malt was a relatively small accomplishment, it was the first thing she had bought and paid for herself. For the first time since arriving in this century, she had accomplished something entirely on her own. Perhaps she could find her way in this new world after all.

Leaving the ice cream shop, she crossed the street and continued down the other side. Three young men wearing baggy pants and black T-shirts were standing outside of a liquor store. They all looked her up and down as she approached. One of them whistled at her.

"Hey, pretty mama," another one called. "You're lookin' mighty fine today."

The third one nodded in agreement and then, as she drew closer, he reached for her arm.

Brenna murmured a quick incantation as his fingers closed over her arm. With a cry of pain, the young man jerked his hand away, yelping as if he had just touched a hot stove.

Grinning inwardly, Brenna kept walking.

When she reached the end of the block, she looked both ways and then crossed the street and started back the way she had come. And then she saw it, a large black sign in the shape of a pointy black hat. The words The Wiccan Way Coffee Shop and Bookstore were painted on the hat in neat white letters.

Quickening her step, Brenna hurried down the street. She hesitated at the entrance, then, taking a deep breath, she opened the door and stepped inside.

It took a moment for her eyes to adjust to the rather dim interior. The walls were a creamy white, the floor was done in square tiles of black, white, and gray. Looking to her right, she saw a wall of glass shelves that held an assortment of crystals, goblets, and dragons made of glass and pewter. Another shelf held small pots of herbs. To her left was a floor-to-ceiling shelf filled with books on witchcraft, paganism, folk magic and medicine, urban legends, Celtic traditions, astrology, tarot, spell casting, channeling, and psychic development, as well as a numbers of almanacs and calendars.

A glass-fronted cabinet held many items that were basic to the practice of witchcraft. The first shelf held a variety of pentagrams, some plain, some with colored points. There were a number of pentacles in gold, silver, or copper. The second shelf held a variety of censers, some with feet to keep them from scorching the surface they rested on. The third shelf held a basket of feathers, bundled sticks of incense, several mirrors, bottles of oils, and pots of ink.

An arched doorway hung with beads in all the colors of the rainbow separated the bookstore from the adjoining coffee shop. Glancing through the archway, Brenna saw perhaps a dozen small round tables. Half of them were covered with white cloths, half with black. Green candles burned in the center of each table. A long black counter lined with bar stools ran along the far wall. A pretty young woman with long black hair was waiting on several customers seated at the counter. A woman wearing a long gray dress and a floppy-brimmed black hat sat at one of the tables reading a newspaper.

"May I help you?"

Brenna glanced over her shoulder to see a tall, painfully thin woman with eyes the color of topaz smiling at her. The woman wore an ankle-length black dress and a pair of high-heeled black boots.

"Are you looking for something specific?" the woman asked.

"No." Brenna shook her head. "I was just . . . just curious."

"Of course," the woman said, smiling. "Many people are curious about the paranormal and the occult these days, some seriously, some just because it's the in thing at the moment. Some are into crystals, others into palm reading or tarot. A few are into voodoo and black magick. There are others who are searching for something to believe in, something to hold on to in these days of unrest and trouble. Some are turning their backs on established religion and seeking new paths to follow."

"Like witchcraft?" Brenna asked hesitantly.

"Wicca," the woman corrected. "It's witchcraft of a sort, but it's also a religion, a way of living and believing."

Brenna nodded. "Is it all right if I just look around?"

"Of course. I'm Myra Kavanaugh. I own the shop. Let me know if you need anything."

"Thank you."

The woman smiled at her again. "Blessed be."

Alone once more, Brenna turned to the bookshelf. Although many of the words in the books were familiar to her, there were others that were unknown, and others that, though familiar, were not spelled the way she knew them. Still, she was able to make sense of most of what she read.

She thumbed through a book about rituals for modern pagans, including the history of the goddess Lilith. Brenna had never heard of Lilith and found the information quite interesting. Lilith was a seductress, tempting men with forbidden pleasures and desires. Strangely, she was also known as a night hag, hardly the description of a seductive maiden. According to the book, modern witches considered Lilith to be the patroness of witches, while others described her as an alluring siren, a seductive vampire, and the ultimate sex goddess.

With a shake of her head, Brenna replaced the book on the shelf and withdrew a book of spells. It was amazing to her that she was standing in a store that made no secret of selling books and charms for witches. How times had changed! In her day, men and women suspected of witchcraft had been hanged. Now they owned coffee shops and mingled with their friends and neighbors without fear.

She glanced at the owner of the shop. Was she a witch? And what of the patrons in the coffee shop? Were they all witches, or merely ordinary people who liked the excitement of mingling with those who believed in the occult?

Turning her attention back to the book in her hand, Brenna read the ingredients for a spell to repel troublesome ghosts. It called for dried rosemary leaves, sea salt, garlic powder, and dried black beans.

Brenna grunted softly as she read the directions. Black beans were, indeed, an ancient charm against ghosts and everyone knew that black was the best color for banishing. Another section dealt with the making of magick wands. She thought regretfully of the wand she had left behind. She had fashioned it herself from a willow branch and painted it in shades of blue and green. The wand was like a conduit, an extension of her will, used to help focus and direct power, cast a magical circle, or stir ingredients in a cauldron. Perhaps it was time to think about making a new one.

She was about to put the book back on the shelf when she heard footsteps coming up behind her.

And then a deep voice asked, "Is this your first time here?"

Turning, Brenna found herself face-to-face with a man a few inches taller than she was. He had short blond hair, pale blue eyes, and a thin mustache. He wore a light blue sweater and a pair of charcoal gray trousers and was, she thought, very nearly as handsome as Roshan, though they were complete opposites. Light and dark, she mused. Sunshine and shadow.

He smiled at her, displaying even white teeth and a dimple in his left cheek. "I'm sorry, I didn't mean to startle you." He held out a slender hand. "I'm Anthony Loken."

She hesitated a moment before placing her hand, briefly, in his. "Brenna Flanagan." Turning away to hide her nervousness, she replaced the book on the shelf and then, taking a deep breath, she turned to meet the stranger's gaze once more.

"May I buy you a cup of coffee?" he asked politely.

"No, thank you."

"Please, change your mind." He smiled disarmingly and then, apparently sensing her uneasiness, he said, "You're perfectly safe here. It's a public place, after all."

Myra smiled at the two of them as she passed by. "Tony's harmless," she told Brenna with a wink. "Just don't believe anything he says."

"You'd better be nice to me, Myra," Loken said with a wry grin, "or I'll take my business elsewhere."

Myra waved a dismissive hand in the air. "No, you won't. Try the Almond Amaretto, you two. Darlene just put up a fresh pot."

Loken turned to Brenna. "So, what do you say?"

"All right."

He smiled at her, then stepped back so she could precede him into the coffee shop. Brenna chose a table near the window. Loken held her chair for her, ordered two cups of Almond Amaretto from the waitress, and then leaned back in his chair.

"I take it you're interested in magick and the like," he remarked, crossing his arms over his chest.

"Yes," she replied cautiously. "Since you are also in here, I gather you are, too."

"Oh, definitely."

Brenna bit down on her lower lip, wondering if she dared ask him if he was a witch. He solved the problem for her.

"This is a well-known meeting place for those who dabble in magick. Of course, we get outsiders from time to time, but most of Myra's customers are serious practitioners." He leaned forward. "Are you by chance a witch?"

She shook her head, unable to voice the lie.

He settled back in his chair again. "Were you looking for anything in particular?" he asked. "Or are you just curious?"

"Just curious," she said. Although Anthony Loken seemed gentlemanly enough, she was reluctant to trust him, though she couldn't say why. She certainly had no intention of telling him that she was interested in finding a cure for vampirism. She wasn't even sure why she was looking for one. Roshan had never said anything about wanting to be mortal again.

"Thanks, Darlene," Loken said, smiling at the pretty serving girl who brought their order.

Darlene smiled back, a blush rising in her cheeks. "Would you like a cinnamon roll or a tart?" she asked. "Nicole just made some fresh."

"Nothing for me," Loken replied. "Miss Flanagan, would you care for anything?"

"No, thank you."

With a last adoring look at Anthony Loken, the waitress left the table.

"So," Loken said, stirring a bit of cream into his coffee, "are you new in the city?"

Brenna nodded. Picking up her cup, she sipped it slowly.

"I didn't think I'd seen you in here before," Loken remarked. "I must say, I hope you're here to stay. We can always use another pretty face."

"That is very kind of you to say," Brenna replied politely. "But you should not pay me such compliments."

He studied her for several moments. "You're not from around here, are you?"

"No."

"And not very talkative." He lifted his cup and took a drink. "I can tell you're wondering if I'm a practitioner. Well, I am. I specialize in channeling and cartomancy."

"You don't care that people know you're a"—she lowered her voice—"warlock."

He shrugged. "Why should I care? This isn't seventeenth-century Salem. No one cares about witchcraft anymore. There are too many other scary things going on in the world for people to worry about witches and warlocks, even if they believed in them."

Though he spoke openly of being a warlock, she couldn't bring herself to tell him that she was a witch. She had spent too many years hiding what she was to share such personal information with a man she had just met. Back home, the villagers had thought of her as a healer, or so she had foolishly believed, until the night her neighbors came to accuse and condemn her.

"You are not into the dark arts, are you?" Brenna asked. Black magick was used to bring harm to others and reeked of negative energy. White magick, intended for doing good to one's self or others, was always positive. If there was one thing Granny O'Connell had instilled in Brenna, it was the law of threefold return. Any witch who used her power for evil could expect to reap three times the amount of whatever harm she caused another.

"No," Loken said. "We only practice white magick here. Healing, finding lost objects, things like that." He leaned forward again. "Do you need help with something, lessons in witchcraft, perhaps? I'd be happy to instruct you."

"No, I was just taking a walk through the city, finding my way around, as it were."

"So you just stumbled in here by chance?"

"Yes. And I really should be going," Brenna said. "Thank you for the coffee."

"My pleasure." He rose when she did. "I'll walk you to the door."

With a nod, Brenna left the coffee shop, conscious of Anthony Loken walking at her side. She stopped at the door that led to the street. "It was nice to meet you, Mr. Loken."

"Please, call me Anthony," he said. "I'd like very much to see you again. Perhaps I could take you out to dinner one evening next week?"

"Thank you, but I cannot."

"I see. Who is he?"

"He?"

"My competition."

"I do not understand."

"I'm assuming the reason you can't go out with me is because you have a steady boyfriend."

She started to deny it and then decided it would be easier to let him think just that. "Yes," she said, "and he can be very jealous."

Loken laughed good-naturedly. "Well, perhaps we can have coffee together again."

"Yes, perhaps. Good day to you, sir."

She left the shop, conscious of Anthony Loken's gaze on her back. She didn't relax until she was in the car and headed back to the relative safety of Roshan DeLongpre's house.

CHAPTER 12

Roshan woke as the setting sun slipped behind the horizon. One minute he was caught in the web of the death-like sleep of his kind, the next he was fully awake and alert. He knew, with his first in-drawn breath, that he was alone in the house.

Throwing back the quilt on his bed, he sat up. A moment later, the overhead lights which were hooked up to an automatic timer came on, illuminating his lair. It was a large rectangular room, usually furnished with little more than his bed and a comfortable chair. However, since Brenna's arrival, he had moved his clothing down here. At the moment, his entire wardrobe was arranged in several neat piles on the floor. Since it looked like Brenna was here to stay for awhile, perhaps it was time to think about furnishing one of the empty bedrooms upstairs so he wouldn't have to carry his clothes back and forth from his lair to the shower.

On the other hand, he might be wise to wait. She had taken his car and left the house. Who was to say she would return? And if she didn't, who could blame her? Even though she had said she wasn't afraid of him, what woman in her right mind would want to live here, with a creature like him?

Rising, he collected a change of underwear, a pair of slacks, a sweater, and a pair of black leather boots. Unlocking the door, he made his way up the winding staircase to the portal that opened onto the first floor.

He unlocked that door, as well, ducked into the hallway, then locked the door behind him. Bent on a shower, he bypassed the small half bath on the main floor and went up the stairs to the master bathroom, noting, as he passed by, that the door to Brenna's bedroom was closed.

He thought about her as he turned on the water in the shower and stepped under the spray, surprised at how empty the house felt without her. How empty *he* felt without her. He hadn't shared a dwelling with anyone since he became a vampire and yet, in a matter of weeks, Brenna Flanagan had moved into his house and into his heart.

Stepping out of the shower, he wrapped a towel around his waist, ran a comb through his hair, brushed his teeth.

He knew the moment she entered the house. Moments later, he heard a gasp from the doorway. Glancing over his shoulder, he saw Brenna standing there, gaping at him. She wore a pair of jeans that outlined the sweet curve of her hips and a white sweater that clung to the swell of her breasts. No one, looking at her, would ever guess that she had been born in another time and place.

"I . . . I'm sorry," she stammered, her eyes wide, her cheeks rosy. "I . . . I didn't know you were in here. I was just . . ."

Her gaze moved over him, her cheeks growing redder by the minute. Looking up, she met his eyes, then turned and fled.

Roshan stared after her, his emotions tumbling over themselves as he listened to her footsteps hurrying down the hall to the bedroom.

So, she had come back after all.

The thought brought a smile to his lips.

Brenna shut the bedroom door, then leaned back against it. Seeing Roshan wearing nothing but a towel was as close as she had ever come to seeing a naked man. It was an image she would not soon forget. Placing her hand over her heart, she took a deep, calming breath. She had never known a man's body could be so beautiful or so finely sculpted. And he was beautiful, from his broad shoulders and stomach ridged with muscle to his long legs.

She jumped when she heard a knock at the door. It could only be Roshan.

"Brenna?"

She felt the heat climb in her cheeks again. Was he dressed now, or still clad in nothing but a towel? "Yes?"

"Are you all right?"

"Yes, of course, why do you ask?"

There was a moment of taut silence. She pictured him standing on the other side of the door, his long black hair damp from his shower, drops of water glistening like dewdrops in the curly black hair on his chest.

"I'm going downstairs," he said quietly. "Will you join me?"

"Yes, if you like."

"I'll be waiting."

Sitting on the bed, she removed her boots and socks, then paced the floor for a few minutes. Finally, after taking several deep breaths, she opened the door. Her heart was pounding as she made her way down the stairs.

She found Roshan in the living room, standing in front of the fireplace. A cheery blaze crackled in the hearth. It provided the only light in the room. Soft music filled the air.

"It's going to storm," he remarked as she sat down on the sofa.

"How do you know?"

"I feel it coming." And even as he spoke the words, lightning flashed across the skies, closely followed by the low rumble of distant thunder. "So," he said, sitting down on the other end of the sofa, "how did you spend your day?"

"I went into the city."

He nodded, his gaze intent upon her face as he waited for her to go on.

"I did not go to the mall," she said. "Instead, I explored some of the shops along the street. There are so many of them! And I had a chocolate malt," she said, grinning.

Roshan smiled at her, pleased by her excitement, and by her courage to go exploring in a new city on her own.

"And then," she went on, her green eyes sparkling, "I went into a bookstore. But not just any bookstore. It was for witches!"

"Imagine that," he said, a smile evident in his tone.

She nodded vigorously. "Imagine! It was right out there in the open. Oh! And I met a warlock."

Roshan sat up straighter. "Go on."

"He was very nice. He bought me a cup of coffee. Never have I tasted anything like it."

"Indeed?"

She frowned. "I do not remember what the coffee was called, but it was quite good. I think I shall have to go back and see if I can buy some to bring home."

"Perhaps the warlock will be there."

She shrugged, as if it was of no consequence. "Perhaps. Wait until you taste—Oh! I am sorry. I forgot."

He dismissed her apology with a wave of his hand. "Do you want to see him again?" he asked, his voice gruff.

"No, though he did ask if I would."

Roshan clenched his jaw, startled by the tidal wave of jealousy that swept through him at the idea of Brenna going out with another man.

Brenna seemed totally unaware of his agitation. "So," she said, curling one leg beneath her, "tell me more about you. I know so little. You live in this large house. What manner of work do you do?"

He shrugged. "I have no need to work."

"Did someone leave you a great deal of money, then?"

"In a way," he said with a wry grin. "When I was first made vampire, I robbed the homes of the rich to provide for my material needs, which were few."

"Where did you live?"

"I had no home. I slept in my coffin, and sometimes in the earth."

Her eyes widened. "You mean . . . under the ground?" She shuddered at the mere idea. "How awful."

He grunted softly. "It wasn't as bad as you might think. In truth, the earth makes quite a comfortable bed. In those days, I didn't trust myself to mingle with mortals, so trying to earn a living was out of the question. And so I robbed from the rich, saving what I didn't spend."

"Were you never caught?"

"No. It was ridiculously easy to slip into their homes and help myself to whatever caught my fancy. I'm not proud of what I did, but at the time it was necessary. After awhile, it became a game. As time passed, I saved enough to buy a small house, and then a larger one, and then a larger one, still. I made a profit each time I sold one of the houses. I saved the money, and later, when I had gained a little more knowledge of the world and how it worked, I began to invest in one thing and another until . . ." He shrugged. "Today I have enough money to allow me to live quite comfortably."

She nodded. Leaning back, she gazed into the fire, then blushed when her stomach growled. "I guess I should go fix something to eat."

"I could take you out, if you don't feel like cooking, and then, if you'd like, we could go dancing."

"I do not know how to dance."

"That's all right. I do. What do you say?"

"Should I change my clothes?"

"It's up to you."

She glanced down at her jeans, then looked at Roshan, who was wearing black slacks and a black sweater. "I think I should change."

"Take your time. I need to go out."

"Oh." The tone of her voice said it all.

"I am what I am," he reminded her quietly.

"Does it hurt your . . . what do you call them, the people you . . . um . . . you know?"

"I think prey is the word you're looking for. And no, it doesn't hurt them, any more than it hurt you."

"But you take more from them, do you not? You said you took only a little from me."

"Yes, I take more. But not all."

"And it is all right for you to do this? They never complain?"

"They never remember."

"Why not?"

"I wipe the memory from their minds when I'm done."

Brenna shook her head. "So, you are a vampire, a sorcerer, and a hypnotist, as well?"

"Just a vampire."

She looked at him for a moment and then, to his surprise, she began to giggle.

"What's so funny?"

"Just a vampire? Just a vampire?" Her giggles turned to full-blown laughter. "You say it as if it is so . . . so . . . ordinary." Her laughter trailed off as she lifted a hand to her neck.

Roshan went suddenly still, his gaze following the movement of her hand, watching as her fingers probed the skin behind her ear. The scent of her blood, flowing like a crimson river through her veins, filled his nostrils; the sound of her heartbeat echoed in his ears. The hunger stirred within him.

"Have you taken blood from me before and wiped the memory from my mind?"

"No." But now that she had planted the idea in his mind, he wondered if he would be able to resist doing just that. "You were going to go and change your clothes," he reminded her, his voice ragged. "Do it now."

She stared at him a moment. Whatever she saw in his face drove her to her feet and out of the room.

Upstairs, Brenna locked the door, even though she

knew it would not keep him out. For a moment, she stood in the middle of the room, her heart pounding. How could she have been so foolish? She should have known better than to bring up the subject of how he fed, should have known it would arouse his hunger. But he had discussed it so calmly, and she couldn't deny being fascinated by it, and by him. Worse, she had almost asked him to drink from her again. What was the matter with her, that she was curious about such a repulsive act?

Her stomach growled again, reminding her that she was supposed to be changing her clothes to go out to dinner with Roshan. That was what he was doing now, she thought with morbid humor, going out to dinner. Who did he prey upon? How did he decide?

Putting the thought from her mind, she went to the closet and opened the door. She stood there a minute, trying to decide what to wear, and finally settled on a gauzy white blouse with a scoop neck and full sleeves, and a white skirt that was longer in the back than in the front. She wished there were a full-length mirror in the room so she could see how she looked. Perhaps the next time she went out, she would buy one. Perhaps Roshan would not mind. She wondered what it was like for him to look into a mirror and not see his image reflected back. She tried to imagine how she would feel in his place. Would it make her feel as if she didn't exist? Was that how it affected Roshan? Was that why there were no mirrors in the house?

Sitting on the edge of the bed, she pulled on a pair of silky nylons and a pair of high-heeled white boots. She had never worn shoes or boots with such high heels and she wobbled a little as she walked into the bathroom to brush her hair.

Forty minutes later, she heard Roshan's knock on the door. He whistled softly when he saw her, chasing away any doubts she might have had about how she looked.

He took her to dinner at a quiet restaurant located in an upscale neighborhood.

Brenna glanced at her surroundings, marveling at the plush carpets, the beautiful paintings on the walls, the abundance of greenery, the distinct lack of mirrors.

Moments later, they were seated at a cozy table in a secluded corner near the back. The table was covered with a dark blue cloth. A small vase held three red roses.

Sitting across from Roshan, she opened the menu, and then she glanced at him. "I thought you did not eat . . . food?"

He glanced briefly at her neck. "I don't."

Wordlessly, she turned back to the menu. "I cannot decide what to have."

"I'm afraid you're on your own." It had been centuries since he'd dined on anything but a warm liquid diet.

When the waitress returned, Brenna ordered prime rib. Roshan ordered a bottle of red wine.

"If you can't eat food, how can you drink wine?" Brenna asked.

He shrugged. "A few sips is all I can tolerate."

"What happens when you eat?"

"You don't want to know." He had tried to eat a slice of brown bread smeared with butter and honey shortly after he had been made vampire. It had made him violently ill. He had not eaten solid food since, though there had been times when he had been tempted to try again. But that had been long ago. The thought of food no longer held any appeal. "So, what did you do today, besides go to the bookstore?"

"I began making a new wand, to replace the one I left behind. I cut a branch from one of the trees in the yard. I hope you do not mind."

"Of course not. Take anything you need."

"Thank you."

He sipped from his glass now and then while she ate.

Brenna felt guilty for eating in front of him, and even more guilty for enjoying the meal. She couldn't believe he never tired of drinking blood. Even if he found it palatable, as he had claimed earlier, to dine on the same thing every night must surely grow tiresome after the first hundred years! As much as she loved chocolate malts, she wouldn't want to have to subsist on chocolate malts and nothing else for the rest of her life.

It was still raining when they left the restaurant. Brenna lifted her face to the rain and licked the drops from her lips. Had she been back home, she would have shed her clothes and danced naked in the downpour.

Roshan helped her into the car, then slid behind the wheel. Moments later they were driving through the rain, the only sound the swish-swish of the windshield wipers and an occasional clap of thunder.

A short time later, he pulled into the driveway of his favorite Goth hangout, a small dance club called the Nocturne. A valet clad in a black suit and hooded cloak handed Brenna out of the car, then Roshan was there, taking her hand in his. They walked under a black canopy, then down a flight of stairs that led to a door that was carved with runes and magical creatures.

He opened the door for her and followed her inside. The place was crowded even though it was after ten o'clock in the middle of the week. Brenna glanced around, her eyes wide as she took it all in. The first thing she noticed was that she was the only one not wearing black. Masks of all kinds decorated the walls, from voodoo masks to ancient Indian burial masks. Black candles flickered in wrought iron sconces, casting eerie shadows over the faces of the crowd. It was rather frightening, being in the midst of so many men and women clad in black. Most of them had black hair; a good number wore cloaks or capes with hoods. A woman at the bar laughed out loud, displaying shiny white fangs. Brenna couldn't help staring at the couples dancing on the floor, their bodies pressed close together as they swayed back and forth, their movements slow and sensual.

"Are all these people vampires?" she whispered.

"No, they're just pretending," he replied. "All but that small dark-haired guy in the corner."

"What about that girl over there? She has fangs."

"They're fake."

"How do you know?"

"I just know."

Roshan found a table in the corner and he ordered drinks, a strawberry daiquiri for Brenna, wine for himself.

"Do you come here often?" she asked.

He nodded. "I can be myself here. No one suspects my true nature. Here, I'm just another wanna-be vampire playing a role. Come," he said, "let's dance."

She shook her head but he paid her no mind. Taking her by the hand, he led her onto the dance floor.

"I cannot," she said, glancing at the other couples. She tried to pull her hand from his, but to no avail.

"Trust me," he said, and drew her into his arms.

Never before had she danced with a man. Never before had she realized how pleasurable it could be. Though she didn't know any of the steps, Roshan held her so closely she had no trouble following his lead. The music seeped into her, a low, steady beat that echoed the beat of her heart, a slow, sensual rhythm that made her think of the heated kisses she had shared with Roshan earlier. His arm was strong and sure around her waist; his body brushed against hers as they moved in a slow circle around the dance floor. The other couples faded into the distance until she was aware of nothing but the music and the tall, dark man holding her in his arms. His lips moved in her hair, his breath fanned her cheek. She risked a glance at his face and saw her own need mirrored in the depths of his eyes.

In her time, there had been those who considered dancing a sin, a prelude to all manner of lasciviousness. Being in Roshan's arms, swaying back and forth, she was all too aware of his body against hers, of the sensual heat that flowed between them.

He met her gaze, his deep blue eyes almost hypnotic in their intensity. She could see nothing but him, wanted no one but him. She leaned into him, feeling as though she was being drawn into his very soul.

She reminded herself that he was a vampire, that there was no way they could have a life together, and that even though she was attracted to him like no other, it would never work, but somehow, with his arms around her, none of that seemed to matter.

It took her a moment to realize the music had ended. Roshan smiled down at her, the affection in his eyes warming her clear to her toes.

The music changed, becoming hard and fast. Taking her by the hand, Roshan led her off the dance floor.

They were on their way back to their table when someone called her name.

"Brenna Flanagan, is that you?"

Glancing over her shoulder, she saw Anthony Loken striding toward her.

Roshan's hand tightened on hers as his steps slowed, stopped.

"Good evening, Mr. Loken," she said politely.

"Anthony," he reminded her with a smile. "It's wonderful to see you again."

"Thank you." She looked up at Roshan. "This is the man I told you about, remember?"

"Ah, yes, I remember," Roshan said, his voice cool.

Loken stuck his hand out. "You must be the competition," he said, grinning good-naturedly. "It's nice to meet you."

Roshan took Loken's hand, felt the unspoken challenge in the other man's grip. "Loken." Roshan had never met a warlock before but he could sense the other man's power. It crawled over his skin like dead leaves over a freshly turned grave.

Releasing Loken's hand, Roshan took a step back. "Come, Brenna."

She smiled fleetingly at Loken. "It was nice to see you again."

"And you."

Roshan guided Brenna back to their table, acutely aware of the other man's gaze on his back. Was it mere coincidence that Anthony Loken was here tonight, Roshan wondered. And yet, what else could it be? Bringing Brenna here had been his own decision, reached only a few hours ago. There was no way Loken could have known Brenna would be here, and yet . . .

He didn't know who or what Anthony Loken was, but he was more than a mere witch. Much more.

Their drinks were waiting when they returned to their table. When they were seated again, Brenna looked at Roshan, her expression troubled. "You are angry with me."

"No. But I want you to stay away from him."

"Why?"

"There's something not right about him."

"Not right?" A strange accusation, she thought, coming as it was from a vampire! "What do you mean?"

"I'm not sure. Just stay away from him."

Her chin went up defiantly. "You are not my father, Roshan DeLongpre. You cannot tell me what to do or who to see, or expect me to spend my days waiting for you to rise. Mr. Loken offered to be my friend, nothing more."

It didn't matter that she had already told Anthony that she couldn't see him again. She would not let Roshan tell her who she could and couldn't see. In the last few weeks, she had read a number of women's magazines, watched *Oprah* and *The View*. While the well-dressed women on television discussed much that Brenna didn't fully understand, one thing she had learned was that the women in this century demanded equality in every facet of their lives. Brenna smiled inwardly. Granny O'Connell would have been proud of her for speaking her mind, for demanding that she be treated as an equal.

A muscle twitched in Roshan's jaw. It hadn't taken Brenna long to assert her independence, he thought irritably. A few weeks of living in the twenty-first century and she was ready to take on the world. Life had been easier when women did as they were told.

Drawing on his preternatural powers, he leaned forward, his gaze capturing hers. "You will not see him again." He kept his voice low and hypnotic as he endeavored to bend her will to his.

Brenna stared back at him, her eyes narrowing as she drew on her own power to resist the enthralling sound of his voice, the mesmerizing look in his dark eyes. Focusing her energy, she threw it out toward him, parrying his hypnotic thrust as a swordsman might ward off the blow of a rival. "I will see whoever I wish, whenever I wish."

Roshan swore under his breath. Even as a young vampire, he had been able to compel others to do his will when it suited him. Why was it that this slip of a girl had the power to thwart him when no one else did? Were her own powers that strong, or was it just that she was the most hard-headed, stubborn woman he had ever met?

"The man is evil," Roshan said. "Can't you feel it? See it?"

She glanced in Anthony Loken's direction and then back at Roshan. The warlock looked like an angel of light with his close-cropped blond hair and sky blue eyes, while Roshan looked like the Dark Prince of legend with his long black hair and midnight blue eyes.

"I see only a handsome man who treated me with kindness and respect," she said coolly.

Thoroughly frustrated, Roshan sat back in his chair. For a time, he considered locking the gates against her again, but the thought of facing her wrath was less than appealing and would gain him nothing. He wanted her trust and her respect, not her anger. Still, short of locking Brenna in her room, and that option was sounding better all the time, there was no way to keep her from seeing the warlock if she chose to do so.

Nor, apparently, was there any way to keep her from dancing with him. Roshan couldn't believe the gall of the man, but there he was, standing by their table, asking Brenna to dance. Roshan was not at all surprised when Brenna said yes, even though he knew she had agreed just to prove he couldn't tell her who she could and could not see.

It was his first hard lesson in the contrary ways of modern women.

CHAPTER 13

The atmosphere in the car on the ride home was so cold Roshan wouldn't have been surprised to see frost forming on the inside of the windshield. He and Brenna had left the club shortly after Brenna's dance with Anthony Loken. She had not spoken a word to him since then.

Now she sat beside him, her back rigid as she stared out the side window, apparently watching the rain.

Women! Was there ever a man on the planet, mortal or otherwise, who understood them? He had warned her against the warlock for her own good. Dark power and negative energy radiated from the man. He was surprised that Brenna hadn't sensed it. Either Loken practiced black magick or he possessed some other dark power. Was it possible that the warlock was a vampire as well as a witch? It seemed unlikely, since Brenna had seen the man in the bookstore in the middle of the day. If Anthony Loken was indeed a vampire, then he was one of the Ancients. Only the oldest of the undead were able to hide their true nature from others of their kind, or walk in the sun's light without fear.

Anger and a growing sense of frustration roared through Roshan. His foot grew heavy on the gas pedal. The car increased speed. Forty miles an hour. Fifty. Sixty.

He glanced at Brenna out of the corner of his eye. She was sitting very straight, her eyes wide, her feet braced against the floorboard. One slender hand clutched the edge of her seat, the other was fisted around the door handle.

He nudged the Ferrari to sixty-five and then goosed it up to seventy.

Flashing lights appeared in the rearview mirror, accompanied by the wail of a siren.

Muttering an oath, Roshan slowed the car, pulled off the road, and rolled down the window.

Moments later, a police officer shrouded in a yellow slicker stood beside the window, flashlight in hand.

"May I see your driver's license, sir?" the officer asked, shining the light in Roshan's face, and then Brenna's.

With a nod, Roshan reached for his wallet. Withdrawing his license, he handed it to the officer, then captured the man's gaze with his. "I wasn't speeding, was I?"

The officer, a clean-shaven man in his late twenties, shook his head. "No, sir, of course not."

"So I can go?"

"Of course." The officer returned his license. "Have a pleasant evening, Mr. DeLongpre."

"Thank you, Officer Miller. Good evening."

With a friendly wave of his hand, the officer returned to his patrol car.

Tossing his license and his wallet on the dashboard, Roshan put the car in gear, checked the rearview mirror, and pulled onto the road.

"I guess you do not get many tickets," Brenna said, disapproval heavy in her voice.

He glanced at her, one brow arched. "Are you speaking to me now?"

"Are you trying to get us killed?" she demanded. "Or should I say trying to get *me* killed?"

She was right. He was behaving like an empty-headed lout. While he would likely survive any accident save for one that drained him of so much blood he could not recover, Brenna could easily be killed. He forgot, sometimes, how fragile mortals were, how little it took to deprive them of life.

"I'm sorry," he said gruffly.

Her demeanor relaxed ever so slightly at his apology. Afraid to say anything that might set her off again, he remained silent for the remainder of the ride.

At home, he pulled into the garage, switched off the engine, then ran up to the house and opened the door for her. Turning, he saw that she wasn't behind him. Instead, she was standing in the yard in her stocking feet, her arms flung out at her sides, her face lifted toward the heavens as she twirled round and round, like a child at play. Clad all in white, her skirt swirling around her ankles, she looked almost ethereal.

He watched her, enchanted by the sound of her merry laughter and the joy that made her eyes sparkle like emeralds. What a rare and wonderful creature she was! She danced in the rain with the innocence and exuberance that came with youth and a clear conscience.

A hiss told him that Morgana was standing beside him. He glanced down at the cat, who was staring up at him, her back arched.

"There's no love lost between the two of us, is there?" he said to the cat. But they both loved the woman.

His gaze was drawn toward Brenna again. She was standing with her arms lifted toward the heavens, her head thrown back, her lips moving. Was she singing, he wondered, or praying?

Oblivious to the rain that quickly drenched him from head to foot, he descended the porch steps and crossed the yard toward her.

Lightning forked through the clouds. Seconds later, thunder rolled across the lowering skies.

Another clap of thunder rocked the earth as Roshan drew Brenna into his arms. Her gaze met his, her eyes widening, then closing as he lowered his head and covered her mouth with his.

It was strangely erotic, kissing her in the midst of a storm. Overhead, thunder rolled and lightning sizzled across the skies, but it didn't matter. Nothing mattered but the woman in his arms. She tasted of the meal she had eaten earlier, of sweet red wine and raindrops. And woman. It was a potent combination.

"You've bewitched me, Brenna Flanagan," he murmured, and kissed her again.

And yet again.

She was like a flame in his arms, her lips like the sweetest nectar, her skin like wet silk. He showered her with kisses as he slowly lowered her to the ground. The grass beneath her was cold; he warmed it with a look.

He kissed her until kissing wasn't enough, until she was mindless, breathless with the same urgent need that drove him. Their clothing disappeared as if by magick, his or hers, it didn't matter.

She looked up at him, a low moan of pleasure rising from deep in her throat as he worshiped her beauty with his eyes and his hands, large hands that caressed her ever so gently, demanding nothing, asking for everything.

There was no hesitation in her now, no hint of maidenly modesty, no murmur of halfhearted protest. In spite of the rain and the cold, her skin was warm, heated by the desire that burned within her. She was a woman, with a woman's needs, and he fanned the embers of her desire until she was ready for him, until she cried his name, her voice thick with passion and a hunger that could no longer be denied.

And he took her, there, upon the wet grass.

Took her innocence, and her blood, and in so doing, he bound her to him for as long as either of them drew breath.

CHAPTER 14

Brenna slept late the following morning and woke with a smile in her heart. Strange, she thought. Back in her own time, she had always been an early riser. Of course, living with a vampire, one tended to keep late hours.

Turning onto her side, she looked out the window. It was still raining, but she didn't mind. She had always loved the rain. It called to something inside her, something earthy and wild and uninhibited.

She had certainly acted wild and uninhibited last night! She could scarcely believe what a wanton she had been in his arms. What must he think of her? She knew what Granny O'Connell would think! Granny would be shocked and horrified at her granddaughter's lascivious behavior.

Brenna let out a sigh. The only good thing was that there was no possibility of conceiving a child out of wedlock. The thought didn't comfort her as it should. Instead, she spent several minutes thinking how wonderful it would be to have Roshan's child—a little boy with thick black hair and deep blue eyes.

"Roshan." She whispered his name. Excitement hummed deep within her, bubbling up until it escaped in a happy sigh. Was this what it was like to be in love, this sense of wonder and discovery?

Morgana stirred at the foot of the bed. Meowing loudly, she yawned and stretched, then approached her mistress and patted Brenna's cheek with her paw.

"I know, you want to go out," Brenna said. Rising, she pulled on her bathrobe and went downstairs. Morgana kept pace at her side, meowing plaintively all the while.

Brenna opened the back door, then stood there a moment, watching the rain. Morgana sniffed the air, laid back her ears, then streaked down the steps and disappeared around the corner of the house. Brenna grinned. Morgana hated the rain as much as her mistress loved it.

Leaving the door open a crack for the cat's return, Brenna filled a kettle with water and put it on the stove. She pulled her favorite mug from the shelf, dropped a tea bag inside, then sat down to wait for the water to boil.

When the water was hot, she filled the cup, then sat there, her chin cupped in her hands, while the tea steeped.

When it was done, she added a spoonful of honey, then carried the cup into the living room. After opening the drapes, she sat on the sofa and watched the rain drizzle down the window, remembering yet again what it had been like to be in Roshan's arms last night. She had never realized that making love could be so explosive, or so satisfying, physically and emotionally, even spiritually. Roshan had tapped a well of passion she had never known she possessed, taken her to heights she had never dreamed existed. Made her hunger for his touch . . .

She lifted her fingertips to her lips, remembering the heat of his kisses, the way his hands had moved over her, as if he wanted to memorize every curve. Sometimes his touch had been gentle, sometimes bold. He had explored every inch of her body. She felt her cheeks grow hot as she recalled that she had done the same to him.

It had been a magical night. In spite of the cold and the rain, the grass beneath her had been warm and dry. Overhead, the thunder and the lightning had combined to play her a symphony; the lyrics had been the love words and endearments Roshan whispered in her ear. She had seen rainbows in the clouds. Truly, a magical night, she thought again, and over much too soon.

Just thinking of him and of the night past made her yearn for the sun to set quickly. Her heart beat faster just thinking of him. Liquid heat pooled in the deepest part of her. She stirred restlessly, wondering how she could endure the hours without him. Never in her life had she felt like this, aroused and anxious at the same time.

And then, like a bolt out of the blue, she realized that he must have used his preternatural powers to entrance her. It was the only explanation for the way she was feeling now, and for her wanton behavior the night before. She had been angry with him when they left the Nocturne, annoyed at the high-handed way he had forbidden her to see Anthony Loken again. And yet, less than an hour later, she had gone willingly into Roshan's arms, had shamelessly let him make love to her out in the open.

But how? How had he entranced her? And when?

She frowned. Always before, she had sensed when he tried to use his preternatural powers against her. Sensed it and blocked it. What had he done differently last night?

She sipped her tea, trying to remember everything that had happened after they left the club.

He had watched her dance in the rain. And then he had kissed her. One soul-shattering kiss, and she had stopped fighting her desire for him. One kiss, and she had surrendered her virtue without a qualm, without a thought. Blinded by needs she had resisted for too long, she had returned his kisses with a fervor she had never known she possessed.

His kisses. They were far more potent than any spell or enchantment ever devised. One kiss had burned away all thought of right or wrong.

She licked her lips and then, with a gasp, she lifted a hand to her neck. He had taken her blood. How could she have forgotten that, or the exquisite pleasure that it had given her? And she had tasted his. Quite by accident, she had thought at the time. His fangs had pricked his lower lip and she had tasted his blood in his kisses. Tasted it and yearned for more. Was that the reason Roshan was the only thing she could think of today? The reason she was so anxious for the moon to chase the sun from the sky?

Would she become what he was, now that she had tasted his blood?

Rising, she hurried up to her room. She took a quick shower, pulled on a pair of black pants, a heavy sweater, and a pair of boots. Grabbing her handbag and the keys to the Ferrari, she ran out of the house.

A short time later, she was driving toward the city and the bookstore.

* * *

The rain had slowed by the time Brenna reached the city, and stopped altogether by the time she entered the bookstore.

Myra looked up from behind her desk and smiled. "Nasty weather we're having," she remarked. She made a gesture that encompassed the rest of the store. "Bad for business, too. So, what brings you out on a day like this?"

"Do you have any books on vampires?" Brenna asked, shaking raindrops from her hair.

"We carry one or two. They're over there, on the bottom shelf. You'd probably find a better selection at the library."

"Thank you." Brenna grunted softly. What had she been thinking? She didn't need a library. Roshan had hundreds of books, perhaps thousands. But would a vampire have books on vampires?

"Are you looking for anything in particular?" Myra asked, coming around the desk.

"No. I . . . uh, saw a movie about vampires the other night and I wanted to find out more about them." She laughed self-consciously. "Not that I believe they exist or anything."

"You should talk to Anthony. He's writing a book about them."

"Really? Maybe I will. Thanks, again."

Brenna found three books on vampires, one on werewolves, and one on shape shifters, none of which were very helpful. Waving good-bye to Myra, who was again at her desk, Brenna headed for the door and came face-to-face with Anthony Loken.

"Well, hello," he said.

"Hello."

"Must be my lucky day, finding you here."

"I was just leaving."

"You can't go now," he said with a smile. "I just got here. Come on, let me buy you a cup of coffee to warm you up before you go back out in the rain."

Since she couldn't think of any plausible reason to refuse, and because she really did want another cup of that wonderful coffee, she let him guide her into the coffee shop.

They sat at the same table beside the window.

Anthony ordered two cups of Almond Amaretto, then leaned back in his chair. "So, what are you doing out on a day like this? You should be curled up in front of a fire with a good book."

"Myra says you're writing a book. About vampires."

"Did she? Well, she's right."

"Why are you writing about vampires?"

"Why not? They're fascinating creatures."

"But surely you do not believe they are real?"

"Aren't they?"

"Are they?"

"I believe they are. I believe they hold the key to something man has been searching for since Adam brought death into the world. Eternal life."

He murmured his thanks as the serving girl brought their order. "Can I get you anything else, Mr. Loken?"

"No, thank you, Darlene."

Brenna waited until the girl moved away before asking, "Even if they existed, how would you find one?"

He tapped his fingers on the edge of the table. "Therein lies the problem." He leaned toward her, his gaze intent upon her face. "You don't know where I could find one, do you?"

Every instinct Brenna possessed warned her to tread

carefully. "Me? How would I know? I have only just arrived here."

"Yet you were at the Nocturne last night."

"So were you." She picked up her cup and took a sip, then set it aside. Yesterday, the coffee had tasted delicious; today, it tasted flat and bitter, like betrayal.

"Just so," Loken replied. "Tell me more about the man you were with."

"He is just a friend," she replied, careful to keep her voice neutral. "I hardly know him." Her words mocked the memory of what had happened between them in the yard the night before.

"And why did he take you there?"

She shrugged. "He said it was an interesting place, filled with people pretending to be vampires. I thought it might be amusing."

He didn't believe her. She could see it in his eyes.

"And if you found a vampire," she asked, "what would you do?"

"Ask for his cooperation, of course. We would need to do some blood tests, isolate whatever agent it is in the blood that allows a vampire to survive hundreds of years and gives them their remarkable ability to heal themselves of practically any injury. Once we isolate it, we would have to do some extensive testing to see if it could be duplicated. Think of what it would mean to mankind," he said earnestly. "The hundreds, perhaps thousands, of lives we could save."

She listened to his words, the tone of his voice, and knew he was lying. He wasn't interested in helping mankind. He was interested in finding a way for Anthony Loken to live forever. She was certain of it. And yet she found it odd that a warlock would wish for such a thing. Granny O'Connell had believed that the only way to perfection was for the soul to be reborn again and again, that in each lifetime, the soul was to learn something it needed to know and teach something that needed to be taught, something no other could teach. To live the same life forever would be to stagnate. Brenna wasn't sure she believed in reincarnation, though a part of her hoped it was true, and that someday in the future she would be with her grandmother again, in another life. There were those who believed that souls traveled from life to life in family units, so that in one life Granny O'Connell might be her grandmother, but in another life, Granny might be her daughter or her mother. But reincarnation was a discussion for another day.

"Why do you not just advertise for a vampire in the newspaper?" Brenna asked.

Loken snorted. "Can you imagine the number of idiots who would answer such an ad? Every nutcase in the city would be pounding on my door." He shook his head. "Better to frequent the places they might congregate, like the Nocturne. If they exist, I'll find one."

"Well," Brenna said, "I wish you luck. I really must go now. I . . . I have an appointment."

"You haven't finished your coffee."

"Oh." Picking up the cup, she gulped it down. "Thank you."

He rose when she did. "Good day, Brenna Flanagan. I hope to see you again soon."

With a nod, she fled the bookstore.

Outside, she took a deep cleansing breath. Roshan had been right. Seeing Anthony Loken again had been a big mistake. Why had she never sensed the negative energy that hovered around the warlock? Had it always been there? How could she have missed such a thing?

Back at home, she went through Roshan's bookshelves,

searching for anything she could find on vampires. She finally found what she was looking for in one of the bookcases upstairs. There, on the top shelf, she found a dozen or so books on vampires and other supernatural creatures.

Blowing the dust off the tops of the books, she stacked them in a pile beside the chair, then sat down and began to read.

Roshan stood in the doorway, his gaze moving over Brenna. She sat in his chair, one leg curled beneath her, thoroughly engrossed in the book in her lap. He perused the titles scattered on the floor, noting they all had to do with vampire lore. Morgana slept underneath the chair, her tail twitching.

Beautiful Brenna, with her sea green eyes and a wealth of russet-colored hair. She was truly a witch, he mused. He had been completely under her spell since the night he saw her dancing outside her cottage. Did she regret what had happened between them last night? If he crossed the room and swept her into his arms, would she surrender or slap his face?

She looked up just then, her eyes widening when she saw him standing in the doorway. "Roshan! How long have you been there?"

"Not long." He gestured at the books. "Are you looking for anything in particular?"

"Not really, but you cannot blame me for being curious." He looked nothing like the vampires described in the books she had just read. According to those who professed to know, true vampires were skeletal creatures with pallid skin and sunken red eyes. Their nails were long, their breath exceedingly foul, their skin cryptcold to the touch.

"Indeed? And what is it, exactly, that you're curious about?"

"Everything."

"I would think that living here, under my roof, would give you all the answers you need."

The memory of their lovemaking flickered in her eyes and pinked her cheeks, but she wasn't ready to acknowledge what had happened, let alone discuss it with him, or, he saw to his regret, repeat it.

She shifted in the chair. "You don't look like a vampire."

"No?"

"No. Is how I see you the way you really look?"

He laughed softly. "Do you think this is some sort of vampire glamour, that underneath my outward appearance I'm nothing but a rotting corpse?"

Her eyes widened. "Are you?"

He dismissed her fear with a wave of his hand. "Most assuredly not."

"I did not really think so," she said, relief evident in her tone as well as her expression. "So much of what I read sounds like foolishness."

"For instance?" He braced one shoulder against the doorjamb, willing to give her all the time she needed.

"Well, one of the books said that if you want to find a vampire, you should take a horse, either all white or all black, into the graveyard and let it walk among the graves. If the horse refuses to step over a grave, then the body inside is a vampire."

Roshan nodded. He didn't know if that was true or not, but he knew from experience that animals avoided him.

Brenna shook her head. "The book also suggested having a virgin boy ride the horse because, being pure, both boy and beast would recoil in horror from the evil rising from the grave.

"Another one of the books said that if I was to scatter seeds on the ground, you would have to stop to count them, either that, or pick them all up. And this one"— she gestured at the book in her lap—"says that if a vampire finds a rope tied in knots, he would have to untie every one." She frowned. "Another part says vampires can't see themselves in mirrors because they have no soul." She glanced up at him, her expression troubled. "Is that true?"

"I don't know. Some say it's because we're no longer mortal; that, in essence, we no longer exist in the real world, therefore we have no reflection."

"Does it bother you, that you cannot see yourself?"

"Not anymore."

"But it used to?"

"It was a little unsettling at first," he admitted. "To tell you the truth, I've almost forgotten what I look like."

"Did it make you feel as though you did not exist?"

He nodded.

"I thought it would."

"You've given it some thought?" he asked, surprised.

"I was thinking of buying a mirror a few days ago, and I wondered how I would feel if I were you, and I could not see my reflection." She looked up at him, her expression thoughtful. "Have you truly forgotten how you look?"

"Pretty much. Not that it matters."

"Maybe we could find someone to paint your portrait," she said, thinking aloud. "Or we could buy one of those cameras that they advertise on the television."

Roshan grunted. "I'm not sure vampires photograph."

"Oh. Well, you are very handsome, you know."

"Am I?"

She nodded.

"I'm glad you think so."

Flustered by the turn of their conversation, she glanced down at the book in her lap. "Can you turn into a wolf? Or a bat?"

"A wolf, if I wish. I'm not sure I could make myself small enough to become a bat, nor can I think of any reason why I would want to."

"But you can turn into mist. I saw you, the night the mob came for me."

"Yes, though it took me some years to master that particular trick."

"And will you turn to ash in the sun?"

He nodded, remembering his recent encounter with the dawn, the excruciating pain that had seared his flesh and burned his eyes.

She gestured at the book again. "How am I to know what is fact and what is fable?"

"Does it matter? I am not mortal, I am not truly immortal, nor am I human in the usual sense. But I am still a man, capable of joy and sorrow, pain and pleasure."

"If you gave your blood to someone who was sick, would it make them better?"

"I don't know. Why do you ask?"

She shrugged, her gaze sliding away from his. "I was just . . . just curious."

"You're a terrible liar, Brenna Flanagan. What's this all about?"

"Does it hurt to become a vampire?"

"Not exactly."

"What does that mean, not exactly? Either it does or it does not."

"It's not particularly painful, but it can be frightening if you don't know what's happening or what to expect. Dammit, Brenna, what are you trying to find out? Are you sick? Do you want me to bring you across?"

"Have you ever made anyone a vampire?"

"Just once." It was something he rarely allowed himself to think about.

"Where is he? Or was it a she?"

"It was a woman." He lifted a hand, hoping to still any further questions.

"Did you love her?"

"No, but she fancied herself in love with me. To this day, I don't know how she discovered my true nature, but discover it she did. From then on, she begged me to make her as I was." He began to pace the floor. "I tried to avoid her, but I lived in a small village. And I was still a young vampire, impulsive, foolish. One night, to my eternal regret, I did as she asked." He took a deep breath. "It was a mistake, one I have never made again."

"Why was it a mistake? Was she sorry after it was done?"

"Not everyone is strong enough to endure the Dark Trick. Lilly Anna was not. She was such a gentle creature. She had no heart for the kind of life required of a vampire. She took no joy in the hunt. She anguished over every drop of blood she took, regretted every act of violence. After a few years, she went quite insane."

"What happened to her?"

It was the one question he had hoped she would not ask, the one question he didn't want to answer. "I set her free."

"You killed her?"

Pain shadowed his eyes. "I brought her across. She was my responsibility."

Brenna stared at him, unblinking. Unbelieving. "How could you?"

"How could I not?"

She heard the anguish in his voice. "I am truly sorry, Roshan. That must have been very difficult for you."

"Yes."

"You said she found no joy in the hunt. Do you?" Her eyes were very wide and very green as she stared up at him, waiting for his answer.

He loosed a heavy sigh, wishing she were not quite so curious, that her questions did not touch upon areas he would rather not discuss, facets of being a vampire that he would rather she didn't know. But he couldn't lie to her.

"I am a predator," he said candidly. "We all enjoy the hunt."

"And killing?" She grasped the edge of the book in her lap, her knuckles white. "Do you enjoy that, as well?"

He stared back at her, wondering how best to answer such a question, wondering if the truth would drive her away. But he wanted no lies between them, not after last night.

"I've killed in the past," he replied quietly. "As a young vampire, it is very nearly impossible not to. The thrill of the hunt, the scent of fear rising from the prey, your own feeling of invincibility, it's a heady thing, something you can't begin to understand unless you've experienced it for yourself. And when you catch your quarry, and his blood is running hot from the chase, it's hard to remember that the puny mortal in your grasp is more than prey, hard to remember that once you were as weak and human as the creature trembling in your grasp."

He looked down at her, his hunger rising at the images conjured by his words. Her scent filled his nostrils, reminding him of nights long ago, when it took more than a few sips to quench his thirst and ease the pain. But he had never killed any who were innocent or helpless, never preyed upon children, or those who were young and vulnerable.

He took a deep, calming breath, then moved to stand in front of her. "What the hell is this all about?"

She stared up at him. He looked very tall and forbidding standing there, his dark eyes focused on her face.

"Anthony Loken," she said. "He is writing a book about vampires."

"You were with him today?" He didn't need her to confirm it; he could smell the faint scent of the other man. He wondered that he hadn't noticed it before.

"I went to the bookstore, to look for a book about vampires. It was only when Myra told me I'd probably have better luck at the library that I remembered how many books you have here."

"And where did you meet Loken?"

"I did not 'meet' him. He arrived at the bookstore as I was leaving and insisted I have a cup of coffee with him."

"And you couldn't refuse?"

Her chin went up defiantly. "At the time, I did not wish to."

"Why is he writing about vampires?"

"He said they are fascinating creatures. He thinks that vampire blood might be a cure for some diseases, and that it might be a way to extend human life, or even conquer death."

"I see. And he wants to do this for the good of mankind?"

"That is what he said, but I do not think he cares about anyone else. I think he wants only to find a way to live forever. He said he is looking for a vampire to help him with his research. That was why he was at the Nocturne last night."

Remembering the young vampire in the club, Roshan swore softly, hoping the kid was smart enough to keep his identity a secret. Once made, most vampires seemed to know instinctively that it was to their best interests not to divulge their true nature. Of course, they also knew enough to stay out of another vampire's territory. Had Roshan been alone last night, he would have invited the young vampire to leave the city or face the consequences.

Brenna looked at him a moment, then her eyes widened. "Do you think Loken knows about the other vampire? Do you think he wants to use him for some kind of research?"

"He was the only other vampire in the place."

"Loken asked me about you," she said, looking worried. "Do you think he knows what you are?"

"No."

"We must warn the other vampire," Brenna said earnestly, "before it is too late."

"It might already be too late."

"Then we must go to the Nocturne now, tonight." She rose, the book in her lap falling to the floor. "Hurry!"

There were only a few other customers at the Nocturne when they arrived. One couple sat at the bar talking to the bartender, another couple sat at one of the tables, intent only on each other.

The young vampire sat at a booth in the far corner. His hair was dark brown, as were his eyes. His lips were thin, his nose was crooked. He was perhaps medium height, with the lean physique of a runner. He held a drink cradled in his hands. A sniff told Roshan it wasn't wine.

The young vampire sensed the presence of another as soon as they entered the club. He looked up, his eyes narrowing as he focused on Roshan. Lifting his glass, he took a long swallow, regarding Roshan over the rim.

Roshan slid into the booth across from the young vampire. Brenna sat beside Roshan, her hands folded in her lap.

"What do you want?" the young vampire asked sullenly, his gaze darting from Roshan to Brenna and back again.

"I might ask you the same question," Roshan replied quietly.

"What do you mean?"

"This is my city. What are you doing here?"

"Hey, man, I didn't know you were here."

"Now you know. Who are you?"

"Jimmy Dugan."

"Where are you from?

"I was born in Florida. That's where I was made."

"Who brought you across?"

"Mara."

Roshan grunted softly. He had never met Mara, but her name was legendary among vampires. Had their kind a queen, Mara would have worn the crown. "Why are you here?"

Dugan stared into his glass. "I wanted to get as far away from home as I could."

"How long have you been one of us?"

"Just a few months."

Roshan nodded. "Do you know a man named Loken?"

Dugan looked up. "Sure, I met him here last night. Why?"

"Don't trust him," Roshan said bluntly. "And get out of my city."

"Wait! I'm supposed to meet him here later tonight."

"If you're smart, you'll be gone before he gets here." Roshan glanced at Brenna. "Let's go."

She slid out of the booth, and he followed her.

"Wait!" Dugan called, a note of panic in his voice. "I need help."

"Indeed?"

"There's so much I don't know. Mara, she didn't tell me hardly anything."

"Then ask her for help."

"Dammit, man, you can't just turn your back on me. We're . . . we're brothers."

"No," Roshan replied coldly. "We are enemies. And you are in my territory."

"I don't want this life!"

"Then end it."

"Roshan." Brenna placed her hand on his arm. "He needs your help. Remember how it was for you?"

He glared at her a moment, and then relented. "Come with me, Dugan."

Roshan didn't wait for a reply, didn't wait to see if the young vampire followed him. Taking Brenna by the hand, Roshan left the club.

CHAPTER 15

Jimmy Dugan grabbed his jacket and hurried after the vampire and his woman. He had known Roshan was one of the undead the moment the man stepped into the Nocturne. He had felt it in the deepest part of him. But the woman . . . she puzzled him. She wasn't a vampire and yet he had sensed there was something different about her, a subtle hint of supernatural power that was similar to, but not quite as strong as, the power he had sensed in the warlock who had approached him last night. Was she also a witch?

His pace slowed as he stepped out onto the sidewalk. Was he making another mistake? How did he know he could trust Roshan? Trusting people was what had gotten him into this mess in the first place. His mother had always warned him that he was too gullible, that he saw good in everyone. Lord, if she could see him now! She had cried when he called her last night. She had begged him to come home, promised to help him out of whatever trouble he was in. But how could he go back? He didn't trust himself to be around those he loved, not now, when the lust for blood was so strong, when he didn't know his own strength. He had spent one night with a beautiful woman and it had cost him his family, his job, and his girl. Damn! He didn't want to be a vampire. He had gone to the Nocturne in hopes of finding a way to regain his humanity. What good was living forever if you couldn't live with the people you loved the most?

He glanced up and down the street, his preternatural senses pointing him in Roshan's direction.

He found the vampire standing in the parking lot beside a sleek black Ferrari. The woman was already in the car. She looked at him through the window with a reassuring smile.

"Where's your car?" the vampire asked.

"Over there," Jimmy said, pointing at a silver Intrepid.

"Follow me."

"Where are we going?" Jimmy asked, but the other vampire didn't answer.

Moving to the driver's side of the Ferrari, the vampire opened the door and slid behind the wheel. A moment later, the engine purred to life.

With an exasperated sigh, Jimmy hurried to his car, certain the vampire wouldn't wait for him to catch up.

He followed the Ferrari for about forty minutes before the vampire pulled off the road.

Jimmy pulled up behind the other car, his gaze darting right and left. They were in a rest area located at the south end of the city limits. He grunted with wry amusement, thinking he felt like some young gunslinger being escorted out of Dodge.

"There's nothing to be afraid of," Jimmy muttered as he got out of the car. "You're a vampire, for crying out loud!"

The other vampire helped the woman out of the Ferrari. Standing side by side, they waited for him.

"Now what?" Jimmy asked. He glanced around. There was no one else in sight. Again, he wondered if he had made a mistake in coming here.

"We talk," the other vampire said. "What do you want to know?"

"I know sunlight will kill me. And fire. Are they the only things I have to worry about? I mean, I've seen all the movies, but all that other stuff is just a lot of crap, right?"

"Wrong. A wooden stake through the heart will destroy you. A good hunter will stake you, cut off your head, and bury the pieces in separate graves sprinkled with salt or holy water."

"You mean vampire hunters really exist?" Jimmy lifted a hand to his neck. He liked his head right where it was, thank you very much.

"You'd better believe it. One of the best of them is Tom Duncan. If he turns up where you are, leave the place as soon as you can."

Jimmy listened intently as the vampire explained more of what he needed to know. Much of what he said were things Jimmy had heard before or seen in movies. Funny, he had never considered that any of the vampire lore he had heard was based on fact. Hell, he had never believed that vampires or vampire hunters even existed. And now, impossible as it seemed, he was one of the undead, and all because he had let a beautiful woman seduce him. Served him right for cheating on Cathy, he thought bitterly.

Jimmy glanced at Brenna. She didn't look much older than he was, or any more worldly wise. He shook his head, thinking they were both mixed up in something they would be better off without.

"Is there anything else you want to know before you leave town?" the vampire asked.

Jimmy shook his head, already reeling under the weight of everything he had just learned.

"Why were you meeting Loken tonight?" the vampire asked.

"I never wanted to be a vampire. He was going to help me reverse the effects of the Dark Trick."

The vampire looked at the woman. "I thought you said he was looking for the secret of eternal life?"

"That is what he told me. Mayhap he has also found a cure." She looked at Jimmy. "He told you he could do that, that he could make you mortal again?"

Jimmy nodded. "He said it involved some blood tests, and then a blood exchange, a transfusion, you know? Out with the bad blood, in with the good."

The woman and the other vampire exchanged glances.

"There's no cure for vampirism," the vampire said flatly.

Jimmy stared at him. "I don't believe you."

"Whether you believe it or not doesn't matter. There is no cure except the destruction of your body."

Jimmy's shoulders sagged in defeat. "Loken was my only hope," he murmured, his voice thick with despair. "I'll never see Cathy again."

"Is Cathy your wife?" Brenna asked.

"My girlfriend. We were gonna to be married at the end of the year, but I told her we'd have to postpone it for a while. She thinks I'm in Chicago looking for a new job."

That's what he had told his mother, too, but she'd always been able to tell when he was lying and he hadn't fooled her for a minute.

"Why can you not see her?" Brenna asked.

"Why not?" he cried, his voice rising. "Why not? I'm a vampire, that's why not!"

Brenna shrugged. "Roshan is a vampire."

Jimmy stared at her. "So?"

"So, he goes out and mingles with people and no one is the wiser. Can you not do that as well?"

Jimmy shook his head. "No. I saw Cathy soon after Mara brought me across. I looked at Cathy and all I could think of was how much I wanted to . . ." He looked at Roshan. "You know how it is, man. I don't trust myself to be alone with her."

The vampire nodded. "It is difficult, at first. But it grows easier, with time."

"We can't have a life together," Jimmy said dully. "She wants to get married, have kids. It's better to end it now before I . . ." He looked at the other vampire, his eyes filled with misery and bitter regret. "Before I kill her, too."

"You killed someone?" Brenna asked.

Jimmy nodded. "I didn't want to." He looked pleadingly at the other vampire. "You know how it is. I tried to stop, man, but I couldn't!"

Roshan nodded.

Judging from the expression on Roshan's face, Jimmy knew the other vampire understood all too well.

"I've told you all I can," Roshan said. "The rest is up to you."

"I don't know what to do, man, where to go. I don't have a job. I'm almost out of money. How am I supposed to live?" He laughed, a short humorless laugh. "Live! That's a good one!"

"If you need money, you can find a job working nights," Roshan said, annoyed by the boy's self-pity. "You can live your life as a vampire the same way you lived as a mortal, if that's what you want. Many humans work nights and sleep days. It's an adjustment you have to make. With time, the lust for blood becomes easier to control."

"I just feel so lost."

"Like everything else," Roshan said, not unkindly, "that will pass, in time." Reaching into his pocket, Roshan withdrew a couple of one hundred–dollar bills and placed them in Dugan's hand.

"Hey, man, I don't want your charity."

"Think of it as a loan. Between brothers."

"Thanks, man," Jimmy said, turning away before the vampire could see the tears of gratitude in his eyes. "I'll pay you back."

Deep in despair, Jimmy walked to his car and slid behind the wheel. He couldn't live like this any longer. He missed Cathy. He missed his mother and his old man. If there was any chance that he could be human again, he was prepared to take it, even if it meant seeing Anthony Loken one more time.

It might be risky to see the warlock again, but it was a risk he was willing to take.

CHAPTER 16

Brenna glanced out the rearview window as Roshan pulled onto the road. "Do you think he will be all right?"

"That's up to him."

"How can you not care what happens to him?" she asked, frowning.

"I can't play nursemaid to the world. If he listens to what I said, he'll be fine. If he doesn't . . ." He shrugged. "I've got all I can handle just worrying about you."

She wasn't sure what to say to that. He had saved her from a horrible death, had made love to her in the most tender, incredible manner, but it had never occurred to her that he worried about her. It was a nice feeling. No one had worried about her since her grandmother passed away.

"What if it is possible?" Brenna mused. "What if Loken really has found a way to make Jimmy mortal again?"

"It isn't possible," Roshan replied. "Being a vampire isn't a disease. You can't cure it like an infection."

"But what if you could? Would you not like to be mortal again?"

It was a question he had never truly considered. He had known the only cure for the Dark Trick was to willingly end his existence. He had accepted that fact and moved on. There was nothing to be gained in wishing for something that could never be. Now, he found himself pondering Brenna's question: what if? Did he want to be mortal again? Would he accept such a transformation if it was offered to him? What would it be like to walk in the sun's light after so many years of darkness, to enjoy a full-course meal in a fine restaurant, to live a normal life, father a child? As a vampire, such ordinary pursuits were forever out of reach. On the other hand, he didn't have to worry about sickness or disease, aging, dying, or any of the other ills that plagued humankind.

"Well?" Brenna prompted.

"I don't know." Would he willingly give up the supernatural powers that were second nature to him now? Being mortal meant being weak, vulnerable.

"I do not understand your hesitation," Brenna said.

"I doubt I could explain it to you. To be a vampire is both a curse and a blessing. In centuries past, we were hunted like animals, killed without compunction or regret. Since we were not considered human, it was assumed we had no feelings. Things have changed for the better, with time. Most people no longer believe in vampires, and so we live in the shadows of the night, careful to hide our true nature from the rest of the world."

"It still seems a lonely life to me," Brenna said. "What good is long life without love, without family, without children?"

Roshan nodded slowly. All that had been taken from him when Atiyana died, had been forever denied him when he succumbed to Zerena's dark kiss. He looked at Brenna, young and vibrant with life, her skin radiant with good health. He had made love to her last night, buried himself in her sweetness. Now, suddenly, it seemed like sacrilege that one such as he had dared to touch her, dared to hope he could love her and that she might love him in return. What right did he have to take pleasure in her embrace? What right did he have to defile her?

He thought of Jimmy Dugan. What if the boy was right? What if the warlock had found a way to return vampires to mortality? In his heart, Roshan was sure that such a thing was impossible, but what if he was wrong?

He looked at Brenna again and knew he would willingly give up his dark powers for the chance to share one lifetime in her arms.

The attraction that ever hummed between them grew stronger when they reached home.

Brenna stood in the living room, shivering a little. She was about to spell the fire to life when Roshan did it with a wave of his hand.

She tensed as he came up behind her, acutely aware of his nearness as he slipped her coat off her shoulders and tossed it over the back of a chair. His breath fanned her cheek, his hands rested lightly on her shoulders, then slid down her arms. She shivered with pleasure at his touch, felt a sharp pang of regret when he moved away from her.

Slowly, she turned to face him, wishing she had the courage to ask him if they were going to make love again.

"It's late," he said quietly. "You should get some sleep."

She nodded, disappointment sitting like a lead weight on her heart.

"Promise me you won't go near the bookstore or Loken unless I'm with you."

"I promise," she said. "But only if you promise me you'll help Jimmy Dugan."

"What else do you want me to do?"

"I do not know. Just do not turn him away if he comes to you again."

"All right. I'll do whatever I can." His gaze moved over her, hot and hungry. And then, unable to resist when she was so near, he drew her into his arms and kissed her. The hunger rose quickly within him, clawing at his vitals, reminding him that he had not fed this night. A seductive voice in the back of his mind whispered that there was no need for him to go out for sustenance, not when she was in his arms, warm and vibrant with life.

Abruptly, he released her and turned his back to her. "I'm going out," he said, his voice gruff. "Lock the door after me."

Before she could reply, he was gone from her sight.

He hunted with single-minded intensity, refusing to think of Brenna, refusing to think of anything but the hunger that must be fed.

A scream from outside an apartment building drew his attention. When he arrived, he saw a man and a woman thrashing around on the ground. At first glance, they appeared to be in the throes of passion, but then the woman cried out again, her voice filled with fear and loathing.

"Shut up, you whore!" Sitting back on his heels, the man struck the woman across the face, splitting her lower lip. The scent of fresh blood wafted through the air.

"Let me go!" she shrieked. "Help me! Someone, please help me!"

The man cursed as Roshan's hand closed around his shoulder. After dragging the man off the woman and spinning him around, Roshan drove his fist into the man's face. There was a satisfying crunch as the man's nose broke. Blood sprayed through the air. Roshan inhaled deeply, then tossed the man aside like so much rubbish.

The woman stared up at him, her eyes wide, no doubt wondering if he had come to her rescue, or if he intended to finish what the other man had started.

"Are you all right?" Roshan asked.

She nodded. "Y-yes, I think so."

His gaze moved over her. She was in her early thirties, with brown hair and blue eyes, one of which was already turning black from where she'd been hit. There was a nasty bruise on her left cheek; blood oozed from the cut on her lower lip.

"Do you live here?" he asked, nodding at the apartment building behind her.

"Yes. I was just coming home from work. I'm a nurse . . ." She recoiled when he offered her his hand.

"I'm not going to hurt you." He kept his voice low, reassuring. Hypnotic. "Do you live alone?"

He was a stranger. It was in her mind to lie, to say she lived with a roommate, but she couldn't lie to him, not when his gaze was locked with hers.

"Yes, alone."

Taking her by the hand, he drew her to her feet, then picked up her handbag and offered it to her.

"Come," he said. "I'll see you safely home."

"Yes," she said. "Safely home."

She lived in a modest one-bedroom apartment that, while small, was clean and neat. There were several paintings on the walls. Vases of dried flowers on the mantel and the table.

Once inside, Roshan closed and locked the door, then took her by the hand and led her into the bedroom. Sitting her on the bed, he went into the bathroom. He found a washcloth, wet it, then went back into the bedroom and wiped the blood from her face. He offered her a drink of whiskey that he found in the kitchen cupboard, then drew her into his arms, his mind melding with hers, wiping away her fear. He fed quickly, then erased his memory from her mind. Tomorrow, she would remember only that she had fought off an attacker.

Leaving her sleeping peacefully, he left the apartment building and returned to the Nocturne. He paused at the entrance, sniffing the air until he picked up Anthony Loken's scent.

It led him to a large one-story brick building located on a patch of weeds on the outskirts of town. The windows were covered with boards on the inside and barred on the outside. No light showed through the cracks.

Anthony Loken's scent was strong here, and so was that of Jimmy Dugan.

Roshan circled the building, noting that there was only one entrance. It, too, was barred. Had this been Loken's home, Roshan would have been unable to cross the threshold without an invitation, but this was an abandoned place of business and the threshold had no power over him.

Dissolving into mist, Roshan slipped under the narrow opening beneath one of the boards. Once inside, he resumed his own shape. Though the building was dark, his vampire sight allowed him to see everything clearly, though there was precious little to see—a wooden chair, a metal desk, a file cabinet.

An open door led to a long hallway flanked on either side by doors that opened into empty rooms. A narrow staircase was located at the far end of the corridor.

Roshan paused at the head of the stairs. Loken's scent was still strong, and mingled with it was the scent of blood and fear. And violent death.

Treading softly, Roshan descended the stairs.

And the scent of death grew stronger.

There was only one door at the bottom of the stairs. Roshan tried the handle, knowing instinctively that it would be locked.

Again dissolving into mist, he floated under the crack beneath the door. He hovered there a moment before taking on his own shape once more.

The scent of blood was overpowering now, awakening his hunger in spite of the fact that he had just fed.

The room was a laboratory. Metal shelves crowded with glass jars, test tubes, beakers, flasks, funnels, slides, and vials lined one wall. A rack held several test tubes filled with blood. Another shelf held several books on witchcraft, anatomy, and hematology. There was a small refrigerator on a long counter, along with a microscope and an incubator. A large gray metal file cabinet stood on one side of the door, a desk with a state-of-the-art computer and printer was on the other side. A circle of power had been drawn on the floor in the center of the room. And in the center of the circle there was a stainless steel operating table that held Jimmy Dugan's remains. His arms and legs were bound to the table with silver manacles. A thick wooden stake protruded from his chest. A long rubber tube was attached to the boy's left arm, slowly siphoning the blood from his body into a large glass container.

Walking toward the table, Roshan felt a whisper of dark energy as he stepped inside the circle. So, Anthony Loken was not only a warlock but something of a scientist, as well.

Roshan stared at Dugan's body. "Foolish boy," he muttered. "Why didn't you get the hell out of town while you had the chance?"

Turning away from the table, Roshan walked over to the desk, quickly perusing the warlock's notes, most of which he found indecipherable.

Roshan glanced at what was left of Jimmy Dugan. Had the boy's blood provided Loken with any of the answers he was searching for? Would it enable him to come up with a formula for eternal life?

Dissolving into mist, Roshan flowed out of the laboratory. Dugan had trusted the wrong man and it had cost him his life.

Materializing outside the lab, Roshan stared up at the sky, at the millions of twinkling stars that faded away into infinity. Until now, even though he had known it was impossible, he hadn't realized how badly he had been hoping that Jimmy Dugan had been right, and that Loken had found a cure for the hunger that plagued him.

Without conscious thought, he followed the warlock's scent across the city to a house located on a hill. A high wrought iron fence surrounded the yard. Lights shone in the windows. A plume of blue-gray smoke rose from a red brick chimney.

Roshan stared up at the house for several minutes, then, lost in thought, he turned and headed for home.

He had told Brenna to go to bed, but he found her curled up on the sofa in the living room, waiting for him. Morgana slept in the crook of her arm.

"You're up late," he said, dropping into the chair beside the sofa.

"I could not sleep. I kept thinking about Jimmy Dugan. Do you think he will take your advice and leave town?"

"He's dead."

Her eyes widened. "Dead? How do you know?"

"I saw his body."

"But . . . what happened? How did he die?"

"I'm not sure, but Loken's draining the blood from the boy's body."

Her face paled. For a moment, he thought she was going to be sick. "You saw him?"

He nodded curtly.

"Poor Mr. Dugan. If only he had listened to you."

Roshan grunted softly, surprised by his regret at the boy's death. Usually, the lives of others, especially mortals, meant little to him. He fed on them when necessary. Until Brenna entered his life, he had cared little for humanity's woes collectively or individually. But Jimmy Dugan hadn't been mortal. He had been a vampire, and though Roshan had scoffed at Jimmy's notion that they were brothers, he felt an uncharacteristic need to avenge the boy's death.

"Well," Brenna said, gathering Morgana in her arms, "I think I will go to bed. Good night."

"Good night."

He watched her leave the room, his gaze lingering on the sway of her hips. His little witch had changed his life in ways he had not imagined, made him yearn for things he had thought forever behind him. Now, looking at her, he found himself wanting to spend his life with her, to plant his seed within her, to watch her womb swell with new life.

Simple dreams for a mortal man.

Impossible dreams for a vampire.

CHAPTER 17

She was walking down the street outside the Wicca Way Coffee Shop and Bookstore when Anthony Loken fell into step beside her. Smiling, he took her hand in his and led her down the street. They walked until the city was far behind them. She frowned as they approached a large brick building. As they drew closer, she began to shiver as all her instincts warned her not to enter the building. The door was made of steel. The windows were boarded up on the inside and barred on the outside.

She could smell death inside.

With a cry, she tried to wrest her hand from Loken's, but his fingers tightened on hers as he dragged her inside the building and shut the door. Desperate to escape him, she tried to gather her will around her in order to repel his hold on her, but her magick was useless against him.

An evil laugh rose in his throat as he dragged her down a flight of stairs to the basement. He opened a door and flipped a switch, flooding the room with light, light that did little to dispel the blackness that gathered around her, a darkness so thick she could feel it crawling over her skin.

A long metal table stood in the middle of a magick circle. Jimmy Dugan's corpse lay on the table, obscene and withered in death. A stake had been driven into his heart. His body had been drained of blood.

She turned to look at Loken, her insides going cold with terror when she saw him, really saw him, for the first time. He was neither man nor warlock but some creature out of a nightmare. His eyes were blood red, his ears long and pointed, more like horns than human ears. His teeth were white and sharp.

She looked back at the table, her eyes widening when she found herself staring into Jimmy Dugan's eyes. And then, to her horror, the young vampire's appearance began to change. His hair turned from brown to black, his eyes from dark brown to the deep blue of midnight. His shoulders grew broader, his legs longer, and suddenly it wasn't Jimmy Dugan's body chained to the cold metal table but Roshan's.

A scream rose in her throat, echoing off the walls, the floor, the ceiling. She screamed until her throat ached. Screamed with terror and revulsion. And mingled with her screams was the sound of Anthony Loken's satanic laughter . . .

She woke with a start, her face and body bathed in sweat.

Scrambling out of bed, she threw back the curtains and opened the window, then stood there drawing in deep breaths of fresh air.

A dream, it had been nothing but a bad dream, and yet she couldn't shake off a feeling of impending doom.

Sometimes dreams were just dreams, and sometimes they were glimpses into the future.

Hurrying downstairs, she went into the kitchen. She pulled a heavy silver bowl from the cupboard and filled it with water, then placed it on the table, her fingertips tapping impatiently while she waited for the water to form a smooth surface.

Passing her hands over the bowl, she stared into the water, murmuring, "Secrets hidden, dark and deep, show me where my love doth sleep."

Slivers of color spiraled up from the bottom of the bowl, swirling across the face of the water until they formed a picture of Roshan. He was lying on his back on a large bed with a carved wooden headboard. A dark blue sheet covered him from the waist down. His skin looked very pale against the bedding. Eyes narrowed, she stared at him. He didn't move, didn't twitch, didn't breathe. She shivered in spite of herself. He did, indeed, sleep like one who was dead. But at least he was safe!

Now, if she only knew the whereabouts of his lair.

Even as the thought crossed her mind, the water shimmered, the colors running together and then painting a new image on the face of the water, and now she was looking at the hallway that ran from the front entryway to the living room. The focus of the picture narrowed until it showed a small door located near the entrance to the living room.

Brenna frowned. She had searched the house from top to bottom trying to find where he slept. How had she missed that door?

Memorizing the location, she ran her fingertips through the water, erasing the image. She poured the water down the sink then went into the hallway. She walked the length of the corridor but there was no sign of a door.

Standing at the end of the entryway, she gathered her powers around her.

"A hidden door is here today, bring me the Sight, show me the way."

There was a ripple in the air, blue motes gathered around her, then outlined a small narrow door located on the left side of the hallway. She stooped in front of the portal. There was no latch. Dropping to her knees, she ran her hands over the door, murmured, "Ah-hah!" when the door opened inward, revealing a long staircase that led down, down, into darkness. At her touch, the blue motes faded and then disappeared.

Returning to the kitchen, she found a candle, then made her way back to the hidden doorway. A quick incantation lit the candle.

She hesitated a moment, then, one hand braced against the wall and the other holding the candle out in front of her, she crawled through the doorway, then walked down the stairs.

She paused at the bottom. At first, she thought she was in the basement, but the basement was much larger and filled with old furniture and boxes. She glanced around, seeing nothing until she used the Sight again. And then she saw it, the faint outline of another door. This one was average size. Once again, there was no discernable latch; once again, she ran her hands over the front and sides but this door refused to budge. She tried several incantations, but to no avail. The door refused to open.

With a sigh of discouragement, she turned and went up the stairs. What would she have done if the door had opened? Did she really want to see Roshan lying there, unmoving? Had she been able to get close to him, she would have been unable to resist touching him. Would his skin have felt cold, lifeless? Would he have known she was there?

When she reached the head of the stairs, Morgana was sitting there, waiting for her. The cat regarded her through narrowed yellow eyes, her expression clearly stating that breakfast was long overdue.

After closing the door, Brenna bent down to scratch Morgana's ears, then went into the kitchen to prepare breakfast for herself and the cat.

Deep in his lair, awareness stirred through the sleeping vampire, roused by the uncanny feeling that someone had been watching him. Yet he sensed no threat to his existence, no immediate danger. And then Brenna's scent was carried to him on a fleeting breath of air. She had been in the outer chamber of his lair. He had only a moment to ponder such a remarkable occurrence before the Dark Sleep dragged him down into oblivion once again.

Anthony Loken stood in the doorway of his laboratory, his brow furrowed as he regarded the body on the table. Such a foolish boy, to believe that anyone could produce a cure for the Dark Trick.

With a shake of his head, Loken removed the tubes from the limp, pale arms, then, careful to make sure the stake remained firmly buried in the boy's chest, he lifted the body into his arms and carried the bloodless corpse up the stairs. Opening the front door, he glanced right and left to make sure there was no one in sight and then tossed the vampire's body out into the yard. There was a faint sizzle as the sun's light fell on preternatural flesh and then, in the blink of an eye, the body of Jimmy Dugan went up in flames.

Loken stared at the patch of barren ground where the boy's body had been. Nothing remained to show that Jimmy Dugan had ever existed. Efficient, Loken mused. Most efficient.

Closing the door, Loken returned to his lab. In all his years of searching, Dugan was the first genuine vampire he had found. A good sign, he thought. At last, fortune had smiled on him.

He opened the small refrigerator where he had stored the vampire's blood and withdrew one of the vials. Now that he had what he needed, perhaps he would finally be able to discover what it was about the blood of the undead that allowed vampires to heal almost immediately from any wound, to change their shape, to travel great distances in a blur of movement. But it was the vampire's ability to survive for centuries that Loken craved. Why should he be subject to the few years of a mere mortal life span? He was a man of intelligence and power, a warlock without equal, yet he was subject to the ravages of age, disease, and death. True, some wizards lived to a vast old age, but he did not intend to grow old and weak. His lifelong goal had been to find a way to enjoy a vampire's power without a vampire's cravings or limitations. And now, at last, that goal was within his grasp!

He pulled the microscope from the shelf and placed it on his desk. After pulling on a pair of gloves, he prepared several slides with the blood of the vampire.

He placed the first one under the microscope, and then, quivering with excitement, he bent his head over the instrument and stared into the eyepiece. For several moments, he forgot to breathe but simply stared at what he saw. He had spent years studying hematology, yet nothing in his experience enabled him to interpret what he now saw, a constantly shifting mass of red blood cells so dark as to be almost black, cells that appeared to devour one another until only a few remained, and these, to his complete astonishment, quickly began to multiply, and then the whole sequence started again.

Shaking his head, he removed the first slide and replaced it with a second, and then a third.

What did it mean? If he was to inject himself with the vampire's blood, would it endow him with the vampire's power? Or would the vampire's blood consume his own until nothing remained?

A guinea pig, that was what he needed.

He quickly put everything away, wiped a bit of dried blood off the examining table, removed his gloves, and turned off the lights. A guinea pig shouldn't be too hard to find. One of the gullible pseudo-vamps from the Nocturne. A bum off the street. A runaway teen. One of the unemployed young men who gathered near the bus stop in the south end of the city looking for work. He had only to take his pick.

Whistling softly, he left the lab, making sure to lock the door behind him.

Roshan found Brenna in the kitchen fixing dinner and talking to the cat. He stood there a moment, admiring the softly rounded shape of the woman, the silky sheen of her hair, the way her jeans molded to her slim shape, the sound of her voice.

She blushed when she glanced over her shoulder and saw him standing in the doorway.

"Don't let me interrupt your conversation," he said. "Morgana looked quite interested in what you were saying."

"How long have you been standing there?" Brenna asked, her blush deepening to a most becoming shade of pink.

"Not long enough."

Morgana glanced from Brenna to Roshan, then darted out of the kitchen.

"I don't think she likes me," he mused.

"She will, in time."

"I doubt it. Few animals will tolerate my kind."

"I am sorry. I do not know what I would do without Morgana. She is all the family I have," she said wistfully. "All I have left of my past."

"You were looking for me today." It wasn't a question. "You were in my lair."

She looked at him, her silence an admission of her guilt.

"Why?"

She lifted her chin defiantly, refusing to be intimidated even though she knew she was in the wrong. "I was curious," she said, and then frowned. "How did you know I was there?"

"I felt your eyes watching me."

"'Tis not possible!"

He lifted one brow. "No?"

She shook her head. "How could you?"

"You admit it then? You were spying on me?"

"I summoned your image in my scrying glass."

Clever girl, he mused. "And what did you use for a mirror?"

"A bowl of water."

He recalled the conversation they'd had earlier when

she had told him she had been thinking of buying a mirror. He had assumed she wanted a mirror for the same reason as any other woman. But she wasn't like any other woman. Still, there was no reason why she couldn't have a small mirror for scrying, if that was what she wanted. No reason why she couldn't have a full-length looking glass in her bedroom. Just because he avoided them, there was no reason why she couldn't have a couple if she wished.

And then, drawn by her scent, by the warmth of her living flesh, he forgot all about mirrors and witchcraft. Closing the distance between them, he took her in his arms. His body quickened immediately, every cell and nerve ending remembering the night they had made love.

She looked up at him, her green eyes luminous.

"Ah, Brenna," he murmured helplessly, and lowering his head, he kissed her.

She went up on her tiptoes, her arms twining around his neck, her body molding itself to his.

The heat of her body warmed him, the sweetness of her lips enflamed him. He held her closer, tighter, felt his fangs lengthen as his hunger stirred to life. The memory of making love to her rose in his mind, tempting him to sweep her into his arms and carry her upstairs, to lay her down on the bed and make love to her until the sun crept over the horizon. Temping, so tempting. Only his guilt at ravishing her the first time, and his fear that he might indulge in more than the pleasure of her sweet flesh, kept him from putting thought into action.

Muttering an oath, he released her.

She blinked up at him, her gaze unfocused, her lips swollen, stained with a single drop of blood where his fangs had broken her tender skin.

A low growl rose in his throat as her tongue slid over her lower lip to lick the blood away.

"I'll be back later," he said gruffly, and hastened out of the house and into the night.

Lifting her fingertips to her lips, Brenna stared after him. One kiss, that's all it took, she thought. One kiss, and she was ready to let him carry her upstairs to bed. She had known him only a short time, yet she could not imagine her life without him. It was as if she had known him all her life, as if they were bound together by invisible cords, as if, in some strange metamorphosis, he had become an integral part of her and she had become an integral part of him. Was that what happened whenever two people made love? Did it happen to everyone, that sense of belonging? She knew making love to Roshan without the blessing of the church had been wrong. It was immoral, a terrible sin, and yet, right or wrong, all she could think of was being in his arms again, making love to him again. Even now, she felt bereft, lost without him. Even the house felt different when he was away.

Would it be so bad, being married to a vampire? True, there was much they could not share, but there was ever so much more that they could. She enjoyed his company, his caring. He was kind and patient, he would protect her, help her learn her way around in this new place. Though her days would be her own, her nights would be his. Best of all, he wasn't afraid of her witchcraft, nor was he intimidated by her power. Quite the contrary, he seemed pleased by it, proud of her abilities, limited though they might be.

Of course, she was taking a lot for granted. Just because they had made love didn't mean he wanted to marry her. If there was one thing she had learned, it was that a good number of people in this century had no qualms about living together, or having children together, out of wedlock. But, accepted or not, she knew it was wrong. Children deserved a mother and a father, a home secured by the bonds of marriage.

Perhaps it is time you became like him, whispered an insidious little voice in the back of her mind. *If there is no cure, if he can never be mortal, then perhaps you should embrace the Dark Gift. It is the only way you can truly share his life, the only way he can share yours.*

She thrust the disquieting thought from her mind. To be a vampire was a life against nature. It meant giving up the sun's light and all hope of ever having a child. It meant giving up her humanity, living in the shadows, existing on the blood of others.

It was not a life she would willingly choose for herself or anyone else.

And yet the seed had been planted. Repellent as it was, it took root in a distant corner of her mind.

Leaving the house, Roshan willed himself to the Nocturne. Clad all in black, he quickly blended in with the rest of the crowd, his hunger growing as the sound of a hundred beating hearts called out to him. His nostrils filled with the scent of prey, ripe and ready for the taking.

A young woman moved toward him, threading her way through the crowd on the edge of the dance floor, her hips undulating, her breasts thrust out. Her dyed black hair fell long and straight over her shoulders.

"Dance with me?" Her voice was low and husky. Looking up at him through eyes that promised more than a dance, she ran a black-painted fingernail across his chest. "Well?"

"Sure." He pulled her into his arms and swept her onto the dance floor.

"I've seen you here before," she purred.

"Indeed?"

"I was watching for you tonight, hoping you'd come alone."

He smiled down at her. "Then I'm glad I came."

"So am I." She studied him intently for a moment. "You don't look like the other guys that hang around here," she remarked. "Or act like them."

"Oh?"

She shook her head, her brow furrowed in thought. "Maybe it's because they're all just little boys at heart. But you, you seem much older."

He laughed softly. "You have no idea, Carrie, my sweet."

Her eyes widened. "How do you know my name?"

"As you said, I'm not like the others." He drew her closer, one hand sweeping her hair from her neck. "Look at me, Carrie, only me."

She stared up at him, her lips slightly parted, a trace of fear in her eyes.

"See only me," he murmured. "Hear my voice, only my voice."

"Yes," she whispered. "Only you."

Slowly, he lowered his head. To anyone watching, it would seem he was kissing her neck as he turned her slowly around the floor. He drank quickly, taking only what he needed, and quickly sealed the two tiny puncture marks left by his fangs.

He lifted his head just as the music ended.

"Carrie?"

She blinked up at him, her gaze unfocused.

"Thank you for the dance."

"You're welcome." Frowning, she lifted a hand to her neck, then blinked at him again.

He kept his arm around her waist. "Are you all right?"

"I don't know. I feel a little dizzy."

"Come," he said, taking her by the hand, "let me buy you a drink."

Roshan was leading Carrie toward the bar when he saw Anthony Loken sitting at one of the tables toward the back. The warlock saw him at the same time and animosity flowed between them, a palpable sense of malice so strong that Roshan was sure the others in the room felt it without knowing what it was.

At the bar, Roshan ordered Carrie a tall glass of orange juice. Standing beside the woman, he was careful to keep Loken in sight.

The warlock turned his back to him, his attention again centered on the young man who shared his table.

Using his preternatural hearing, Roshan eavesdropped on their conversation. The young man was tired of pretending to be a vampire and he had come to the Nocturne in hopes of finding one of the undead. Loken nodded sympathetically. Leaning closer to the young man, he told him that his search was at an end. He, Loken, was a vampire. If the young man was sincere, he had only to come to Loken's lair to begin the transformation. The young man, whose name was Roger West, quickly agreed. Loken paid the check and the two men left the table, heading for the rear exit.

Roshan swore softly as he watched them leave the club. He had seen the results of Anthony Loken's last experiment.

He stood there a moment, undecided. It was of no consequence if Loken killed West. The young man meant nothing to Roshan. Mortals, in general, meant little to him other than their ability to satisfy his hellish thirst.

He danced with another one of the women in the club, drinking from her as he had from the first. Leaving her at the bar, he was about to go home when, on a totally inexplicable impulse, he found himself headed for Loken's laboratory on the outskirts of town.

CHAPTER 18

Roger West whistled softly when he saw Anthony Loken's car. "Nice," he said, running his hand over the top of the Lexus.

Grinning, Loken unlocked the door and slid behind the wheel. As soon as West was in the car, he pulled out of the parking lot, tires squealing as he turned onto the road and headed for home.

"Hey, buddy, slow down," West said, grabbing the armrest. "I'm not immortal yet."

Loken flashed him a smile. "All in good time." A whispered incantation gave him green lights all the way home.

"Is this your place?" West asked as Loken parked in front of a large house and killed the engine.

"It is indeed." Opening the door, he exited the car.

"You must be rich as hell," West muttered as he followed Loken up the stairs to the front door.

"Almost," Loken said. He smiled wolfishly as he opened the door. "Come in, won't you?"

"So," West said as he crossed the threshold, "how long does it take? To become a vampire?"

"Not long."

West nodded. He gasped, startled, as lights began coming on in the room.

Loken grinned at him. "A little magick, nothing for you to worry about."

West swallowed hard. "Vampire magic, right?"

"Not exactly."

"No?" West frowned. "What kind, then?"

"I'm a warlock, actually. A wizard, if you will."

"But I thought . . . you said you were a vampire."

"Yes, I did, didn't I? I'm afraid I lied."

"What the hell's going on here?"

"I'm sorry, Mr. West, but I'm sure you've told lies from time to time. It's a fact of life that we sometimes have to lie to get what we want."

West glanced at the front door. "What do you want?"

"You. For a little experiment."

"No way! I'm outta here!" With a shake of his head, Roger West started toward the front door, only to find that he no longer had control over his body. He looked back at Loken, his eyes wild and scared.

"Come along," Loken said, beckoning to him with his forefinger.

West shook his head. "I'm not going anywhere with you," he retorted, but his feet were following the warlock down a long dark hall, down a flight of stairs, into the basement.

"Climb up on the table," Loken said.

"Damn you!" West cried as he obeyed the warlock's bidding. "Let me go!"

"Lie down. This won't take long."

Roger West stretched out on the table, his heart

pounding. No matter how hard he tried, he couldn't move, had no control over his own movements. Sweat broke out across his brow, gathered under his arms. "Please, let me go."

"Too late." Loken pulled a vial out of his coat pocket and removed the seal.

Pulling a syringe from the drawer of a large tool chest, he filled it with blood.

West stared at him in horror. "What . . . what are you going to do with that?"

"It's a test. For all I know, it just might turn you into a vampire. Then again, it might kill you," he said with a wicked grin. "Or give you eternal life. But we won't know until we try."

Loken wrapped a strip of rubber around West's upper arm, then poked around for a vein. Finding a good one, he inserted the needle and pushed the plunger home.

West stared at the blood flowing into his arm, and then looked at Loken. And then he screamed, his body writhing in agony as the vampire's blood seeped into his bloodstream.

"Shut up!" Loken said. "Tell me what you feel."

"It burns, it burns," the young man said, whimpering. "Make it stop . . . make it . . ."

He stared up at Loken, saliva dripping from a corner of his mouth. His body convulsed one last time and then lay still.

"Dammit!" Grabbing the boy's wrist, Loken felt for a pulse. It was strong but irregular.

Dropping the boy's arm, Loken sat down to wait for the final outcome.

* * *

Roshan prowled the outside of the warlock's laboratory, his senses testing the night. Loken had been there earlier that evening but there was no indication that Roger West had been with him.

Where had Loken taken the boy?

Frowning, he dissolved into mist and entered the building. The laboratory was empty. Jimmy Dugan's body was gone, though the smell of fear and blood and death lingered in the air.

Leaving the building, Roshan regained his own shape. If Loken wasn't here, then he must have taken Roger West home. But why there and not here?

A thought took him to the warlock's house. As soon as he neared the front door, he caught the heavy scent of the boy's fear. They were here.

He was wondering how he might gain access to the house when he heard a faint scream from the direction of the basement. Roshan cursed softly as a second scream reached his ears. It was a cry of such torment that it seared his soul. And then it came again, a wordless cry of agony, a heartrending plea for help.

Even knowing he couldn't enter the warlock's house without an invitation, Roshan couldn't resist the urge to go to the boy's aid. Using his preternatural powers to unlock and open the door, he took a step forward, only to be repelled by the power of the threshold and the wards the warlock had set around the entrance.

Roshan swore softly; then, knowing there was nothing he could do to save the boy, he transported back to the Nocturne and called the police.

Roger West's head rocked back and forth as Loken's knife cut into his flesh. The stink of his own waste filled his nostrils, mingling with the scent of his blood. Nausea roiled in West's stomach. So much blood. So much pain. He tried to summon the energy to move, the strength to free himself from the warlock's power, but it was futile. He could only lay there, helpless and afraid.

Loken watched through unblinking eyes as blood flowed from the deep gash he had made in the boy's forearm. "The wound isn't healing. It appears an injection doesn't work," he said, thinking aloud. "Perhaps the blood has to be ingested."

Pulling another vial out of his coat pocket, he lifted the boy's head and held the vial to his lips. "Drink this."

Unable to resist, Roger West opened his mouth and swallowed the thick red fluid, only to vomit it up again. It ran down his chin and chest, sprayed over Loken's shirt, dripped from the table to the floor.

Cursing, Loken jumped out of the way. "You will drink this and you will keep it down," he said, and pulling a third vial from his pocket, he held it to the boy's lips.

"Damn you," West said weakly. But he drank the contents of the vial.

"We'll give it a chance to work," Loken said, glancing at his watch. "Perhaps an hour or two." Tearing a strip of cloth from the boy's shirt, he used it to gag the boy, then strapped his arms and legs to the table. "Rest while you can," Loken said, and turning off the lights, he left the basement.

Returning to the living room, he was about to go into the kitchen for a bottle of beer when he felt a draft. Walking toward the entry, he saw that the front door was open.

Frowning, he gathered his power and murmured an

incantation. A moment later, a shadowy image took shape on the porch. He recognized it instantly. Roshan DeLongpre.

Loken grunted softly. What had DeLongpre been doing here?

He was still considering the possibilities when a police car pulled up in the driveway. Two policeman, both young, got out of the car.

Loken stepped out onto the porch. "Good evening, officers," he said with a congenial smile.

"Mr. Anthony Loken?"

"Yes."

"We had a report that screams were heard coming from this house."

"You must be mistaken. I've been here all night and I've heard nothing."

"Do you live alone, sir?"

"Yes, I do." He smiled again. "The only screams heard here tonight came from my television set."

"Do you mind if we look around?"

Loken shook his head. "Help yourself." He took a step back, allowing them entrance.

One of the officers went to search the house. The second policeman stayed with Loken, one hand resting on the butt of his revolver.

"Can I offer you something to drink?" Loken asked. "A cup of coffee, or a soda?"

"No, thank you."

Loken nodded. He listened to the footsteps of the first officer as he moved through the house. There was nothing to worry about. The door to the basement was invisible, protected by a recent enchantment no mere mortal could detect.

Perhaps five minutes passed before the first officer

returned to the living room. "Let's go, Frank, there's nothing here. Sorry to have bothered you, Mr. Loken."

"That's quite all right." Anthony followed the two officers to the front door and watched them leave. He even waved as they pulled away from the curb.

And then he closed and locked the door.

Something would have to be done about Mr. Roshan DeLongpre, he mused. Something permanent. And painful.

And then he smiled. Perhaps Mr. DeLongpre could take the boy's place in the basement.

Whistling softly, he went downstairs to see how his latest experiment was coming along.

CHAPTER 19

Brenna waited up until after midnight and still Roshan didn't come home. It never took him this long to feed. Where was he? She didn't like the answer that came to mind. He was a handsome man gifted with the preternatural allure of a vampire. Women looked at him wherever they went . . . She shook her head, refusing to entertain the thought that he might be with another woman.

Moving through the rooms downstairs, she turned off all the lights but one, then went upstairs to get ready for bed. Morgana trailed at her heels, meowing reassuringly.

Undressing, Brenna pulled her nightgown over her head, then slipped into bed. Morgana curled up beside her, one paw resting on her arm.

Turning on her side, Brenna gazed out the window, one hand idly stroking Morgana's head. Even though she was growing used to life in this century, Brenna sometimes wished she were back home. Life had been so much simpler there. Harder in many ways, but simpler nevertheless. There was still so much in this century that she didn't fully understand. Wars in places she had never heard of. Diseases that were unknown in her time. Inventions like the washing machine that made doing the laundry easier but somehow robbed her of the satisfaction of washing her clothes by hand. The dryer dried her clothes quickly but they lacked the fresh smell of clothing dried in the sun. With so little to do, the days seemed longer.

Perhaps she needed to find a job.

The more she thought about it, the more she liked the idea of earning her own money. But what could she do? She wasn't qualified to work in an office. She didn't have a college education, but surely there was something she could do. "What do you think, Morgana?"

With a shake of her head, Morgana rolled onto her back.

"Perhaps Myra would give me a job at the bookstore," Brenna said, thinking aloud. "Maybe I could sell books or wait tables. Of course, *he* would not like it." She scratched Morgana's tummy for a few minutes, and then smiled a conspiratorial smile. "Of course, there is no need for us to tell Mr. DeLongpre." Her smile faded. "Perhaps the bookstore is not the right place to look for employment. Mr. Loken visits there all too often."

Thinking of Anthony Loken brought Jimmy Dugan to mind. She was certain that the young vampire had died in Loken's pursuit of eternal life.

Thinking of Jimmy Dugan brought tears to her eyes. Though she had known very little about him, it was sad to think that he had died so young.

Sniffling, she closed her eyes, only to open them again a moment later, certain that she was no longer alone in the room. "Roshan?"

He materialized beside the bed, his black clothing blending into the darkness of the room. "I thought you would be asleep by now."

She shook her head. "I was thinking of Mr. Dugan."

Roshan grunted softly. "I'm afraid Loken has another victim."

"Oh, no! Who?"

"A young man he met at the Nocturne tonight."

She stared up at him, her green eyes filled with concern. "Is there nothing you can do?"

"I called the police, for all the good it did. They searched his house but didn't find anything. I should have known they wouldn't."

"At least you tried. That is all you can do."

He nodded, thoughts of the unknown young man's fate receding as Brenna's nearness filled his senses. She was here, in his house, in his bed, and he wanted her.

Sitting on the edge of the mattress, he murmured her name.

Brenna shivered as his voice moved over her. She heard the question he didn't ask. Sitting up, she drew him closer, her kiss the unspoken answer to his unspoken question.

Roshan drew back a little. "Are you sure?"

"I doubt if I have ever been more sure of anything in my life."

"Sweetheart!"

He dragged her onto his lap, his mouth covering hers, his arms so tight around her she thought her ribs might be in danger of breaking, but then she was kissing him back, pain and pleasure mingling together, until there was nothing in all the world but his mouth on hers. Excitement fluttered in her stomach. Anticipation made her pulses race. His tongue was warm against her throat, his hands gentle as he caressed her.

Closing her eyes, she surrendered to the wealth of sensations that he aroused in her. Somehow, his clever hands managed to undress both of them, and then he was stretched out on the bed beside her. She had not intended for this to happen again and yet she had known, in her heart of hearts, that it was as inevitable as the sunrise.

Colors and images flooded her mind, shattering into rainbows of shimmering crystal as his body merged with hers. Her body arched to receive him more fully. Her nails raked his back. She felt his teeth graze her neck and she turned her head to the side, giving him better access to her throat. She moaned softly, her senses overwhelmed with sensation. How could something that should have filled her with revulsion feel so wonderful? In a distant part of her mind, she realized that she was feeling everything that he did, his yearning, not only for their physical joining, but for the sense of belonging that he found in her arms, as she found it in his. Pleasure engulfed her until she felt as though she were drowning in pure bliss, a pleasure so intense it was almost painful, and then she plunged over the edge into ecstasy, and at last fulfillment unlike anything she had ever experienced.

Rolling onto his back, Roshan drew Brenna up against his side, his arm holding her close. He had no reason to ask if she was all right, not when she was looking at him through heavy-lidded eyes, her expression that of a woman who had been well and truly loved.

"Is it this way for everyone?" she asked.

"No."

"How do you know? Have you taken many women to bed?" It was a foolish question. He had lived for hundreds of years. No doubt he'd had hundreds of women.

"Not so many, all things considered," he replied. "Certainly none like you." He brushed his knuckles over her cheek. "None so beautiful, or so tempting. None that I loved."

Her eyes widened. "You love me?"

"More than you can imagine."

"I do not know what to say."

"Say that you love me."

"Oh, I do," she murmured fervently. "I do love you." A soft smile played over her lips. "More than *you* can imagine."

"Then you'll stay with me?"

"Where would I go?"

"Anywhere you wish," he replied soberly. "Anytime you're not happy here, you have only to say the word. I'll buy you a house of your own, if you wish, anywhere you want to live."

"Truly?"

He nodded. "Truly."

"That is most generous of you."

"It's little enough to give you in return for what you've given me."

Her eyes widened in surprise. "I have given you nothing."

"Oh, but you're wrong, my sweet Brenna. You gave me hope and a reason to go on living." He brushed a kiss across her lips. "You've given me the most precious gifts any woman can give to a man. Your innocence, your love, and your trust."

Turning onto her side, she wrapped her arms around him. "I do love you. So very, very much."

He kissed her gently. "Can you accept me as I am, Brenna? All of me?"

"Yes. I want to share your life, as much of it as I can."

He crushed her close, his heart overflowing as he rained kisses on her cheeks, her eyelids, the curve of her throat, the tip of her nose. "Promise me you'll never leave me."

"I promise."

It was a weighty promise, one he didn't expect her to keep but, for now, it was enough.

They made love again, more slowly this time, and then Roshan carried her into the shower and washed her from head to foot. They might have gotten out of the shower before the water grew cold if she hadn't taken the soap from his hand and returned the favor. Her soapy hands moving over his body was an erotic sensation he had never known before, one that had the expected results.

It was the cold water that finally drove them out of the shower and down the stairs. Roshan lit a fire in the hearth, then drew her down on the rug, his arm around her shoulders.

Brenna leaned against him, sleepy-eyed and content as she watched the flames. No doubt Granny O'Connell would be turning in her grave if she could see her granddaughter now, sitting naked on the floor in the arms of a vampire, her virginity well and truly lost.

Glancing up, she met Roshan's gaze. "Are you going to marry me?" She hadn't meant to ask the question but, once spoken, there was no taking it back.

"Is that what you want, Brenna?"

"Only if you do."

"And if I said no?"

Her heart seemed to drop to the floor. If he didn't want to marry her, what then? Could she stay here, in his house, as his mistress? Would it be so different from what she was doing now? She knew it would be, though she was reluctant to admit it. It was one thing to succumb to a night of passion in a man's arms, quite another to make a conscious decision to live with him without benefit of marriage even though, in this time and place, no one seemed to think there was anything wrong with it.

"You said you loved me," she reminded him, her voice barely audible.

"I do."

"But you do not wish to marry me?"

"I never thought to marry again," he replied slowly. "I never thought any woman would want me, or be able to accept me as I am now." He gazed deep into her eyes. "Have you thought it through, Brenna? Are you sure this is what you want?"

"Only if you do," she said again.

"I would be honored to have you as my wife," he said quietly. "I will love you as long as you live."

As long as she lived. The words hit her like a blast of cold air. In time, she would grow old and feeble. Her skin would wrinkle, her hair would turn gray, her hearing and eyesight would grow dim. But time had no claim on Roshan. In twenty years or a hundred, he would be as he was now—strong and healthy and vigorous, a man forever in his prime.

Roshan watched the play of emotions on her face, the doubts that rose in her eyes. He didn't have to use his preternatural senses to know what she was thinking. A moment later, her words confirmed his suspicions.

"Will you still love me when I am no longer young?" she asked, her gaze searching his. "How will you feel when I am old and you are not? When that time comes, will you leave me for someone else? Someone younger?"

"I will never leave you, Brenna, I swear it. Young or old, I will love you as much as I do tonight."

Easy words for him to say, she thought. How would she feel when her youth was behind her? Would she resent all that she had given up to spend her life with him? Would she look back and be sorry that she had given up the chance to be a mother? Would her arms forever ache for the children and grandchildren she had never had? When she was an old woman and the fires of youth and passion no longer burned within her, would she grieve for the life she had given up, for the posterity that had never been born? Would she hate him then because he did not age? Would her hatred destroy the love she felt for him now?

You do not have to grow old. The seductive words crawled through her mind. *You have only to become as he is.* If she became a vampire, she would stay as she was. They could be together forever. But did she want to be a vampire? To exist only at night, to survive on the blood of others?

Unbidden, Anthony Loken came to mind. Perhaps there was another way . . .

"Brenna?"

"Yes, Roshan DeLongpre, I will marry you."

"Name the day, my sweet."

"Can we have a big wedding?"

"As big as you wish, though I fear the guests will be few."

She had not considered that. Strange, she hadn't really missed having friends in this place, she thought. And then she smiled. What need had she for friends when she had Roshan? He filled her every thought, waking or sleeping.

"I have no need for guests as long as you are there."

"Only name the day and the place."

"Oh!" The smile faded from her face and she bit down on her lower lip.

"What is it? Have you changed your mind already?"

"No, but . . . that is . . . I should like to be married in a church and . . . can you . . . you won't . . . ?"

"Go up in a puff of smoke?" he asked with a wry grin.

She nodded, a faint blush pinking her cheeks.

"A church will be fine," he assured her. "You find yourself a pretty dress and a church you like and leave everything else to me."

Lying in bed later that night, though she supposed it was actually morning, since the sky was turning light, Brenna thought about all that had happened during the night past. After talking about the wedding, they had made love again, and then Roshan had carried her upstairs. They had taken a quick shower and then Roshan had put her to bed, tucking her in as though she were a child instead of a woman grown. Whispering that he loved her, he had kissed her good night, then left the room.

Brenna ran her fingertips over her lips, remembering the sweetness of his kiss, the light in his eyes when he told her he loved her. It all seemed unreal somehow. Everything that had happened since the night she first saw him seemed impossible, like something out of a dream. How could she be here, in this place, in this time? If not for Roshan, she would have died at the stake, dead these past three hundred and thirteen years. Instead, she was living in a house unlike anything she had ever known, and she was going to marry a vampire. Strange, how none of what she had believed about vampires seemed to be true where Roshan was concerned. He wasn't a monster with no conscience who killed indiscriminately. He wasn't a horrible creature with foul breath and a misshapen body. Quite the contrary. He was tall and handsome, more handsome than any man she had ever met.

And he loved her.

The knowledge filled her with an inner warmth that made her heart glow and brought a smile to her lips.

He loved her.

It was her last thought before sleep carried her away, and her first thought when she woke seven hours later.

Flinging the covers aside, she slipped out of bed and went into the bathroom. She brushed her teeth, washed her face, then dressed quickly in a pair of jeans, a peacock blue sweater, and a pair of boots.

Going downstairs, she ate a quick breakfast. Grabbing Roshan's car keys and the money he had left for her, she hurried out of the house and headed for the mall. She was going to be a bride, and a bride needed a dress.

She'd had no idea that finding a dress would be so time consuming, or so much fun. She tried on dozens of gowns, surprised and pleased by the fashions of the day. There were racks and racks of dresses, long white gowns of satin and silk and taffeta. Some were quite daring. Cut low, they bared her arms and her shoulders and an expanse of cleavage that, in her time, would have been considered scandalous. Others, with modest necklines and long sleeves, were so demure that even Granny O'Connell would have approved. Brenna tried them all on, long and short, modern and old-fashioned, finally settling on a silk gown with a beaded bodice, long sleeves, and a slim skirt with a short train.

Next, she tried on veils. Some were shoulder-length, others trailed gracefully down her back to the floor. They came with a variety of headpieces, some elaborate, some simple in their elegance. The veil she decided on was shoulder-length, the headpiece a simple beaded circlet.

Looking at herself in the mirror, she wondered what Roshan would think. Would he have preferred a more revealing gown? Something with a lower neckline and a shorter skirt?

Brenna looked at the saleslady. "Do I look all right?"

"Oh, my dear, you look like a princess out of a fairy tale."

Brenna smiled at her reflection. "I'll take it," she said, for her life was nothing these days if not a fairy tale.

CHAPTER 20

Anthony Loken prowled through his laboratory, his brow furrowed. His experiments on Roger West had proved most disappointing. Having the boy drink the vampire's blood had not proven any more successful than injecting it straight into the boy's veins. In the end, West had died a rather gruesome death. His body had violently rejected the vampire's blood and he had slowly shriveled up until, at the end, he had looked rather like a human dried apple.

Loken had tossed what was left of West's body into the hearth. The ensuing stench had been most unpleasant.

Loken filled several clean vials with the vampire's blood and placed them on a rack, which he then placed in the refrigerator, along with the rest of the vampire's blood.

The examination table was clean.

The blood was ready.

All he needed now was a new guinea pig.

CHAPTER 21

Brenna paced in front of the hearth, sat down, and stared at the images on the television screen, only to rise and pace again.

Where was Roshan? She was eager to see him, eager to share her day with him. Why, tonight of all nights, did he have to be so late?

Sensing her apprehension, Morgana meowed loudly from her perch on the back of the sofa.

"He will be here," Brenna told the cat. "He probably went out to . . . you know. Eat or drink or whatever he calls it."

"Indeed, he did."

Whirling around at the welcome sound of his voice, she flew across the floor into Roshan's arms.

"Miss me, did you?" he asked as she showered him with kisses.

"Maybe a little," she confessed.

He lifted one black brow. "Only a little?"

"All right, more than a little." Taking him by the hand,

she led him to the sofa. Sitting, she drew him down beside her. "Where have you been?"

"Just where you think. It's not so easy to find prey in the early part of the evening. Far easier to hunt late at night."

"Then why did you not wait until later?"

"Because I don't trust myself to be alone with you when I've not fed," he replied candidly.

"Oh."

"So, tell me about your day."

"It was wonderful!"

He smiled at her, charmed by her exuberance and the way her eyes sparkled with excitement. "Indeed? What did you do that put that glow in your eyes?"

"I went shopping, of course. Oh, Roshan, I bought the most beautiful gown! Wait until you see it! And shoes. And a veil. And underwear," she added, her cheeks turning pink. Such scanty undergarments, hardly more than a few scraps of white lace sewn together.

"If it makes you blush, I can scarcely wait to see it."

"There is not much to see." The admission made her cheeks grow hotter.

He laughed softly. "Did you find a church, as well?"

"Not yet."

"We can look this evening, if you wish."

"Will they not be closed at this time of night?"

He lifted one dark brow.

Brenna grinned ruefully. Of course. He was a vampire. Locked doors meant little to him.

"Have you eaten?" he asked.

"Yes."

"Shall we go then?"

She had expected to take the car, but he assured her he knew a quicker means of travel. With his arm wrapped around her shoulders, he transported them to one of the churches in the city. And when it wasn't to her liking, he took her to another and then another.

In spite of Roshan's assurances that he wouldn't go up in flames, she watched him carefully every time they crossed a threshold. She had been told that vampires couldn't enter churches, that crosses repelled them. More falsehoods, she thought.

"But what about holy water?" she asked as they walked down the center aisle of a beautiful Catholic church.

"Holy water burns, if you'll pardon the expression, like the very devil, and renders me helpless for a short time."

She laughed in spite of herself. It seemed wrong to laugh in such a place. Even the statue of the Virgin Mary seemed to be frowning her disapproval as the sound echoed eerily off the walls and the vaulted ceiling.

"So?" he asked.

She shook her head. "It is beautiful but cold."

Moments later, he had transported them to a small chapel far from the city.

Brenna loved it immediately. The altar and the pews were carved from oak. Moonlight shone through a stained glass window above the altar. The carpet was a deep blue. But it was the sense of peace that she found most appealing.

"I had a feeling you'd like this one," Roshan remarked.

"Then why did we come here last?"

"Because I knew you wouldn't be happy until you'd seen them all."

"Oh, you think you are so smart!"

Drawing her into his arms, he hugged her. "No, but I do think I know you pretty well."

She looked up into his eyes. Desire sparked between them and only the fact that they were in a church kept him from making love to her then and there.

Leaving the building, they walked hand in hand in the moonlight. It was a pretty spot. Tall trees and lush greenery surrounded the church, which looked almost ghostly in the light of the full moon. The air was filled with the fragrant scent of evergreens and rain-dampened earth. Night birds called to each other, their cries combining with the chirp of crickets and the croaking of a bullfrog to create a midnight symphony.

"Where will we find a priest to marry us?" Brenna asked as they followed a narrow trail through the trees.

"I know someone," Roshan replied.

"A vampire," Brenna guessed.

"Yes. He was a priest before he was turned. I'm not sure the marriage will be legal in the eyes of the state."

"It is more important that we be married in the eyes of the Lord," Brenna replied, then frowned. "I thought you said you did not have any friends among the vampires."

"I'm not sure Father Lanzoni qualifies as a friend. I haven't seen him in the last thirty or forty years."

"Mayhap he will not wish to perform the ceremony."

"Not to worry," Roshan said, squeezing her hand. "Just name the day." He grinned at her. "Or should I say the night?"

"Would tomorrow night be too soon?"

"I don't think so. I'll call Father Lanzoni when we get home."

Brenna's heart swelled with excitement. Tomorrow night she would be Roshan's wife. Mrs. Roshan DeLongpre. "Oh! Will we not need someone to stand up with us to witness our marriage?"

Roshan grunted softly. "I suppose so."

"I have no friends in the city save for Myra at the bookstore. Would it be all right for me to ask her?"

"Sure, if that's what you want."

"Who will stand beside you?" Brenna asked.

"That's a good question. Perhaps Father Lanzoni knows of someone."

"Mrs. Brenna DeLongpre," she murmured. "It sounds pretty, does it not?"

"It sounds perfect," he said, drawing her into his arms. As always, she pressed herself against him, her face lifting for his kiss, her eyes shining with love and happiness.

He gazed down at her a moment, wondering at his good fortune in finding her. Had it been the hand of fate that made him chose *Ancient History and Myths, Fact or Fiction* from the shelf the night he had been thinking of destroying himself? Was it possible that he and Brenna were always meant to be together? Had Zerena cursed him with the Dark Trick so that he would be able to travel back in time to save Brenna from the flames?

He shook his head, amused by the turn of his thoughts.

"What are you smiling at?" Brenna asked.

"I was thinking about us," he said.

"That always makes me smile, too."

He laughed softly, his hands lightly kneading her shoulders and then, unable to wait any longer, he lowered his head and kissed her.

Sweet, he thought, sweeter than the wine of the gods. Sweeter than the barely remembered taste of his mother's plum jelly. He ran his tongue along Brenna's lower lip, savoring the taste, the softness, before plundering the sweetness within. Desire sparked between them and he cupped her buttocks in his hands, pressing her body closer to his.

She moaned softly, her tongue dueling with his. She ran her hands over his chest, down his arms, reveling in his strength, marveling that a man as strong and powerful as Roshan could be so tender, so very, very gentle. His strength excited her, made her feel small and helpless, but in a good way, because they both knew she wasn't helpless.

With a sigh of regret, Roshan put her away from him.

Brenna made a soft sound of protest deep in her throat. "Why did you stop?"

He shrugged sheepishly. "I don't know. It just seems wrong to ravish you the night before we're to be married."

She made a face at him. "But it was all right last night?"

"Indeed it was, but don't ask me why."

She smiled up at him. "I had no idea you were so gallant," she said, linking her arm with his. "I wonder what else I shall discover about you in the nights to come."

"I can't imagine," he muttered.

Walking back to the church, he couldn't help thinking that marriage to Brenna Flanagan was likely to be a great deal of fun, something that had been sorely missing in his life these past two hundred and eighty-six years.

Brenna arrived at the bookstore shortly after it opened the following morning.

Myra greeted her warmly. "You're early today." She tilted her head to one side. "You look as if you've swallowed a piece of the sun. Tell me, what has put that glow in your eyes?"

"I came to ask you a favor."

"Well, as long as it isn't illegal, consider it done."

Brenna bit down on her lip. Roshan had said the marriage wouldn't be recognized by the state.

"You're not planning a bank heist or anything are you?" Myra asked.

"No, I am getting married."

"Well, no wonder you're grinning like the Cheshire cat. Congratulations! Who's the lucky man?"

"His name is Roshan. I do not know anyone in this city and I . . . well, I need someone to stand up with me, and I was wondering, if you are not busy, if you would . . . ?"

Myra took Brenna's hands in hers. "My dear, I'd love to."

"Oh, thank you."

"So, when's the happy occasion?"

"Tonight, at nine." She had found a note from Roshan on her bedside table this morning. In it, he had told her that he had spoken to Father Lanzoni and the priest had agreed to marry them that night.

"Tonight!" Myra exclaimed.

Brenna nodded. "I know it seems rather sudden but . . ." She felt herself blushing. "We did not want to wait any longer. I know I should have given you more notice, but"—she shrugged—"neither Roshan nor I have any family, and . . ."

"I quite understand," Myra said, patting Brenna's shoulder. "Young love and all, but my dear, that hardly gives me time to find a dress, let alone shoes! Sarafina," she called, "cover for me, won't you? I'm going shopping."

After giving Myra directions to the church and bidding her farewell, Brenna returned to the house. Too excited to sit still, she dusted the furniture, vacuumed the carpets, did a load of wash, put away the dishes in the dishwasher, and still she had hours to wait until sundown.

Finally, she sat down on the sofa and turned on the television, hoping to find a movie that would distract her. After flipping through the channels, she settled on a movie she had seen before. She knew the title now: *Ladyhawke.* There was something haunting about the story of a gallant knight and a woman who had been cursed by an evil clergyman.

Moments later, Morgana jumped up on the sofa, demanding her attention.

Brenna smiled at the cat as she scratched her ears. "Do you know that I am getting married tonight?" she murmured. "Think of it. I will be Mrs. Roshan DeLongpre."

The mere idea made Brenna's heart skip a beat. Of course, it would mean some changes in her lifestyle. She would have to adjust her sleeping habits to his so that they could spend as much time as possible together, and after awhile she might get tired of eating all her meals alone. Maybe he would sit with her in the evening from time to time. But these were trivial matters.

Soon, she thought happily, soon she would be his wife.

Roshan woke with the sun's setting. His first breath carried Brenna's scent to his nostrils. His first thought was that before he slept again, she would be his, though in his mind, she was already his in every way that mattered. Mortal laws no longer had any sway over him, but the marriage was important to Brenna, and that made it important to him, as well.

Rising, he left his lair, eager to see his bride. He found her in the kitchen. She was standing at the stove, stirring something in a pot. He wrinkled his nose against the smell of corn and roasting chicken.

On silent feet, he moved up behind her. "Good evening, my love," he murmured, nuzzling her nape.

She leaned back against him, turning her head for his kiss.

"You've not changed your mind?" he asked.

"Never."

He drew her into his arms so he could kiss her more fully, his senses filling with her nearness. Tonight she would be his, always and forever his. From this night forward, he would share his life with a woman he loved. It was a heady thought, the fulfillment of a wish he had never acknowledged, a hope he had never expected to obtain.

Reluctantly, he released her. "I'll be back soon," he promised.

She nodded. She did not have to ask where he was going. She knew him well enough now that she could tell when he had fed and when he had not.

He kissed her again, quickly, and then he was gone.

Anthony Loken stood over the remains of his latest victim. Like the last four, this one no longer resembled anything remotely human. Hands clenched at his sides, Loken stared at what had been a healthy young man only a short time ago.

Damn! Filled with a growing sense of defeat, Loken paced the lab from one end to the other. He had tried infusing the vampire's blood into the human system in every possible way he could think of. None of them had been successful. Always, the subjects had shriveled and died, sometimes in minutes, sometimes in hours. How did vampires survive when their blood seemed to be toxic? He had tried mixing the vampire's blood with the blood of his subjects, he had tried diluting it with a variety of liquids, but to no avail. He had experimented with the temperature, making the blood warmer and then colder. The results had been the same. The subjects had shriveled and died, most of them screaming in an agony he could only imagine. He had increased the white blood cells. He had decreased the white blood cells. He had mixed the blood with holy water, thinking it might counteract the deadly effects of the vampire's blood. He had tried adding a small amount of salt. No matter what he had tried, the results were always the same.

He slammed his fist into the wall, a wordless cry of frustration and rage rising in his throat. He would not be defeated. He struck the wall again and yet again and then came to an abrupt halt, oblivious to the blood flowing from his knuckles. Frowning, he stared at the empty vials on the counter. Perhaps there had been something amiss in the blood of the vampire. Or perhaps he had been using the wrong subjects . . .

Of course! He was no mere mortal. He was a warlock of almost unequaled power. His mistake had been in experimenting on puny humans when what he needed was a witch.

Licking the blood from his knuckles, he turned off the lights and left the laboratory. Myra would know where he could find a witch. She would, in fact, have been his first choice had her powers not been greater than his own.

Yes, he thought, his confidence restored. All he needed

was a witch and the secret of eternal life and good health would be his.

But before he went hunting a witch, he needed a vampire. And a supply of fresh blood.

CHAPTER 22

Because it was quick and easy, Roshan went looking for prey at the Nocturne. There were only a few people in the club this early in the evening. It made hunting dangerous, but then it was always dangerous to hunt when the prey wasn't alone, more so at this time of the night. Better to seek prey when the hour was late and mortals were more susceptible to preternatural forces. But tonight he had no choice. He must be at his best when he stood at the altar beside Brenna. He wanted no trace of his hellish thirst lurking in his eyes, no hint that he was thinking of anything other than his bride.

Unbidden came the memory of the day he had wed Atiyana. How young they had both been, innocent and eager and a little afraid. He had never known a woman. She had been a maiden, untouched and untutored. Together, they had learned the ways of love, discovered the pleasures of the marriage bed, waited with joyful hearts for the birth of their first child . . . His sweet

Atiyana, in heaven these many years. What would she think of him if she could see him as he was now?

A movement in the far corner caught his eye. Glancing sideways, Roshan saw Anthony Loken. He was dancing with a pretty girl wearing a pair of skintight black leather pants and a black midriff top. Her eyes were lined with kohl, she wore black lipstick. Her waist-length, silver blond hair stood out like a shining beacon in a sea of black tresses.

Loken threw back his head, laughing at something she said.

Moving toward the bar, Roshan asked the first single girl he came to if she would care to dance. Leading her onto the dance floor, he drew her into his arms. Careful to keep his back to Loken, he captured the girl's gaze with his. When she was pliant in his arms, he lowered his head, about to drink, when he overheard the voice of the blonde dancing with Loken.

"Why are you looking for a vampire?" she asked in a deliberately throaty voice.

"I'm fascinated by creatures of the night," Loken replied. "Their lifestyle, their longevity, their ability to heal themselves of all but the most fatal of injuries. I'm hoping to find a vampire who will bring me across."

"So, you're in search of the Dark Gift?"

He nodded. "Do you know someone who can bestow it on me?"

"I might."

"Might it be you?" Loken asked.

"No, but I've heard it rumored that a real vampire comes here now and then."

Roshan froze, the girl in his arms momentarily forgotten.

"Does he come here often?" There was no denying the excitement in Loken's voice. "Do you think he'll be here tonight?"

"I don't know. What's it worth to you if I can find out who it is?"

"Honey, if you can do that, you can name your own price."

Roshan swore under his breath. Had someone seen him feeding? Or was the blonde simply telling Loken what he wanted to hear? Damn!

Releasing the girl in his arms from his power, Roshan led her back to the bar, then left the club, his anger rising with his hunger. Damn Loken! The man turned up at the worst times.

He shook his head. He had always been careful when he hunted at the Nocturne. Nevertheless, he would have to find a new place to hunt.

With preternatural speed, he headed for the far side of town. He had little time to waste. Brenna was waiting for him.

It was almost eight o'clock when he returned home. He made a quick trip down to his lair for a change of clothes, then headed for the shower. He noted, in passing, that the bedroom door was closed. He could hear Brenna humming softly inside, felt his desire quicken as he imagined her slipping into the lacy underwear she had told him about.

Twenty minutes later he knocked softly on the bedroom door. "Brenna? Are you ready?"

The door opened and she stood there, a vision in white silk, her red hair like a cloud of silken fire beneath her veil.

She looked up at him, a half-smile playing over her lips as she waited for his reaction.

"Ah, my love," he murmured, "you're beautiful."

"Thank you."

Brenna's gaze moved over the man who would soon be her husband. He looked resplendent in a black tuxedo, so handsome it fairly took her breath away. Even if she hadn't known he was a vampire, she would have known he wasn't mortal. No mere man could exude such power, such inner strength. It was a potent combination.

Careful not to muss her hair or her veil, Roshan drew her into his arms and kissed her lightly on the cheek.

"Come," he said, smiling down at her. "We don't want to be late."

Moonlight rained down on the little church in the woods, giving it an otherworldly aura. Lights shone through the stained glass windows, shedding faint rainbow-colored streaks on the ground. Roshan paused at the entrance, his preternatural senses probing the surrounding shadows and the interior of the building before he opened the door and followed Brenna inside.

Father Giovanni Lanzoni was standing at one side of the altar. The priest was of medium height. He had wavy black hair laced with silver at the temple. His eyes were hazel.

A slender, dark-haired man stood beside the priest. Roshan knew immediately that the dark-haired man was a vampire.

A woman dressed in a deep purple gown and long white gloves sat in the first pew. She was not one of the undead, but supernatural power emanated from her. A witch, he thought, and wondered if his bride knew. The woman rose as Brenna drew near.

"My dear, how lovely you look!"

Brenna smiled. "Thank you. Myra, this is Roshan DeLongpre. Roshan, this is Myra Kavanaugh. She owns the bookstore I told you about."

Myra offered Roshan her hand. "It's a pleasure to meet you."

"And I you," Roshan replied. Releasing her hand, he turned to the priest. "Good evening, Father."

The priest smiled at him. "It has been a long time."

"Too long. Thank you for coming on such short notice."

"As if I would miss an occasion like this one," Father Lanzoni said with an easy grin. "Roshan, this is Vincenzio Fonti. He will be your best man."

Roshan shook Fonti's hand. Power flowed between them. Roshan knew, without knowing how he knew, that Fonti was one of the ancient ones.

"Thank you for coming," Roshan said.

"I am happy to do it," Fonti replied.

Father Lanzoni glanced from Roshan to Brenna. "Are we expecting anyone else?"

"No." Roshan took Brenna's hand in his and gave it a squeeze. "Ready?"

Brenna nodded. It suddenly seemed unreal that she was here, in this church, about to be married to a vampire by a vampire priest. She glanced at Myra, who was staring at Roshan, then at Vincenzio Fonti, who was watching Myra. Brenna clenched her free hand, wondering if Myra suspected something. Did she think it odd that the ceremony was taking place at such a late hour and that neither she or Roshan had any family present? Brenna knew little of what weddings were like in this time and place. In her own village, a marriage had been cause for celebration, with everyone from the oldest patriarch to the newest babe in attendance.

Father Lanzoni took his place in front of the altar and Roshan and Brenna turned to face him. Myra stood at Brenna's left, Fonti at Roshan's right.

"My children," Father Lanzoni began, "we are gathered here this night to join Brenna Flanagan and Roshan DeLongpre in the bonds of holy wedlock, an institution ordained by God for the blessing of His children. There is no secret to a happy marriage," he said, glancing from Brenna to Roshan. "You have only to put your loved one first and yourself second, to treat your spouse as you would be treated, to remember how much you love one another on this day and on every day that follows for as long as God grants you breath.

"I will say the words that bind you together, but the true marriage between the two of you must take place here, in your hearts.

"Brenna, do you promise to love and cherish Roshan, here present, for as long as you shall live?"

Brenna looked at Roshan, her eyes glowing with love. "I do."

"Roshan, do you promise to love and cherish Brenna, here present, for as long as you both shall live?"

He gazed deeply into her eyes. "I do."

"Then, by the power vested in me, I pronounce you husband and wife. You may kiss your bride."

With great tenderness, Roshan drew Brenna into his embrace. At that moment, he was acutely aware of how very fragile she was. As a mortal, she could easily fall prey to sickness; in a few short years, old age and death would come to steal her away.

"I will love you and no other for as long as you live,"

he murmured for her ears alone, and then he bent his head to claim his first kiss as her husband.

Heat flowed between them, not the heat of passion, but the gentle warmth of heart speaking to heart as they sealed their vows with a fervent kiss.

"Well done," Father Lanzoni said with a quiet smile. "Well done."

Roshan kissed Brenna one more time, then, taking hold of her hand as if he would never let go, he turned to face the priest.

"Thank you, Father."

"My pleasure, my son."

Fonti shook Roshan's hand. "Congratulations," he said solemnly. "I hope it works out for you."

"Thank you."

Fonti smiled at Brenna. "I wish you every happiness, Mrs. DeLongpre."

"Thank you for coming."

"A lovely ceremony, just lovely," Myra said, coming forward to give Brenna a hug.

"Thank you, and thanks again for being here."

"Oh, I wouldn't have missed it," Myra assured her. She sent a speculative look at Vincenzio Fonti, and then at Roshan. "No, indeed, I wouldn't have missed this for the world. I've arranged for a small reception at my store," she said, smiling at Brenna. "Nothing elaborate, just a small cake and some champagne. And no obligation, of course, if you've already made other plans."

"I am not sure what Roshan wants to do," Brenna replied, looking up at him.

"Whatever you want is fine with me." He looked at Father Lanzoni and Fonti.

"I am afraid I cannot stay," Father Lanzoni said.

"Nor I," Vincenzio said.

"I'm sorry to hear that," Myra said, and there was real regret in her tone. "But you'll come, won't you?" she said, glancing from Brenna to Roshan.

"Of course," Roshan said, "if that's what Brenna wishes."

"Maybe for just a little while," Brenna said.

"It's settled then," Myra said, beaming. "I'll just go open up the shop and see you there." She gave Brenna's hand a squeeze and hurried out of the church.

"There's something about that one," Fonti said. "She is not one of us, but she has powers. Could she be a witch?"

"A witch!" Brenna exclaimed. "Do you think so?"

Fonti nodded. "Her aura is similar to yours, though not so strong."

Brenna frowned. Was Myra a witch? If so, why hadn't she ever mentioned it? And then, realizing what Fonti had said, she looked at him askance. "You think my powers are stronger than hers?"

Fonti nodded again, then looked at Roshan, a hint of deviltry in his eyes. "Be careful of this one."

Roshan laughed softly. "I have felt her power on more than one occasion."

After saying their farewells, Roshan and Brenna left the church. Excitement thrummed through Brenna as she thought of what lay ahead. They would spend a short time with Myra and then they would go home. She could hardly wait to be in Roshan's arms again. It would not be like the last time, she thought, though that had been wonderful. But this time she would be his wife, with every right to be in his bed, in his arms.

"Wife," she murmured. "What a lovely word!"

Myra was waiting for them at the door when they arrived at the shop. "Come in," she said, stepping aside. "I hope you don't mind, but a few of the girls who work for me were closing up when I got back. They wanted to stay and wish you congratulations."

Brenna glanced at Roshan. "No, I do not mind."

Myra closed and locked the door and turned the sign so that it read "closed," then led them through the bookstore and into the coffee shop. Several women, none of whom Brenna recognized, were talking in low tones when they entered. A small wedding cake sat on a cloth-covered table, along with two bottles of champagne. The women all stopped talking when Brenna and Roshan followed Myra into the room.

"Well, here we are," said Myra. "Ladies, may I present Roshan and Brenna DeLongpre."

Brenna felt suddenly uneasy amid the greetings and good wishes. Something wasn't right. She looked up at Roshan, wondering if he sensed it, too.

There was a loud pop as Myra opened a bottle of champagne. She filled several crystal glasses and passed them around. The ones she handed to Brenna and Roshan had pretty pink bows tied around the delicate stems.

"A toast to the bride and groom," Myra said. "May all your dreams come true."

Brenna hesitated but then, seeing that the others were drinking, she sipped her champagne. The bubbles tickled her nose. She noticed that Roshan did not drink from his glass, but that was not surprising. What was surprising was that no one asked him why he wasn't drinking.

After the toast, Myra cut the cake and passed it around. Roshan refused with a smile, telling Myra that he was allergic to white flour.

Feeling suddenly unsteady, Brenna looked up at him.

She blinked, trying to bring his face into focus. The lights suddenly seemed brighter, the voices around her louder. She reached for Roshan, who seemed to be getting smaller and smaller and then, without warning, everything went black.

Roshan caught her before she hit the floor.

"Oh, my!" Myra exclaimed, one hand pressed to her heart. "I think she's fainted. Poor dear," Myra added sympathetically. "Probably too much excitement for one night."

Roshan stared at Brenna. Her face was pale, her skin overly hot. Her pulse was beating rapidly. He detected a strange, sickly sweet aroma on her breath. Had she been drugged?

Before he could question Myra, he sensed a ripple in the air, a stir of supernatural power. Too late, he realized someone had come up behind him. A hot burning sensation engulfed him as someone wrapped a thick silver chain around his neck and yanked it tight. Pain shot through him and he reeled backward.

Darting forward, Myra pulled Brenna out of his arms.

Freed of his burden, Roshan was about to wheel around and see who was behind him when another chain circled his middle, pinning his arms to his sides. With a low growl of rage, he swung around and came face-to-face with Anthony Loken.

The warlock bared his teeth in a feral smile as he tossed a small bucket of holy water in Roshan's face. The drops penetrated Roshan's clothing, sizzled over his skin, raising huge red blisters everywhere they touched. A few drops splashed into his eyes, blinding him.

"Got him!" Loken crowed, and with the help of one

of the girls, he wrapped several more lengths of thick silver chain around Roshan's body and legs.

Unable to see, no longer able to stand, Roshan dropped heavily to the floor with Brenna's name on his lips.

CHAPTER 23

Anthony Loken looked at Myra, his smile victorious. "Got him!"

"And her," Myra said, a faint note of regret in her voice. "I hope you don't have to kill her, Tony. I've grown rather fond of her."

"How did you know she was a witch?" he asked. "I've been with her several times and never guessed." He had never suspected DeLongpre of being a genuine vampire, either, but he saw no need to let Myra know. It galled him that her magick was stronger than his, though his expertise in the Dark Arts was growing rapidly. The fact that she was the leader of their coven was equally irksome. But once he had achieved his goal, all that would change. He would have powers far beyond hers.

"They both veil what they are very well," Myra remarked, glancing down at the vampire, "but then, I'm older and stronger in the craft than you are. Be careful with the vampire," she warned sharply. "Don't turn your back on him. I'm not sure what he's capable of."

"Don't worry."

"Do you really think you can create this magic elixir that will allow us to live forever?"

"I'm sure of it. Carry the girl out to my car, will you? Serafina, go and open the trunk."

Myra paused in the doorway, looking up and down the street before she carried Brenna out to Loken's car and deposited her on the front seat.

Serafina opened the trunk and Anthony dropped Roshan, none too gently, inside. He stared down at the vampire a moment, noting the ugly red blisters on his face and hands, the bright red welts that appeared wherever the silver touched his skin. So long as the vampire was bound with silver chains and periodically doused with holy water, he would remain as weak and helpless as a newborn babe. Sort of like Superman when he was exposed to kryptonite.

Smiling at the comparison, Anthony closed the trunk.

"Call me if you need me," Myra said.

Loken nodded.

"Are you taking them out to the lab?"

"Just him."

"Be sure to strengthen the wards and wrap the doorknobs in silver, just in case."

"I know what to do," he said somewhat testily.

She smiled disarmingly. "Of course you do. Where are you taking the girl?"

"To my place. It doesn't seem wise to keep them together."

"Perhaps you're right. You will let me know as soon as you learn anything?"

With a nod, Anthony opened the car door and slid behind the wheel. Jamming the key into the ignition, he put the car in gear and stomped on the gas. He glanced in the rearview mirror as he pulled away from the curb. If it wasn't for Myra, he might not have managed to capture both witch and vampire so easily, he thought resentfully, and because of that, she would pay dearly when the elixir was his.

Roshan regained consciousness slowly, aware that the sun had not yet risen. His body felt heavy. Every nerve and cell shrieked with pain. His eyes were swollen and it was an effort to open them.

He recognized the laboratory immediately, grimaced when he realized he was bound to the metal table that had once held Jimmy Dugan's corpse, and that he was naked from the waist up. A thick leather strap ran across his chest, securing him to the table. His hands and feet were secured to the table by heavy silver chains fastened to thick silver manacles on his wrists and ankles. The silver seared his skin. His arms and chest, wet with holy water, burned like the very fires of hell.

Turning his head to the right, he saw a cadaver lying on a table against the far wall. Glancing to his left, he saw Loken watching him, a cloying smile on his face.

"So," the wizard said, pushing away from the doorway. "Awake at last."

Roshan licked his lips. His throat, still bound by silver, felt as if it was burning from the inside out. "Where's Brenna?"

"She's no longer your worry." Loken picked up a syringe from the counter and jabbed it in the large vein in Roshan's left arm.

"What are you going to do with her?"

"I tried infusing vampire blood into several people

with no success, and when that failed, I tried having them drink it." Loken shrugged. "That didn't work, either. And then I realized that I was using the wrong test subjects. What I needed was—"

"A witch," Roshan said, his stomach churning with anxiety.

"Exactly."

"It won't work," Roshan said. He watched with morbid fascination as the warlock filled a glass vial with his blood, then jabbed another needle into the same vein.

"I think it will."

"What . . . what's the body for?" The silver weighed heavily on his throat, making it difficult to speak.

"Ah, yes, the body. Well, it occurred to me that diluting vampire blood with the blood from a corpse might make it less potent and thereby less toxic to mortals," Loken replied with a grin. "Mixing dead blood with dead blood, as it were."

"You can't steal a vampire's powers from his blood. There's only one way to get them," Roshan snarled, baring his fangs. "This way."

Loken jumped back in spite of himself. Angered by his show of weakness, he jabbed another needle in Roshan's vein. "If I'm right, I'll soon know it. If I'm wrong . . ." He shrugged. "Your bride will pay the ultimate price."

A low growl rose in Roshan's throat as he struggled against the chains that bound him to the table. The pain in his body, excruciating as it was, was nothing compared to his fear for Brenna's life. But the holy water combined with the silver did their work all too well. Panting heavily, he fell back on the table. "Damn you—do what you want with me, but let her go."

"How very noble of you," Loken said with a sneer. "I had no idea vampires were so chivalrous."

Roshan glared at him, his hands clenching in impotent rage as the warlock withdrew yet another vial of blood.

Moving to the counter, Loken pulled a tray filled with small glass bottles from the overhead cupboard and proceeded to fill them, mixing the blood he had taken from Roshan with the blood he had taken earlier from the dead man.

"I think that will be enough to start with," Loken remarked, and capping the vials on the tray, he left the room.

Roshan stared after him. Hunger burned deep inside him, made worse by the blood that the warlock had taken from him. His whole body felt as though it were on fire. The hunger burned through his veins; the holy water and the silver manacles seared his flesh.

He tugged against the chains that bound him, groaned softly as the silver bit deeper into his flesh.

"Damn you, Loken!" he roared. "Damn you to hell!"

Concentrate. He had to concentrate. He had to find Brenna and get her out of here before Loken performed whatever experiments he had in mind.

He cursed softly. Never, in all his existence, had he experienced such agony. If he managed to get out of this, Anthony Loken would be a dead man five minutes later!

Concentrate. Make a friend of the pain. Let it strengthen you. He closed his eyes, willing himself to relax as he endeavored to gather his power around him. But he was weak, so weak. He couldn't concentrate, couldn't think of anything but the agony that leeched his strength and clouded his mind.

Concentrate! He had to find a way to escape the chains that imprisoned him.

He had to find Brenna.

He had to feed before it was too late, before the hunger engulfed him, blinding him to everything else . . .

Brenna glanced at her surroundings. She was in a large room, lying on a four-poster bed, still wearing her wedding gown. The walls were a pale sickly green. Curtains of a similar color hung at the single window to the left of the bed. A small square night table held a Tiffany lamp, which offered the room's only light. There were no pictures on the walls. A triple dresser stood across from the bed. Her veil was draped over a corner of one of the mirrors.

Where was she? There was a terrible taste in her mouth. Nausea roiled in her stomach. Her nose itched. When she tried to scratch it, she realized her arms were stretched over her head and her hands were bound to the bedposts.

Fear slammed into her. Where was she? The last thing she remembered was being in Myra's shop, drinking a toast . . .

Brenna licked her lips. Had she been drugged? Where was Roshan?

Dread trapped her breath in her lungs as she heard footsteps approaching. She stared at the doorknob, suddenly afraid that she knew who was on the other side of the door.

The door swung open and Anthony Loken stepped into the room. "So," he said cheerfully, "how are you feeling?"

Brenna stared at the tray in Loken's hand, her gaze

riveted on the small vials filled with red liquid. It was Roshan's blood; she knew it without doubt.

She tugged against the ropes that bound her to the bedposts as Loken closed the door and walked toward her.

"So," he said cheerfully, "imagine my surprise at finding out you're a witch. Why didn't you tell me?" He made a small tsking sound. "And after I shared my secret with you."

She didn't answer, only continued to stare at him, her horror growing with each passing moment. He had said he didn't practice black magick. She knew now that he had lied to her.

"I'd like to say this won't hurt a bit," the warlock said, smiling wolfishly. "Unfortunately, I can't guarantee that."

"What are you going to do?" It was a foolish question. She knew only too well what he was going to do.

"Research, my dear. You remember? I told you all about it."

She nodded, unable to draw her gaze from the tray in his hands.

"I had so hoped to have discovered the secret by now but, alas, I've yet to come up with a successful way to infuse a vampire's blood into a human without killing the human in the process. But," he said, filling a syringe with blood from one of the vials, "I haven't given up hope."

"You cannot do this!" Brenna cried, horrified at what he was about to do. "Please, I beg of you!"

"I'm doing you a favor, my dear. You can't have any kind of life with one of the undead. But if my theory works, you'll be able to live with him forever. Not only that, but you won't get sick and if you get hurt, why, you'll heal overnight. And the best part is, you won't have to drink blood to survive. You'll have all the perks with none of the drawbacks." He frowned thoughtfully. "I'm not sure if you'll be able to tolerate the sun for any length of time, but that seems a small price to pay for immortality, does it not?"

"Are you insane?" Brenna tugged against the ropes that bound her, frantic to free herself before it was too late. "It will never work. You must know that! Please, do not do this!"

"Ah, skeptics have always tried to halt the advance of science. Where would we be today if Pasteur and Salk and Curie had listened to those who told them they were wasting their time?"

"I . . . I do not know what you are talking about," she said, eyeing the needle in his hand.

"Well, it doesn't matter, does it?" Loken replied absently. He laid the syringe on the table beside the bed, then grabbed her ankle to tie it to the bed frame.

Brenna bucked and kicked with all her might. Her heel struck Loken in the face, bloodying his nose.

Muttering an oath, he backhanded her across the mouth. For a moment, she saw stars. When her head cleared, it was too late. She was spread-eagled on the mattress, her ankles bound to the posts at the foot of the bed.

She watched in horror as the warlock picked up the syringe, screamed as he plunged the needle into her arm. Hot bitter bile rose in her throat. Stomach churning, she closed her eyes. What if it worked? What if it didn't? She didn't know which she dreaded most.

She moaned, her body convulsing, as Roshan's blood burned through her veins. She was going to die.

She would never see Roshan again, never feel his arms around her, never hear his voice . . .

She cried his name, sobbing with pain and fear and regret.

Hush, my love . . . don't be afraid.

At the sound of his voice, she opened her eyes, expecting to see him standing at her side.

Instead, she saw Anthony Loken standing beside the bed, watching her carefully through narrowed eyes.

"How do you feel?" he asked, leaning forward. "Does it hurt?"

She blinked at him. Fear coursed through her, but the pain was gone.

Brenna?

"Roshan?" She glanced around the room, searching for him, then realized that the voice she was hearing was inside her head.

"Forget him," Loken said sharply. "Tell me how you feel."

Brenna, answer him. How do you feel?

"I feel wonderful."

Loken looked as if he didn't believe her, as if he was afraid to believe her. "Are you in pain? Do you feel dizzy? Sick to your stomach?"

"No." In fact, she felt stronger than she ever had before. She pulled against the ropes that bound her, wondering if she could break them. "He will kill you for this," she said calmly.

The warlock laughed. "He's in no condition to do anything to anyone."

Roshan, where are you?

In Loken's lab outside of town.

Are you well?

No.

Fear rose within her once again. She glared at Loken, her hands clenching and unclenching. "Where is Roshan? What have you done to him?"

Loken shrugged. "He's well enough for now. It's you I'm interested in. How do you feel now?"

Brenna glared at him, felt her anger turn to rage as she imagined Roshan at Loken's mercy. Was he in pain? No sooner had the thought crossed her mind than she felt as if her skin, her very blood, was on fire. There was a terrible gnawing ache deep inside her, a ravening hunger that could never be quenched. With a gasp of horror, she knew she was feeling what he was feeling. She moaned softly. How did he bear such agony?

Loken's face paled as he stared at her. "Good Lord . . ."

"What is it?" she asked. "What's wrong?"

"Your eyes . . ." He took a step back, his expression one of growing horror. And then he smiled. "It worked!" he cried jubilantly. "By damn, I knew it would!"

Grabbing the tray containing the rest of the vials, he left the room, locking the door behind him.

Brenna stared after the warlock, a sudden sinking feeling in the pit of her stomach. What had he seen when he looked at her? Was she a vampire now?

No, my love, you need not worry. Are you all right?

Yes, he is gone.

Where are you?

In his house, I think. Brenna glanced at the window, trying to judge the time. What would happen when the sun rose? Would Roshan be safe as long as he was inside, or did he have to be underground in his lair?

It's hours until sunrise. Don't worry about me.

How can I help it? She tugged against the ropes that bound her, but they held fast and struggling only caused them to cut deeper into her wrists and ankles. Defeated, she fell back on the bed. She had to get out of here, had to get Roshan out of the lab and safely into his lair before sunrise, but how?

Roshan's voice sounded in her mind once again.

I'm working on it, he said. *If you know any prayers, this would be a good time to say them.*

Anthony Loken could barely contain his excitement as he stood at the bar of the Nocturne, sipping a glass of champagne. At last, he had found the secret! Still, he was determined to make one last test before he tried it on himself, and since he didn't have another witch at his disposal, he had come here. If it also worked on a woman who was not a witch, then he would be certain that it was safe, he thought, and then he frowned. Perhaps he should try it on a man, as well. Yes, that was the ticket. Better safe than sorry . . .

Damn! He knew he had forgotten something. Why hadn't he thought of it before? He had been so elated when Brenna had survived being injected with the vampire's blood he had neglected to see if her powers of healing had increased! If her body healed itself, then he could safely assume that eternal life would also be hers, and therefore, his. He had intended to dispose of the witch but it suddenly occurred to him that he would have to keep her alive a little longer to make sure the results of the injection didn't wear off after an hour or two, or a day or two. And he would also need to make sure there were no side effects.

He swore softly. Myra was always telling him he was too impetuous. Maybe she was right. Well, no matter, he would take care of all the trivial loose ends later. He would dispose of the witch when he had no further use for her. Witch or vampire, she would not survive the flames. But that was a task for another day. For now, he needed another guinea pig. Luckily, they weren't hard to find.

He beckoned at a pretty little dark-haired female. She smiled back, and then she was walking toward him.

Roshan stared at the ceiling. Ignoring the pain that burned through him, he concentrated on summoning his power, drawing it toward him, focusing it on the chain that bound his right wrist to the table. Teeth clenched, he jerked against the restraint with all the force at his disposal. The movement caused the manacle to cut deeper into his skin, but also pulled one of the links apart, breaking the chain so that his right hand was no longer bound to the table.

He lay there panting heavily for several minutes, and then he jerked against the other chain. Once his hands were no longer bound to the table, he removed the leather strap from his chest and sat up. Moments later, his ankles were also free.

Swinging his legs over the edge of the table, he stood up, one hand grasping the edge. Though he was no longer bound to the table, the silver manacles still circled his wrists and ankles. Lengths of chain dangled from each one, but there was no time to worry about that now. His first priority was Brenna.

CHAPTER 24

Weakened by the silver rubbing against his skin, Roshan made his way toward Anthony Loken's house. Though the holy water had dried long ago, his skin still burned, but it didn't matter. Nothing mattered now but getting Brenna away from the warlock before it was too late.

A vile oath exploded from Roshan's lips when he reached the front porch of Loken's house. Pain had dulled his thinking. He was here, with no way to get inside. Had he been at his full strength, he might have tried to cross the threshold in spite of the consequences, but he was too weak to battle the warlock's defenses, and growing weaker by the minute.

Turning, he retraced his steps down the street until he came to another house. He knocked on the front door, waited impatiently for someone to answer his summons.

It was a teenage girl with long blond hair. She wore a red halter top that exposed an indecent amount of skin, and a pair of white shorts that were equally revealing. A small black rose was tattooed on her left shoulder.

"Geez, man, what happened to you?" she asked, looking him up and down.

"I don't have time to explain," he said, trapping her gaze with his. "Come with me."

Without question, she followed him up the hill and onto Loken's front porch.

Roshan handed her a large rock he had picked up along the way. "Break the glass."

She didn't hesitate. Taking the rock from his hand, she tossed it through the narrow window beside the door.

"Now, reach inside and unlock the door."

Again, she did as she was told, her expression carefully blank, even when she cut her hand on a shard of glass. The scent of blood drifted through the air. Without thought, Roshan grabbed her hand and licked the blood from the wound.

"All right,"—he searched her mind for her name—"Jean, I need you to go upstairs and find Brenna. When you find her, you will bring her to me."

"Find Brenna," Jean said. Opening the door, she disappeared inside the house.

Closing his eyes, Roshan rested his forehead against the doorjamb. He was weary, so weary.

In the distance, he heard a woman's voice calling Jean's name.

A few minutes later, Jean appeared in the doorway, leading Brenna by the hand.

"Roshan!" Breaking free of the girl's hold, Brenna ran toward him. "What has that monster done to you?"

"I'll be all right. Come, we don't have time to waste."

Brenna glanced over her shoulder. "Who is this girl? What is she doing here?"

"There's no time to explain now. We've got to go. Jean, close the door, then come with me."

Descending the stairs, Roshan started down the hill, closely followed by Jean and Brenna.

When they were two doors away from Jean's house, Roshan drew the girl into his arms.

"Brenna, turn away."

"No."

"Do as I say." His voice was low, ragged with pain and a hunger that would no longer be denied. "Please, Brenna."

How could she refuse when he was looking at her like that, his voice filled with anguish and pleading, his eyes already turning red.

With a sigh of resignation, she did as he asked, listened as he spoke quietly to the girl, assuring her that he would not hurt her.

Brenna closed her eyes, trying not to imagine him bending over the girl's neck, his lips touching her skin . . .

A bolt of bright green jealousy shot through Brenna. It was their wedding night! If Roshan needed to feed, why hadn't he asked her? She shook her head, appalled at the turn of her thoughts. She was angry because he was holding another woman in his arms, resentful that he had chosen to feed from someone else.

She heard him speaking to the girl again, telling Jean that all was well, telling her to go home and remember nothing of what had happened.

Brenna turned around when she felt his hand on her shoulder. "Let's go."

"Why?" she asked, her gaze searching his. "Why did you feed off her and not me?"

Roshan stared at his bride, unable to believe that she was jealous. Laughing softly, he took her hand. "This isn't the time or the place to discuss it," he reminded her. "Loken could return any time."

She shivered at the mention of the warlock's name. "Let us hurry."

It took the last of his strength to will them home. Inside the front door, he dropped to his hands and knees, then rolled onto his side. He closed his eyes, panting heavily. But it didn't matter. Brenna was safe now. Nothing else mattered.

Brenna knelt beside him. There was a hideously ugly red mark around his neck. His chest and belly were covered with blisters. The skin on his wrists and ankles was raw and angry looking.

Choking back her tears, she stroked his brow. "What can I do? How can I help?"

He lifted one hand. "Get these off me."

With a nod, she ran upstairs to her room. Grabbing the wand she had finished only days ago, she hurried back to Roshan's side. Clutching the wand she focused on the manacle on his right hand.

"Rimuova!"

There was a soft click, and the manacle fell to the floor. She repeated the spell on his left hand and each ankle, then kicked the shackles aside.

She touched his chest with her fingertips, jerked her hand away when he winced at her touch. "Is there anything I can do?" she asked, wishing she had some aloe to apply to the burns.

With an effort, he opened his eyes. "I'll be all right in a few days. If Loken tries to come here, the wards should keep him out. If I don't rise tomorrow night, don't worry . . ."

Her eyes widened. "What do you mean?"

"The Dark Sleep heals me. I may not awake at sunset." He rolled onto his knees then sat back on his heels and cupped her face in his hands. "Not much of a honeymoon, Mrs. DeLongpre," he murmured. "I'm sorry."

"We will just have to wait a few days." She looked at him, her worry evident in her eyes. "Maybe you should go downstairs and rest."

He nodded. "Will you be all right?"

"I am not afraid."

"You're not a very good liar, either," he said with a faint smile. "I love you."

"I love you."

He kissed her, a quick brush of his lips across hers, and then he opened the door to his lair and disappeared into the darkness beyond.

Anthony Loken stared at the empty table in disbelief. The vampire couldn't have escaped the chains. It was impossible. Everyone knew silver rendered the undead weak and helpless. Yet the fact remained that the creature was nowhere in sight.

A shiver slid down Loken's spine. The vampire was far more powerful than he had imagined! And then, stroking the vial in his pocket, he smiled. There was nothing to fear. All it meant was that once he had injected the vampire's blood into his own veins, he would be even stronger than he had hoped. But first he had two more tests to perform.

Glancing over his shoulder, he gestured for the young man and woman to enter the lab.

The girl stared in horror at the body laid out on the table against the far wall. Had she been able, he was certain she would have run screaming from the room, but her mind and her will were no longer her own.

Lifting the body, Loken placed it on the floor in the corner and covered it with a sheet. He would have to dispose of it soon, he thought irritably. It was starting to stink.

When both of his subjects were in place on their respective tables, he removed two vials from the tray. He injected the man with the first vial, held the second to the woman's lips and commanded her to drink. She stared at him, helpless to resist, her eyes wide with fear and revulsion. Almost, he felt sorry for her.

Standing between the two tables, Loken watched them intently.

In moments, they were both shrieking and writhing in pain.

In a matter of minutes, they were both dead, their skin gray and shriveled, their eyes wide and frightened, even in death.

Rage exploded through Loken. A swipe of his hand swept the tray from the counter. The vials shattered on the cement floor. Blood sprayed across the room, painting the walls with streaks of crimson.

With a wordless cry, he drove his fist into the wall once, twice, three times. Pain exploded through his knuckles and up his arm, bringing him back to his senses. Pulling his handkerchief from his back pocket, he wrapped it around his bleeding knuckles. Perhaps he was overreacting. Maybe his first theory had been right after all. Perhaps the deaths of these two subjects just proved that the blood mixture he had used on Brenna was only effective on witches and therefore perfectly safe for him to use on himself.

Looking at the mess on the floor, he swore again. He had just destroyed all the blood samples he had.

Hands clenched at his side, he took a deep calming breath. He had captured the vampire once, he could do it again. He would draw the remaining blood from the first corpse and refrigerate it, then he would dispose of all three bodies. When that was done, he would do the remaining tests on the witch.

It was while he was sweeping up the broken glass that he found a single unbroken vial of the vampire's blood.

Smiling, he tucked the glass tube in his coat pocket. All was not lost.

Brenna sat on the sofa in front of the fire with Morgana curled up at her side. It was early morning, but Brenna couldn't sleep. She had taken a long hot bath, hoping it would relax her, and then gone to bed, but sleep wouldn't come. Every time she closed her eyes, she saw Anthony Loken standing over her, a maniacal gleam in his eyes as he jabbed a needle into a vein in her arm, a needle filled with Roshan's blood and the blood of a dead man. The thought sent a shiver of revulsion down her spine.

Where was Loken now? Had he returned home and found her gone? Would he come after her again?

Earlier, she had gone through Roshan's house, making sure all the doors and windows were closed and locked. She had drawn all the curtains, shutting out the night.

And now she sat here, clad in her gown and robe, staring into the flames, listening to the soft sound of the rain on the roof. Had it not been for Loken, she would have been outside, enjoying the storm, perhaps dancing under the clouds. She jumped as thunder rumbled overhead.

Morgana lifted her head, her yellow eyes glowing in the light of the fire.

Brenna sighed, wishing that Roshan were there beside her. She wouldn't be afraid if he were here, though she doubted he would be capable of protecting himself against Loken, let alone the two of them. Roshan had said there was nothing to worry about, that he would heal in a couple of days.

Did they have a couple of days? Would she ever feel safe anywhere again?

What if Anthony Loken was searching for the two of them, even now? If he was as powerful a warlock as he appeared to be, he would have no trouble finding them. All he needed was something that had belonged to one of them: an item of clothing, a strand of hair, a drop of blood. A simple spell would lead him straight to this place. Her only hope was that the wards Roshan had set around the house and the grounds were strong enough to repel whatever spell the warlock conjured.

She glanced at her arm, at the tiny pinprick left by the needle. What effect, if any, would the blood Loken had injected into her vein have on her? Would she live forever? Would any injuries she might sustain in the future heal with the same preternatural rapidity as did Roshan's?

Overcome with a sense of morbid curiosity, she went into the kitchen and pulled a sharp knife from the drawer. She stared at the blade a moment, then, biting down on her lower lip, she made a shallow gash in the palm of her left hand.

Blood welled from the cut and she wiped it away with a dish towel, stared in disbelief as the edges of the cut drew together until nothing remained but a thin red line, and then that, too, disappeared.

Merciful heavens, what did it mean? She made a second cut in her hand. Again, the wound healed within moments. Was it possible? Had Loken actually found the elixir he was looking for? Feeling suddenly nauseous, she wrapped her arms around her stomach. Merciful heavens, what if she was turning into a vampire?

Brenna glanced at the window. Dawn lurked beyond the curtains. If she went outside, would she burst into flame?

Fear was a hard, cold lump in her stomach, the taste of bile in the back of her throat. Morgana hissed softly and jumped off the sofa, her back arched, her tail at attention.

Heart pounding, Brenna stood and walked toward the back door. Her hand was shaking as she reached for the knob.

Roshan, hear me. Help me.

But only silence answered her plea.

Unable to restrain herself, she opened the back door and stepped out into the pale sunlight of a new day.

CHAPTER 25

Gathering his power around him like a warm cloak, Anthony Loken focused his attention on the oval, silver-backed looking glass sitting on the table in front of him. Murmuring a divination incantation, he gazed into the mirror which slowly grew cloudy and then cleared, revealing a large two-story house located behind a high block wall. Leaning forward, he read the address on the curb—1366 Black Meadow Lane.

"You can run, Brenna Flanagan DeLongpre," he murmured as he passed his hand across the mirror to clear it, "but you can't hide, my little witch, not now, not from me."

He had not been surprised to find her gone when he returned home. Angry, but not surprised. It didn't take a rocket scientist to figure out that the vampire had found her and freed her, though how Roshan had crossed the threshold remained a mystery. But it was daylight now and the vampire would be trapped in the Dark Sleep, helpless to interfere.

It took less than twenty minutes for Loken to reach the vampire's lair on Black Meadow Lane. Parking his car out of sight down the street, he walked up to the driveway. He held out one hand, felt the shimmer of power that surrounded the gates. So, the vampire had placed wards around his home, but that was to be expected.

Pulling his wand from inside his jacket, Loken tried several spells, his agitation growing as each of them failed.

He was a warlock. Save for Myra, he was the most powerful witch in the coven! How could a vampire, a creature who wasn't even human, thwart him?

Fuming inwardly, he conjured another spell, felt it grow within him. With a wave of his wand, he threw his will at the gates. Power sizzled through the air, but to no avail. The gates remained closed against him; the wards prevented him from reaching the other side.

Furious now, he paced along the length of the wall, searching for a way to get past the wards set by the vampire. When none could be found, he reached into his pocket and withdrew his cell phone. It was time to call for backup.

Brenna stepped out the back door, her whole body taut as the sun's light touched her face. There was no pain, though the brightness made her squint.

She stood there for several minutes, weak with relief. She was about to return to the house when a whisper of power danced over her skin. She recognized it immediately for what it was. She had, from time to time, experienced the same sensation when Granny O'Connell practiced her magick in Brenna's presence. It meant there was a witch nearby.

Loken!

Every instinct she possessed told her that the warlock was there, trying to get past the wards set on the front gate.

Whirling around, she ran back into the house. Snatching up her wand, she went into the bedroom, pulled back the curtains, and peered out the window. From her vantage point on the second floor, she could see the driveway and the front of the house, and even as she watched, she saw Anthony Loken approach the front gate. He wasn't alone this time. Myra and Serafina were with him.

She stared down at the three witches, her heart pounding as she watched Myra sweep an area of the sidewalk. Though Brenna couldn't hear what was being said, she knew the witch was cleansing the area, sweeping away any negative energy that lingered there so it wouldn't interfere with whatever spell they planned to conjure. When the area was clean, Myra walked in a circle three times. The first time, she carried a bottle of water, the second time a handful of salt, the third time she swung a smoking censer filled with incense. Next, she pulled a piece of white chalk out of her skirt pocket and drew a large circle on the sidewalk that encompassed the three of them. She touched her wand to the circle to close it, and then the three of them stood facing each other, their arms linked, forming another circle.

Brenna drew away from the window, a shiver of unease running down her spine.

What would she do if they breached the gates? The thought of being at Loken's mercy a second time filled her with dread. The man was insane, driven by his need to find a way to live forever, something mankind had been searching for since Adam and Eve brought death into the world. She wondered if Myra knew what Loken was trying to do. She wondered if he had injected Roshan's blood into himself. If so, then he knew it worked, at least in part, so why was he here? And if he hadn't, the question remained. Why was he here? Had he come to drag her back to his house for more tests?

Either way, she wanted nothing more to do with him.

Letting the curtain fall back into place, she ran downstairs to check the locks on all the doors and windows again.

Anthony Loken felt his power merge with that of the other two witches as they joined arms. Alone, he had lacked the strength needed to break the wards set by the vampire, but with Myra and Serafina adding their magick to his, there was little chance of failure. Myra's voice rose as their power coalesced. Magick rippled through the air, raising the hairs along the back of his neck, causing the air within the circle to crackle with otherworldly energy as Myra gathered their combined power and directed it at the gates.

There was a pop, like a cork being pulled from a bottle, and the gates swung open.

They'd done it!

Reaching into his pocket, Loken pulled out several strands of Brenna Flanagan's hair, as well as a vial of her blood that he had taken for his research. Bending, he placed both of the items on the sidewalk inside the circle Myra had drawn, and then once again linked his arms with the other two witches.

"Brenna Flanagan DeLongpre," he intoned with a wave of his wand, "come to me. As I command, so mote it be."

* * *

Brenna had just checked the lock on the side door and was about to go back upstairs when something drew her toward the front door. She was reaching for the handle when Morgana leaped into the air and scratched her cheek.

With a jerk of her head, Brenna reeled backward.

Morgana let out a long low warning hiss, her yellow eyes glowing, her tail twitching furiously.

Brenna stared at the cat, then at the door, surprised to find herself in the foyer.

Yet even as she tried to turn and go back to the staircase, she found herself opening the door, stepping out onto the porch, descending the steps.

Morgana trailed at her heels, meowing loudly.

Moving woodenly, Brenna walked down the driveway toward the gates, unable to resist. She knew, in the back of her mind, that she was under a spell, but try as she might, she couldn't shake it off.

She tried to call for Morgana, hoping her familiar could help her counter the spell, but words failed her.

And then she was at the gates, walking through them toward the three witches who waited for her on the sidewalk. She stared at Anthony Loken, wishing she could slap the smug smile from his face.

Moments later, she was in the backseat of his car. Glancing out the window, she saw Morgana pacing back and forth in front of the gates.

Brenna stared out the window, unable to move. All too soon, Loken pulled up in front of his house. At his command, she followed the warlock into his home.

A cold chill slithered down her spine as he shut the door behind her.

* * *

"So," Myra said, "show me the results."

Still smiling smugly, the warlock pulled a small knife from his pocket.

Brenna stared from one to the other. Loken had sent Serafina home, leaving Brenna at the mercy of the witch and the warlock who now stood on either side of her. Once again, she was bound hand and foot to the bed in Anthony Loken's house.

She glanced out the window. It was still hours until sunset, hours before Roshan would know she was missing. With a start, she remembered him telling her that he might not rise this night, that he might linger in the Dark Sleep to heal his wounds. There was a very real possibility that he would not rise until tomorrow night.

And by then, it might be too late.

She jerked as Loken made a shallow gash down the length of her left arm. She stared at the blood welling from the wound, felt a bubble of hysterical laughter rise in her throat as she watched the crimson drops fall onto the towel that Loken had spread beneath her arm so as not to stain his sheets. Too bad Roshan wasn't here, she thought morbidly. It was a shame to let all that blood go to waste.

Loken looked at Myra. "Watch now," he said, and taking a damp cloth he wiped the blood from Brenna's arm.

Both witches leaned forward, their eyes fixed on the shallow gash that, even now, was starting to close.

"Amazing!" Myra exclaimed as the wound knit together. "Simply amazing."

She looked at Loken. "You're sure the elixir is safe?"

"Yes, but only for witches," Loken said. "I've tried it on half a dozen mortals. They all died rather quickly."

"I never thought you'd actually do it," Myra said. "Forgive me for doubting you."

"Think of it," Loken said, his voice rising with excitement. "Immortality will be ours. We'll never grow old, never be sick! Imagine what other powers it might impart!"

"Perhaps," Myra said. "But how do you know the effects last? What if they wear off after a time?"

Loken shrugged. "I know the exact ratio of vampire blood to dead blood." He patted his pocket. "I have enough left for one injection."

"Just one?" Myra's eyes narrowed. "And who will be the one to make use of it?"

"Patience, woman," Loken said. "Just hear me out. The sun is high in the sky. The vampire is trapped in sleep. I'll go to his lair and drain him dry, and then I'll destroy him. We'll have enough blood to make a hundred vials, perhaps a thousand."

"Do you plan to share this with the coven?" Myra asked.

Loken's gaze slid away from Myra's. "That, of course, is up to you."

Brenna's gaze darted from Loken to Myra and back again. She had to warn Roshan, but how? Were the wards set on the entrance to his lair stronger than the ones on the gates? If not, he would be easy prey for Loken and Myra.

"Cut her again," Myra said. "Deeper this time."

Staring at the other woman, Brenna shook her head vigorously from side to side, unable to believe her ears. She had thought Myra was her friend. How could she have been so wrong?

Myra returned Brenna's gaze. "Have you something you wish to say to me?" She made a freeing gesture with her hand. "Speak then."

"How can you do this?" Brenna asked.

"I'm sorry, my dear, truly."

Brenna bit down on her lower lip to keep from crying out as Loken made a deep gash in her right arm from her elbow to her wrist. She wanted to be strong. She wanted to be brave. But the pain was too great. She sobbed with pain and fear, her stomach churning as a river of bright red blood ran from the wound. What if it didn't heal this time? What if it did? How much blood could she safely lose? Already, the towel beneath her arm was soaked through.

Again, Loken wiped the blood away. "There! See!" he cried exultantly. "The wound is already starting to heal! Even without the promise of immortality, the elixir is worth its weight in gold. If it heals wounds, it will doubtless provide immunity to diseases, increase one's life span."

"But not yours."

Loken froze, all the color draining from his face as he stared at the gun that had appeared in Myra's hand.

"What are you doing?" he asked hoarsely.

"You're too ambitious, Tony. There's no room in the coven for both of us any longer."

Loken held out one hand, his lips pulled back in a mockery of a smile. "Myra, what the hell are you talking about? We're in this together, remember. You and me."

"I've felt you breathing down my neck for months now. I know how badly you want to be the leader of our coven. I know how it galls you to take orders from a woman. I'm sure my future would be measured in days instead of years if this elixir of yours really works."

Loken shook his head. "No, Myra, you're wrong . . ."

She smiled. It was a look like death. "I'm never

wrong, Tony. You should know that by now. Give me the vial in your pocket."

He took a step backward. "Myra, it doesn't have to be like this."

"Yes, I'm afraid it does." She held out her hand, then eased back the hammer on the gun. "The vial, please."

Brenna glanced from Myra to Loken, her stomach knotting.

With a shake of his head, Loken took another step backward. "If you want it, come and get it."

Myra laughed. "What do you hope to gain by stalling? A few more minutes of life? You fool! I can take it off your body if I have to."

"All right, all right." Conceding defeat, Loken reached into his coat pocket.

"Slowly!" Myra admonished.

Eyes glittering with hatred, Loken's hand delved into his pocket.

And then, in a blur of motion almost too quick to follow, he raised both hands. One held the vial, the other held the knife he had used on Brenna. A single drop of blood glistened on the tip of the blade.

With a shout, he flung the knife at Myra.

Myra let out a shriek. She reeled back as the blade buried itself to the hilt in her chest. Her arm dropped, her finger convulsively squeezing the trigger.

Brenna screamed as white-hot pain exploded through her side.

Myra hit the wall. She stared at the knife protruding from her heart, her eyes wide with disbelief, and then, as her strength began to wane, she slid slowly to the floor, the pistol still dangling from her hand.

"The elixir . . ." she said, gasping for breath. "Give it . . . to . . ."

Her body went slack, her head lolling forward.

"You were right, Myra," Loken said. "The coven isn't big enough for both of us." He laughed as he held the vial up to the light. "I'm invincible now!" he crowed. "I'll be the most powerful warlock the world has ever seen!"

Blowing out a deep breath, Loken put the vial on the table beside the bed.

All he had to do now was coax the location of the vampire's resting place from the girl, and then he would dispose of her body and Myra's. He'd have to come up with a good story to tell the witches at the coven, he thought, staring at the vial, something to explain Myra's abrupt absence from the city, but he would worry about that later.

He glanced at Brenna. She seemed to be asleep. She was a pretty little thing. Too bad she had to die. With a grimace, he looked at Myra. There was nothing pretty about death, he mused. The sooner he got her out of his bedroom, the better. He couldn't just drag her through the house, not without getting blood on the carpets. He thought a moment, then left the room, bound for the garage. He had some large plastic sheeting there. He'd roll her into the plastic and put her in the basement while he searched his spell book for an invocation that would make a body disappear without a trace. Where Myra was concerned, he didn't want any evidence of her death, not even ashes.

Brenna opened her eyes a crack when she heard the door close. Loken was gone, but for how long? She glanced at the dead witch. Myra lay sprawled against the wall like a pile of dirty laundry. Brenna shivered. How long would Loken leave Myra's body lying there? The witch's evil lingered in the room, a dark miasma that was almost tangible. Brenna imagined Myra's spirit hovering over her in a vain effort to steal the last of her life's breath, her ghostly fingers clawing at her arms and legs as Myra tried to veil her spirit in flesh once more.

Brenna looked out the window, willing the sun to set, the night to come quickly. She felt herself growing weaker with each breath. And then she looked at her arm. Blood still oozed from the wound. It wasn't healing. She could feel more blood dripping from the gunshot wound in her side. Roshan had been right. The effects were only temporary.

Please. She sent a silent prayer toward heaven. *Please let me see him one more time . . .*

How could she die without hearing his voice, seeing his face? *Please, one last kiss to warm me through eternity.*

"Roshan, come to me . . ."

CHAPTER 26

As he had every evening for the past two hundred and eighty-six years, Roshan woke with the setting of the sun. But on this night, he didn't rise immediately. Instead, he lay still, taking inventory of his injuries. He felt only marginally better than he had the night before. He hoped Brenna would forgive him for rising just long enough to feed. Though he yearned to see her, be with her, he knew that on this night, he needed blood. And rest. In that order. He would make it up to her tomorrow night.

Closing his eyes, he let his preternatural senses search the house. She wasn't preparing her dinner in the kitchen, she wasn't curled up in a chair in the living room, reading, nor was she anywhere upstairs. He expanded his senses to search the grounds. She was not walking in the gardens, or sitting on the stone bench. Where was she?

A shiver of alarm slid down his spine. Surely, she hadn't been foolish enough to leave the house?

Brenna! Where are you? Dammit, woman, answer me!

Something was wrong. He reached out, his mind searching for her. There was a flicker of life at the gates. Morgana. But no sense of Brenna's presence. He jackknifed into a sitting position. The gates were open!

Cursing softly, he slid his legs over the edge of the bed, stood, swaying on his feet, wondering if he had the strength to make it up the stairs.

He was panting when he reached the top. Taking a deep breath, he opened the door and then, keeping one hand on the wall for support, he made his way down the corridor toward the entry hall, wondering if this was what it felt like to be old.

The front door stood open.

Descending the porch steps, he walked down the driveway to the gates. Morgana was there, pacing back and forth. She looked up at him, meowing loudly, then leaped into his arms.

Startled, Roshan stroked the cat's fur. "Don't worry," he said. "I'll find her."

He carried the cat up to the house and locked her inside, then went to the garage.

He would have preferred traveling through the night with his own preternatural speed, but he was too weak. He needed to save his strength for whatever lay ahead.

He backed out of the garage, down the driveway, and out onto the street. Once again, he sent his senses searching for Brenna. It frightened him that he could not detect her life force.

Certain that Loken was behind her disappearance, he drove toward the warlock's house. Parking the car a short distance away, he exited the vehicle. Several tall trees and shrubs grew alongside the parkway, shielding him from passersby. Drawing on what power he could muster, he summoned Jean to his side.

A moment later, she was walking toward him, clad in a red T-shirt and a pair of cutoff jeans. Taking her by the hand, he pulled her behind a nearby hedge.

Overcome with worry for Brenna, the hunger raging deep within him, he bent his head to the girl's throat, his fangs ravaging her flesh. He drank and drank, his eyes closing in near ecstasy as her life's blood flowed into him, filling him with warmth and heat, easing his pain.

It was only when her heartbeat slowed and her breathing grew labored that he lifted his head. The girl lay unmoving in his arms, her face pale.

Muttering an oath, Roshan bit his wrist and held it to the girl's lips. "Drink," he commanded.

She did as she was told. A few drops of his blood brought the color back to her cheeks. She stared up at him, her eyes widening.

"Who are you?" She struggled against him. "Let me go."

"Jean, there's nothing to fear." He spoke quietly, the sound of his voice soothing her. "We're old friends, Jean, remember? You did me a favor yesterday. I need your help again."

"Help you, yes."

"Good. Let's go."

Obediently, she followed him up the hill, ready to do whatever he required of her.

Brenna closed her eyes when she heard the door open again. Loken was still whistling softly. She heard him moving around the room. Curious, she opened her eyelids a crack and saw him roll Myra's body in plastic. Fear jolted through Brenna. Was that to be her end, as well? Rolled up in plastic and buried where no one would ever find her?

She closed her eyes as Loken stood and turned toward her.

"So," the warlock said, "how are you doing? You might as well answer me," he said impatiently. "I know you're awake."

She yelped as he grabbed her wounded arm.

Swearing prolifically, he untied her wrist and lifted her arm higher so he could examine it more closely. "It's still bleeding!" he shouted. "What happened? What's wrong? Why isn't it healing?" He walked to the other side of the bed, stared in disbelief at the blood trickling down her side.

"I told you . . ." She gasped for breath. "Told you . . . it . . . would not . . . work."

A sound from downstairs drew Loken's attention. Moving to the window, he stared down at the street.

Roshan stood to one side of the door as Jean tossed a rock through the window Loken had repaired. Magick certainly came in handy for home repairs, Roshan mused as Jean reached through the jagged hole, unlocked the door, and then opened it.

Roshan frowned as the door swung open. Taking a step forward, he peered down the hallway. He sensed supernatural power within the house, but there was nothing guarding the threshold, nothing to repel him.

Curious now, he moved closer to the threshold. Taking a deep breath, he stepped into the warlock's house.

Nothing happened. The wizard's threshold no longer had any power over him.

Turning toward the porch, he spoke to the girl.

"Jean, I don't need you anymore. I want you to go home. When you get there, all you'll remember of this night is that you took a walk, nothing more. Just that you took a walk. I want you to get something to drink, and then go to bed."

"Yes, bed."

"Go now." He watched her until she was out of sight, then turned and walked down the hallway. As he did so, his nostrils filled with the scent of death. That explained why he had been able to enter the warlock's house, Roshan mused as he started up the stairs. The house was no longer a home. Murder had been done here, thereby destroying whatever protection the threshold had provided against supernatural powers.

He shook his head ruefully. Had he not been so weak the last time he was here, he would have realized the warlock's wards had vanished. But there was no point in dwelling on that now.

Brenna was here.

He followed the scent of her blood up the stairs, down a narrow hallway, and into a darkened room. She was lying on the bed.

Anthony Loken stood beside her, the gun in his hand aimed at Brenna's head.

"And so," Loken said, "we come to the last act."

Ignoring the warlock, Roshan's gaze moved over his wife. Blood trickled from a wound in her arm, oozed from her side. Her face was as white as the pillow beneath her head, her eyes were dull, her heartbeat slow and erratic.

Rage uncoiled within Roshan like a snake ready to

strike. "You have one chance," he said, his eyes fixed on the warlock's face. "Just one. Put the gun down and I might let you live."

"You have no chances," Loken retorted. "Leave my house or she dies right now."

"The fact that she's still alive is the only reason you're still breathing," Roshan said. "Put the gun down."

Loken shook his head. He opened his mouth to speak, but the words were never uttered. Between one heartbeat and the next, Roshan was standing between Brenna and the warlock. In the next instant, Roshan's hand was locked around Loken's neck.

Eyes bulging, the warlock made a mad grab for the vial on the nightstand.

Roshan beat him to it. He held the tube up to the light. "Is this my blood?"

Unable to speak, Loken glowered at him.

Uncapping the vial, Roshan took a sniff. "Is this the magick elixir that was going to give you immortality?" he asked, his voice deadly quiet. "Well, let's see if it works."

Eyes wild, Loken glanced at Brenna, then shook his head.

A slow smile spread over Roshan's face as he captured the warlock's gaze.

"Drink," he commanded, and poured the contents of the vial down Loken's throat. Tossing the man aside, Roshan turned toward Brenna.

Removing the ropes from her hands and feet, he sat on the edge of the bed and gathered her into his arms. "Brenna? Brenna, can you hear me?"

Her eyelids fluttered open and she stared up at him. "You came." She lifted one hand to stroke his cheek. "One kiss," she whispered. "One kiss before I go to sleep."

"You will not die, Brenna Flanagan," he said fiercely. "I will not permit it."

"You cannot stop it."

He held her tighter, his mind in turmoil, all thought of Loken forgotten until the man screamed. The sound reverberated through the room, a wordless cry of madness and gut-wrenching fear.

Gaining his feet, the warlock staggered drunkenly around the room, his face a mask of agony. Arms clasped around his stomach, he dropped to his knees and rocked back and forth. He stared up at Roshan. "Help me!"

Roshan watched him, unmoved, as he remembered what the warlock had done to Jimmy Dugan and others. They had suffered horrible deaths in the warlock's search for immortality.

"No! No!" Loken's voice rose in terror. "This can't be happening, not to me. Not to me!"

Roshan watched impassively. The warlock's skin seemed to be shrinking, making him look like a living skeleton. His body writhed and convulsed on the floor like a spider on a hot rock. His eyes bulged from their sockets. His skin wrinkled, turning an ugly shade of gray, as his body continued to shrivel up, and all the while a wordless, high-pitched whine rose in his throat until, with a last horrified cry, he toppled over onto his side and lay still.

Rising with Brenna nestled against his chest, Roshan left the house.

Brenna was close to death when they reached home. Her lips were turning blue; her skin was cold to the touch. He lit a fire in the hearth. Sitting on the sofa, he cradled her in his arms, one hand gently stroking her cheek. She was cold, so cold.

"Brenna, tell me what to do," he begged, but she was past hearing.

He stared down at her. They had often discussed what it was like to be a vampire. She had asked how he felt about being one, but they had never really talked about how she felt about becoming what he was. It was one of the things he had intended to talk to her about later, after they had spent more time together, after she'd had time to understand more fully what being a vampire entailed. He had foolishly assumed they had years to discuss the subject. She was so young, there was no hurry for her to accept the Dark Gift. Better she should continue to live a normal life for another ten or fifteen years before she gave up the sun.

But she no longer had twenty years. He doubted she had twenty minutes. He could feel her life force slipping away, and he knew, in that moment, that he could not let her go. Fate had brought them together. He could not lose her now.

"Brenna, forgive me," he whispered, and lowered his head to her neck.

Brenna woke slowly. Eyes still closed, she thought about the dream she'd had. A strange dream, filled with violence and death. She had been frightened, more frightened than she had ever been in her life, as she watched her life's blood drain away. And then she had heard Roshan's voice calling to her, drawing her up out of the darkness.

With a sigh, she turned over on her side. And realized, abruptly, that she wasn't alone in bed, and that she was wearing her nightgown. In that same instant, she realized the bed beneath her felt strange.

Her eyelids flew open and she found herself staring into Roshan's face.

"Oh!" she exclaimed. "You startled me." She frowned as she noticed several things all at once. She wasn't in her bedroom. There were no lights on, and yet, even in the dark, she could see his face clearly, the fine lines at his eyes, the apprehension in his expression. She glanced around. "What am I doing here?"

"Brenna . . ."

She ran her hand over her wounded arm. There was no bandage, no scab, no scar. She touched her side. There was no pain.

"It works," she murmured. She looked up at Roshan. "Loken's elixir, it does work," she said, and then she frowned. She had seen the warlock die a horrible death, but that had been nothing but a bad dream. Hadn't it?

"No, Brenna," Roshan said quietly. "It doesn't work."

"But my arm, my side . . . the wounds are gone."

"Yes."

She was confused by the pain in his voice. Sitting up, she took a deep breath, her senses filling with a myriad of sounds and smells—a car backfiring on the street outside, the hum of the refrigerator upstairs, the scent of Roshan's skin, the faintly musty smell of the bricks.

She squinted as light suddenly filled the room, gasped as a sudden sharp pain knifed through her stomach. She moaned as the pain grew worse.

"What is wrong with me?" she asked. "Does it have something to do with the blood he made me drink?" The thought of dying the same way as Anthony Loken filled her with mind-numbing fear. "Am I going to die the way he did?"

Sitting up, Roshan drew her into his arms. "No, my love."

"Why not? He drank your blood and it killed him, and he . . . he made me drink your blood." She looked at him in wonder. "Why did it not make me sick?"

"Because you'd already tasted my blood," Roshan said, stroking her hair. "Only you got it directly from me. That's the only way it works. That's why your body was able to accept the blood he forced on you."

"Then what's wrong with me?" She looked at him, her heart pounding with fear. "Am I dying?"

"You're not dying, my love." He took a deep breath, his arm tightening around her. "You're just hungry."

"Hungry!" She moaned again. "What kind of hunger hurts like this?" she demanded.

She stared at him, waiting for an answer.

His silence told her everything she needed to know.

CHAPTER 27

Brenna stared at him, not wanting to believe what she knew to be true. Pushing him away, she held up her hands, turning them this way and that, seeing them as if for the first time. Sliding out of bed, she walked a few steps away and turned her back to Roshan. Standing there, she ran her hands over her face and her body. She felt the same and yet different.

And all the while a fierce hunger burned deep inside her. With one arm wrapped around her stomach, she turned to face him.

"What have you done to me?" she demanded. "Tell me you did not make me what you are."

"I couldn't let you die. I couldn't let you go, not when I had the power to save you—"

"Save me! You have condemned me to a lonely hell on earth!"

"What the devil are you talking about?"

"You said it yourself. Vampires are territorial predators, not social creatures. You have condemned me to a life alone!"

"It doesn't have to be that way, not for us. You're not my enemy. I'm willing to share my house, my territory, and my life with you." He ran his hand through his hair, then lowered his arm to his side, his hand curling into a tight fist. "Call me a selfish bastard if you will, but I've been alone too long, love you too much, to lose you now."

"No! I cannot be what you are! I will not be what you are!" She stormed across the room, rage churning inside her. "Let me out of here!"

Rising, he unlocked the door and followed her as she ran up the stairs. He unlocked the second door, followed her down the hallway into the living room, stood in the archway while she stomped through the room, her anger growing with every breath. Grabbing a lamp, she hurled it against the wall. A second lamp followed. She smashed everything breakable in the room, including a chair and a small table. She overturned the sofa and then, chest heaving with exertion, she thundered into the kitchen.

She opened the cupboards and began tossing out the contents—bowls and cups and saucers, plates and glassware. She opened a drawer and tossed it and the silverware it contained through the window, hurled pots and pans against the wall.

And still her rage grew stronger.

She opened the refrigerator, her nostrils filling with the scent of butter and eggs and milk, apples and oranges, mustard and ketchup. And chocolate pie. Placing the container on the counter, she picked up a plate that lay miraculously unbroken in the pile of crockery, grabbed a knife, and cut herself a huge slice of pie.

"Brenna, don't . . ."

She whirled around, daring him to stop her as she took one bite, and then another.

She looked at him defiantly, and then, with a cry, she dropped the plate and ran to the sink as her stomach rebelled.

She stood over the sink, her eyes closed, her hands gripping the edge of the counter. "How could you do this to me?"

He drew her into his arms, held her tenderly as he wet a dish towel and wiped her face, then handed her a glass of water so she could rinse her mouth.

"It's not a bad way to live, Brenna."

"It is not living at all," she retorted, but there was no heat in her words now, only resignation and defeat. "I want you to free me," she said, "the way you did Lilly Anna."

"No! Dammit, don't ask that of me!"

"Yes. Please, Roshan, if you care for me at all, then you must do this for me. I haven't the courage to walk out into the sun. I cannot face the flames again."

He crushed her to him, holding her so tightly she could scarcely move. "Listen to me, my love. I know you're frightened. I know you're in pain. But give it time before you ask me to set you free. A few weeks, at least. Trust me, my love."

Burying her face in his chest, she groaned. "I cannot. It hurts too much."

"Then it's time to hunt."

It was her worst nightmare come true. Holding her hand in his, he took her out into the night. A short time later, she watched Roshan call a young man to him, watched as he held the young man in thrall. He drank briefly, then turned toward her.

"Drink, Brenna."

She shook her head. "I cannot."

"You are no longer human. Do not think like one. Listen to the beat of his heart. Let it call to you, and take what you need."

She thought to feel revulsion, horror, but the hunger within her was too strong to resist. The young man offered no resistance as she took him in her arms. His flesh was remarkably fragile; the blood welling from Roshan's bite was remarkably sweet to the taste, infusing her with heat and warmth.

She looked up, her gaze meeting Roshan's, and in her husband's eyes she saw love and approval and understanding.

And then she bent her head and drank again, until an image of what she was doing rose in her mind. With a wordless cry, she pushed the young man into Roshan's arms and fled down the street.

Roshan watched her go. His first instinct was to go after her, catch her, take her home.

But he didn't move, only stood there and let her go. In bringing her across, he had made the only choice he could. Even knowing she might hate him, even knowing she might never forgive him, it had been the only decision he could make. He stared down the deserted street. He knew only too well what she was thinking, knew the confusion she was feeling as her vampire powers expanded and everything she was seeing and hearing was filtered through her preternatural senses.

He knew how frightening it could be, the sense of disorientation when your body no longer felt like the one you were used to, when every sensation was magnified a thousand times. If she needed time alone, he would give it to her. But if she wasn't back long before dawn, he was going after her. They were linked by an exchange of blood now. There was no way she could hide from him. For as long as she lived, he would be able to find her. Whether she agreed or not, she would be back in his lair before dawn. He only hoped that, in saving her life, he hadn't lost her love forever.

Brenna ran aimlessly though the night, frightened and fascinated by what she saw and heard. Though the skies were dark, she saw everything clearly, as if the sun was high in the sky. There were no shades of gray, no shadows her eyes couldn't penetrate. Even at night, colors were bright and clear. Noise assailed her from every side—a baby's cry from four streets over, a car's engine backfiring, the creak of a house settling, water trickling from a drainpipe, and over all of it the beating of thousands of hearts. Smells she did not recognize filled her nostrils.

She ran tirelessly, amazed at her stamina. No wonder Anthony Loken had wanted the power of a vampire for himself! She felt as though she could run forever and never stop, never grow weary. Her body felt strong, yet lighter than air. Was that because she had shed her mortality, or because she had shed her soul?

The thought gave her pause and she slowed to a walk. Had she lost her soul? She considered that as she made her way across a bridge into a park. Why should she have lost her soul? She had done nothing wrong. She hadn't asked to be made a vampire, that decision had been made for her. She hadn't killed anyone. True, she had stolen a little blood, but surely she could be forgiven for that, if forgiveness was necessary . . .

She stopped beneath a weeping willow tree, lightly

rolling one of the leaves between her thumb and forefinger, amazed at the nuances in the texture of the leaf. How beautiful the tree was! She could hear the whisper of each leaf, hear the sap running through the branches, the creak of the wood as the tree swayed in the breeze. Everything was different when absorbed through her enhanced senses. No wonder Roshan didn't want to give it up. Except for the blood part, being a vampire seemed a wonderful thing.

She picked up her pace until she was running again. Never in all her life had she felt so wonderful, so free! Laughter bubbled up inside her. Why had she made such a fuss earlier? Would she truly rather be dead now? How awful it would be if she could never again catch the scent of rain in the air, or dance in the silvery light of a full moon. And what of Roshan? Would she be happy, even in heaven, if he were not there to share it with her?

She slowed as she reached the end of the park, her earlier enthusiasm waning. She would never have a child now. It was the only true regret she had. Of course, she thought, rationalizing, if he had let her die, she wouldn't have been able to have a child, either.

Roshan. She had spared a thought for little else since the first time she had seen him outside her cottage, and he was all she could think of now. His scent was in her clothes, in her hair. His voice was a welcome echo in her mind. His kisses a memory she would never forget. Roshan. He had told her, in word and deed, that he loved her. And she knew, without doubt, that she loved him. Perhaps she had loved him from the moment his eyes met hers.

Suddenly, she wanted nothing more than to be in his arms, to feel his lips on hers, to hear his voice whispering that he loved her.

Laughing out loud, she turned and ran toward Roshan. Toward home.

He knew the moment she passed through the gates, felt it in the deepest part of his being. He wasn't sure why she had come back, but at least she was here, where she belonged, of her own free will.

Walking through the living room into the kitchen, he shook his head as he glanced at the damage her fury had wrought. Wading through the debris scattered from one end of the kitchen floor to the other, he opened the back door and went outside to wait for her. Morgana sat beside him, a low rumble reverberating in her throat.

He clenched his hands as he watched her walk across the grass toward him. She stopped when she reached the door, and he took a step back so she could enter the house.

Taking a deep breath, he followed her inside, ready to face her wrath or her hatred. Ready to go down on his knees and beg for her forgiveness if necessary.

"Are you all right?" he asked quietly.

She shook her head, her hair swirling like a fiery cloud around her shoulders. "No, I am not all right."

"Brenna, I'm sorry. Please, just listen to me. It doesn't have to be as bad as you think. I'll help you for as long as necessary, teach you everything you need to know."

She arched one brow. "Will you?"

"I'll do anything you ask, spend the next thousand years making it up to you."

"Will you?" she asked again.

He nodded, wondering what penance she would require. "Only tell me what you want."

"What I want!" She frowned at him, her hands fisted

on her hips, her chin raised defiantly. "I will tell you what I want, Roshan DeLongpre. I want the wedding night we never had."

He stared at her, then shook his head, wondering if he'd heard right.

She poked her finger at his chest. "You heard me," she said, a slow smile curving her lips. "We never had a wedding night. Do you not think it is long overdue?"

"Indeed, wife, I do."

"Well, husband, what do you intend to do about it?"

"I intend to make love to you until the sun comes up," he said, swinging her up into his arms, "and when the moon rises, I intend to start all over again. And then," he said, raining kisses over her face and the hollow of her throat, "I expect you to clean up the mess you made."

Laughing softly, Brenna wrapped her arms around her husband's neck, nestling against him as he carried her up the stairs to their bedroom.

Morgana padded after them, complaining all the way.

CHAPTER 28

Roshan glanced at his wife out of the corner of his eye, amazed as always by her beauty, a beauty that had only been enhanced by the Dark Trick. To his relief and delight, she had taken to vampire life as if she had been born to it. With him there to guide her and reassure her, to explain what she was feeling and why, she had been able to control her hunger. At first, she had fed several times a night, but that was no longer necessary.

Brenna lifted her face to the sky. "'Tis a gorgeous night."

"It is that," Roshan agreed, squeezing her hand.

They were strolling along the outskirts of town, on their way home from their nightly hunt. He was a lucky man, he thought. The last five months had been just about perfect. Best of all, after the first night, Brenna had accepted her new life wholeheartedly and never looked back, never expressed any regret or castigated him for his decision.

She had brightened his life, and his home. She had

repainted all the unused bedrooms in the house, choosing light, airy colors, and when that was done, she had bought new carpets and drapes and then picked out a unique style of furniture for each room. He had put up with the mess and the clutter and foolishly assumed she was done when she turned her attention to their lair, declaring it was cold and dreary looking. Since it was true, there was no way to argue with her. She had painted three of the walls and the ceiling a restful shade of sky blue; on the fourth wall she had drawn a mural that depicted a large window looking out on a sunlit garden. She had hung lacy white curtains around the window and covered the floor with dark green carpeting "because it looks like grass."

They were approaching a dead-end street when Brenna put her hand on Roshan's arm. "What is that?" she asked, cocking her head to one side. "Do you hear it? It sounds like an animal in pain."

Roshan grunted softly. "It's not an animal."

"What is it, then?"

He didn't answer. Instead, he turned down a dark alley that ran behind a three-story warehouse. The noise grew louder as they approached a Dumpster.

He'd been right. It wasn't a cat. It was a teenage girl in the throes of childbirth. Deep in a contraction, the girl was unaware of their presence.

"We must help her," Brenna whispered.

Roshan looked at his wife, one brow raised. "What do you suggest we do?"

"Whatever we can."

The girl let out a deep breath, her eyes widening when she realized she was no longer alone. She recoiled when Brenna took a step toward her.

"Do not be afraid," Brenna said quietly. "I am not going to hurt you."

The girl inched backward. "Go away," she said, then cried out as another contraction took her unawares.

"We just want to help," Brenna said. "What is your name?"

"That's none of your business," the girl said curtly. "Get the hell away from me." She cried out, her hands clutching her stomach, as a second contraction came hard on the heels of the first.

Brenna looked up at Roshan. "I think the baby is coming now."

Muttering an oath, Roshan removed his cloak and spread it under the girl. She was too far gone in pain to object.

The contractions came harder, faster. Brenna knelt beside the girl, gently stroking her brow, urging her to push, while Roshan kept watch.

Brenna looked up at Roshan. "I see the head!"

Moments later, a harsh cry erupted from the girl's throat.

Brenna murmured, "Oh, my," as the baby slipped into her waiting hands amid a rush of water and blood.

Roshan turned, his eyes narrowing at the covetous look in Brenna's eyes.

"We need something to cut the cord," she said.

"Here." Reaching into her pocket, the girl withdrew a wicked-looking knife.

Using the girl's shoelaces, Roshan tied them tightly around the cord in two places; then, taking the knife from the girl's hand, he cut the cord between the laces.

Brenna removed her cloak and wrapped it around the baby. "You have a beautiful little girl."

"Take her," the mother said. "I don't want her. I don't want to see her."

Brenna looked up at Roshan, her arms tightening around the infant.

He shook his head. "Don't even think about it."

"But she does not want it."

"Brenna, what would we do with a baby?"

"Love her."

"No. It won't work. There's no way . . ."

The mother glanced at Brenna. "If you don't take her, I'm just going to dump her in a trash can somewhere. I can't take her home with me."

"Surely the baby's father—"

"I don't know who he is." The teenager was pulling on her discarded jeans as she spoke. Taking a deep breath, she stood up, one hand braced against the wall behind her.

"What are you doing?" Brenna asked.

"I'm leaving." A sob rose in the girl's throat. "Do whatever you want with the baby."

"But—"

"Don't try to stop me," the girl said. "You look like a nice lady. You keep her."

Rising, Brenna cradled the infant against her breast. "She will be well cared for, I promise. Do you have somewhere to go?"

With a nod, the girl turned and staggered toward the sidewalk.

Brenna watched until the girl was out of sight, then smiled at the baby in her arms. "Hello, precious."

"Brenna, you know we can't keep it."

"Yes, we can."

He swore softly. "Do you want to tell me how? What are you going to do when she wakes up wet and hungry in the morning?"

"We will find a nanny," Brenna said calmly.

"And what are you going to do until then? What are you going to do when she wakes up hungry and wet tomorrow?"

Brenna frowned. "I do not know."

"Are you determined to keep her?"

"Yes."

He swore again, but how could he deny her the one thing that she had always wanted, the one thing he could not give her? "All right, come on."

"Where are we going?"

"To find someone to take care of her tomorrow."

"But how? Who?"

"Leave that to me. Take her home and clean her up. I'll be back soon." And so saying, he vanished from her sight.

With a shake of her head, Brenna went home.

Carrying the baby upstairs, she filled the bathroom sink with warm water and washed the infant from head to toe. When that was done, she wrapped her in a fluffy towel. The baby gazed up at her through dark blue eyes and then, with a yawn, her eyelids fluttered down and she was asleep.

Going downstairs, Brenna sat on the sofa, the baby cradled in her arms, wondering where Roshan had gone.

A baby! Roshan ran a hand through his hair. She wanted to keep the baby! What the hell was she thinking? Who ever heard of a vampire raising a human child? It was unheard of, unthinkable, impossible.

Shaking his head, Roshan went to the emergency entrance of the hospital and made his way up to the maternity ward. What on earth were they going to do with a baby?

He stopped the first nurse he saw. She frowned at him. "Sir, I'm sorry, but visiting hours were over long ago."

"Yes, I know." His gaze captured hers. "But I need your help, Sandra."

"My help? Yes, of course."

Quickly, he explained what he needed.

Twenty minutes later, she followed him out of the hospital.

Arriving at the house, Roshan found Brenna sitting on the sofa, the baby asleep in her arms. Morgana sat on the mantel, her ears laid back, obviously annoyed by the infant's arrival. Roshan had never realized cats could frown, but Morgana was definitely miffed at the thought of sharing Brenna's time and affection with another. Roshan had to admit that he wasn't too crazy about the idea, either.

"Who is this?" Brenna asked, her gaze darting to the nurse and back to Roshan.

"This is Sandra. She's a nurse in the maternity ward at the hospital. She's going to look after the baby until we can find a nanny."

"But . . . you cannot just bring a stranger here. Surely they will miss her at the hospital."

"I'll worry about that later." He took a large plastic bag from Sandra's hand and handed it to Brenna. "This has everything the baby will need for the next few days."

"But—"

"Stop worrying. As soon as we get a nanny, I'll send the nurse home. She won't remember anything."

"It does not seem right," Brenna said, "to keep her here against her will."

"If you've got a better idea, I'm ready to hear it."

Brenna shook her head.

"All right then." He turned to Sandra. "Your room is

upstairs at the end of the hall. I want you to go to bed now. During the day, you'll sleep when the baby is asleep and wake when the baby wakes."

"Yes," Sandra said.

"And you'll retire when the sun goes down. Do you understand?"

"I understand."

"That will be all. The room at the top of the stairs is yours. Good night."

"Good night," she replied, and left the room.

Humming softly, Brenna laid the sleeping infant on the sofa and sat beside her. Opening the sack, she pulled out a diaper, a little white cotton shirt, a cap, a pair of tiny socks, a blanket. In passing, she noted there were several bottles of formula in the sack, as well as baby wipes and more diapers, bottles of baby powder, lotion, and shampoo.

Roshan stood near the sofa, his arms crossed over his chest, while Brenna diapered and dressed the infant, then covered her with the blanket.

Rising, Brenna slipped her arms around her husband's waist. "You are not angry with me, are you?"

"No."

"She is lovely, is she not?" Brenna asked, smiling down at their new daughter.

"Indeed," he replied, but he was looking at his wife, not the child. "What will you call her?"

"I would like to call her Cara Aideen, after my Granny O'Connell," Brenna said. "If it is all right with you."

"Whatever you want is fine with me."

Finding a nanny proved far easier than Roshan had expected. He put an ad in the local newspaper, requesting that those interested in applying for the job do so after six P.M. They hired the first woman who came to the door. Her name was Charlotte Ray, and she was a wonderfully cranky grandmotherly type. She wore her gray hair in a tight bun at her nape and viewed the world through bright blue eyes that were both worldly wise and compassionate. Roshan installed her in the apartment above the garage. She had accepted the DeLongpres' strange lifestyle without question, but then, Roshan had offered her a great deal of money, enough to silence her curiosity and assure her loyalty.

Life, indeed, was good, made so by the lovely woman who had bewitched him one moonlit night. Brenna. She had given him love. She had given him laughter. She had given him a child.

Indeed, his little witch had given him everything he had thought forever lost to him.

And then she was there, smiling up at him, and he knew he would ask nothing more of his existence than to wake with her beside him for as long as he drew breath.

Murmuring her name, he swung her into his arms.

"Are you going to have your wicked way with me?" she asked, grinning as he carried her down to their lair.

"Yes, ma'am," he replied. "Every way I can."

And he did.

EPILOGUE

Four months later

Brenna sat on the curved sofa in front of the hearth, her daughter cradled in her arms while Roshan read aloud from a book of old Irish poems. She loved the sound of his voice, so deep and rich. It never failed to amaze her that words written by a poet long dead still had the power to speak to her heart and her soul.

She glanced at the portrait hanging over the fireplace. It had been painted a month after their marriage. Roshan had been reluctant, but Brenna had insisted. "So we can always remember how we looked when we fell in love," she had said, knowing he would be unable to refuse her. Soon they would have to have another one painted, she thought, one that included their daughter.

The baby tugged at a lock of Brenna's hair, and tugged at her heart, as well.

After feeding the baby and changing her diaper, Brenna carried Cara Aideen upstairs to the nursery. Once a room that held only books, it now held everything a new baby required, and more. The walls were painted a soft pink; a carpet of a deeper shade covered the floor. White lace curtains fluttered at the window. A white crib stood against one wall, a matching dresser on the other. Angelic cherubs danced on the ceiling. There was a padded rocking chair in one corner, a huge stuffed teddy bear in another.

"Sweet dreams, my angel," Brenna murmured as she put her daughter to bed.

Looking up, Brenna saw that Roshan had followed her into the room. Moving up beside her, he placed his arm around her shoulders.

"She grows more lovely every day, does she not?" Brenna asked.

"Indeed," he replied, kissing her cheek, "and so does her mother."

"I still cannot believe she is really ours."

Roshan nodded. Adopting the baby had been relatively easy. He'd had to use his supernatural powers on more than one occasion, but he'd had no qualms about doing so. And though the means had been less than totally honest, Cara Aideen was legally theirs. He had expected the infant to make drastic changes in their lives, and she did, but not in the ways he had thought. By the time she was a week old, he was her slave and her champion, willing to do anything to keep her safe.

He knew they would have some difficult days ahead when Cara Aideen started to wonder why she never saw her parents during the day, why they never ate together as a family, why they insisted that her birthday parties be held at night, why they missed school picnics and went swimming only after dark. In time, they would tell her the truth. In time, perhaps she would join them. If not, well, that was a worry for another day.

Drawing Brenna into his arms, he kissed her gently. "You've put our daughter to bed, my sweet wife," he said, kissing the tip of her nose. "Is it my turn now?"

"Would you like me to tuck you in and kiss you good night?" she asked with a teasing smile.

"Indeed, I would."

Laughing softly, she took him by the hand and led him out of the nursery and down the hall to their bedroom. She dimmed the lights with a look, then slowly began to undress him, letting her fingertips explore the width of his shoulders, the hair that curled on his chest, the ridges in his stomach. And when he stood gloriously naked, she slid her robe over her shoulders, let her nightgown pool at her feet.

"I will love you as long as we live," he whispered.

"And I you."

His gaze moved over her, filled with aching tenderness and the promise of forever as he carried her to bed. And as he covered her body with his, a chant whispered long ago rose in Brenna's mind.

Light of night, hear my song, bring to me my love, ere long.

Clasping her husband close, she thanked the Fates for granting her heart's desire and making her every dream and wish come true.

And turn the page for a sneak peek at
Amanda's newest book,
NIGHT'S MASTER,
coming in October from Zebra . . .

"Would you like to go for a drive?"

I cleared a throat gone suddenly dry. Every instinct I possessed screamed that going for a drive with a man whose scent was more intoxicating than whiskey straight up was a very bad idea. So naturally I said yes.

Moments later we were flying down the highway at a hundred miles an hour. It was a first for me, and I have to admit that it was exhilarating until I let myself think about what would have happened if the car had skidded out of control and wrapped itself around a tree. It probably wouldn't have hurt Raphael much, at least not permanently. I would have most likely ended up dead.

Before I could ask him to slow down, he eased off the gas and turned on the radio. Kenny G's "Songbird" filled the air, though I didn't pay much attention. I was too busy watching the speedometer. I didn't relax until we were doing a nice, reasonably safe, sixty.

Raphael flashed a grin in my direction. "Sorry, I didn't mean to scare you. Going a hundred miles an hour with my hair on fire has always been my way of letting off steam."

"Really? What are you steamed up about?"

"You."

"Me?" The word emerged from my throat as little more than a squeak.

With a nod, he pulled off the road and put the car in PARK. "You." His dark eyes glowed when he looked at me. "I've wanted you since the first night I saw you."

Mindful that a Vampire could mesmerize a human with little more than a glance, I was careful not to meet his gaze.

"Admit it," he said, and there was a rough edge in his voice. "You feel the same about me."

I started to deny it, but the words died, unspoken, as I recalled the image I'd had of the two of us lying entwined in each other's arms. I wasn't about to admit it, though, especially not here and now.

"Kathy, look at me."

"No way."

"Still afraid of me?"

"Darn right! I know all about Vampires . . ." That was a lie. All I really knew for sure was that they drank blood, slept in coffins, and that the sun turned them to ash in the blink of an eye.

"Do you?" he asked, amusement evident in his tone.

"Well, not all," I amended, "but enough to know better than to look one in the eye." Especially now, when we were parked on a dark, deserted road in the middle of nowhere. I could scream for help until the cows came home, but no one would hear me.

I felt the weight of his gaze on my bowed head, felt the heat of his desire brush my senses like a breath of summer air. It filled the car with an almost palpable energy. I didn't know if it was some kind of Vampire magic or not, but it was all I could do to keep from crawling into his lap and begging him to make love to me. If Vampires had pheromones, his were working overtime.

"I think you'd better take me home."

I shivered as his fingertips slid, slow and sensuous, down my arm. "Is that what you want?"

I nodded. Being this close to him in a confined space was far too dangerous, and far too tempting. I mean, he was the most gorgeous creature, man or Vampire, that I had ever seen, and I'm only human, after all. Add to that the fact that I hadn't been in a man's arms or kissed by anyone other than my mother in a good long time, and well, you get the idea.

"Kathy." He caught my chin between his thumb and forefinger and forced my head up. "Please don't be afraid of me. I won't hurt you. I won't hypnotize you. I swear I'll never do anything you don't want me to do."

There was no safety in that, I thought wildly. I wanted him to sweep me into his arms and make mad, passionate love to me in every way humanly, or inhumanely, possible. I wanted to feel his hands on my body, wanted my hands on him.

I swallowed hard, glad that he couldn't read my mind. "Why me?"

He smiled faintly. "Why not you?"

"But you've been a Vampire for years. You must have had dozens of women . . ." I stared at him. For all I knew, he had a wife waiting at home. "You're not married, are you?" I told myself it didn't matter. He was a Vampire, not a potential husband. But I still wanted to know.

He looked offended. "I wouldn't be with you if I was," he said curtly. "I've never been married, although I came close once."

"Really?" Curiosity drove everything else from my mind. "What happened?"

He snorted softly. "What do you think? When she found out what I was, she called me every dirty name in the book and then she packed up and left town."

"I'm sorry, that must have hurt."

He shrugged, as if it was of no consequence. "It was a long time ago."

But it still hurt. Though he tried to hide it, I could hear the pain in his voice. I resisted a sudden, almost overwhelming urge to comfort him, to stroke the black silk of his hair, to kiss his cheek and whisper that any woman who would walk away from him was a fool. Darn! What was I thinking? Alarmed by the turn of my thoughts, I folded my arms over my chest to keep from reaching for him.